PRAISE FOR
PIANIST IN A BORDELLO

"If only the political milieu of America today was this much fun, our polarized national discourse might be drowned in a sea of chuckles."

—Ask David Reviews

"Pianist in a Bordello is a well-written send-up of contemporary politics. In it, running for office seems less of a civic duty than an outright act of madness."

—Indie Reader

"The satire and wit, mixed with wisdom and knowledge of history and politics formed a successful recipe for a satisfying read!"

—Karla J

"This is just a delicious, silly, fun, fact-filled, sometimes-sexy (which is more implied) wild ride through the times of many people's youth (including this reader!)"

—Susan Loveira

"I was immediately blown away by the cleverness of Mr. Erickson. The first several chapters had me grinning and giggling quite a bit. As the story moved on, things took on a more serious tone, but underlying it all was a wit and intelligence that I found most impressive."

—Raeleighreads

"As a politician I may have taken more than the average reader's pleasure in this wildly funny send-up of our modern electoral mess. As an author I'm simply jealous."

—Cecil Bothwell,
an Amazon "Vine Voice" Reviewer

"I laughed the entire way through the book. I would love to read a sequel to this."

—Julie Baswell

"Brilliance! I love the multi-layers of fun, mystery and political prowess throughout this novel! I'm recommending this read to my literary circle. I imagine our discussion at book end will be very entertaining! Great book! BRAVO!"

—Felicia Wimberly

"Pianist in a Bordello is a rollicking good read because of Mike Erickson's finely tuned sense of an increasingly absurd political process."

—Alan Miller

"Charming, witty, wildly imaginative, well-written & colorful."

—PM Jones

AWARDS AND RECOGNITION:

General Fiction by Northern California
Publishers and Authors.
BRAG Medallion honoree

Top ten percent of indie books by *Publisher's Weekly* and
KIRKUS Reviews

Amazon Reviews (as of 8-31-2015)
43 with an average of 4.7 out of 5.

PIANIST IN A BORDELLO

A Novel

Mike C. Erickson

Tri - Rhyme Publications

Pianist in a Bordello
Mike C. Erickson

Tri – Rhyme Publications
11454 Tunnel Hill Way
Gold River, California 95670

ISBN 978-0-578-15186-1
(e-book ISBN 978-1-4951-3136-3)

Cover design by Katelyn Schirmer
Book design by Christopher Fisher

This edition was prepared for printing by The Editorial Department
7650 E. Broadway, #308, Tucson, Arizona 85710
www.editorialdepartment.com

To Trudy, Nick and Zac

My choice early in life was either to be a piano player in a whorehouse or a politician. And to tell the truth, there's hardly any difference.

—President Harry Truman

PIANIST
IN A BORDELLO

PROLOGUE

Being in politics is like being a football coach. You have to
be smart enough to understand the game, but dumb enough
to think it's important.

—Senator Eugene McCarthy

"DICK, YOU CAN'T BE A GREAT CONGRESSMAN if you never get
elected," Emily said.

"Ah, the conundrum of seeking elected office." I stood up
straight, all six feet two-plus inches of me, and gestured toward
the wide windows and the modest Sacramento cityscape beyond.
In my own mind, I was professorial in tone and as inspiring as
Kennedy at Brandenburg Gate.

Tim frowned. "Emily's right. Your chances of election are
almost nil if you really put *everything* in your book. So what's the
point?"

"It's the truth as I know it," I said. "The first completely honest
political autobiography."

Emily groaned and jabbed her Clintonesque thumb at me.

"Why the hell did I agree to be your campaign manager?"

"You loved my commitment to candor?"

"This isn't candor, it's … it's—"

"It's too close to the election," my legal adviser, Tim Escuella,
said. "It makes you look flippant."

"It's not flip—"

"It's muck," Emily said. "At least let us put a positive spin on it."

That was when Bradford Nayan, my publisher's representative, walked in.

"What's up, Brad?" I said. "Ready for the next chapter?"

"Actually, I was hoping to talk you into a little … fine-tuning."

"How fine?"

"The kidnapping stays, but the yellow submarine—"

"That's the way it happened," I said. "The sub stays."

Brad held up his hands. "It's just that we don't think this book—as it stands now— will help you get elected."

"So your company is jumping on my campaign bus?"

"Look, Dick—you win, your book makes money. You lose, we're lucky to break even."

"Anything else?" I said.

"We'd like you to dial back the sex. More Jimmy Carter, less Bill Clinton."

"Sorry, Brad, no major content changes without my approval— and I don't approve. But you and your company can rest assured I'm going to win."

"That's not what the polls say."

"Allison, give us the latest numbers," Emily said.

"Dick's fallen from eight points up right after the primary to ten points down today—in spite of having a two-to-one advantage over Banks in name recognition."

"Maybe now," I said, "but after my book is—"

"Dick, this book is a really a crappy idea," Tim said. "All of us think so."

"Except Nick," I said as my financial consultant entered the office. "How're we doing?"

"Contributions are down. Please tell me you're not going ahead with that book?"

"He is."

"He won't—"

"*Stop!*" I said,. "Thank you. Brad, what if I agree to personally cover the first hundred grand of your publisher's losses—assuming there *are* losses?"

Brad nodded. "Give me something in writing and I'll take it to the senior editors."

"While you're at it," I said, "remind them that if they don't agree, I'll sue their literary socks off —right, Tim?"

"We'll explore all possible legal remedies." Tim forced his voice down to reasonable-lawyer levels. "You sure as hell don't want Rob Banks voting on stuff like education or immigration, do you?"

"Speaking of immigration," Emily said, "take it out of your stump speech. If someone asks, skirt the issue. It's a huge loser in parts of your district."

Now I was the one struggling to keep my voice down. "Emily, there is no way in hell I'm not bringing up immigration. It's too important. And I'm publishing the book."

That seemed to be the nail in the conversational coffin.

"Is there anything we can do to stop you?" Emily said after a long silence.

"Nope."

"What if I quit?" Tim said. "What if we all quit?"

I walked toward the windows, gazed out at the skyline again, and counted thirty long seconds. Then walked back to the conference table.

"You won't quit."

One by one they caught each other's gaze, and then they turned to me. They all nodded.

Emily checked her cell phone.

"I've got to go. Just remember, Dick, most idealists end up as footnotes in forgotten tomes in the basements of libraries."

"You know, Gandhi—"

"And I *don't* want to hear another one of your fucking Gandhi quotes!"

* * *

5

The next day I picked up Amanda Patina at Sacramento International Airport. As I watched her descend the escalator in all her cosmopolitan splendor, I fell in love all over again.

We caught up over ales at the Red Dog Pub.

"So you're going ahead with your autobiography," she said.

"Voters are looking for candidates with integrity, an aura of probity, and they won't believe I've got it unless I show them everything, scars and all."

"I hope you've kept 'aura of probity' out of your speeches."

"Just trying to impress a Harvard girl."

"Know any Harvard girls?"

"Just you. Anything else to boost my ego?" I asked.

"You're deliciously gifted in bed."

"Hey, a quote for the book jacket. Anything else?"

"Well, your tongue is poetic platinum." Her body began shaking with a repressed giggle. "And didn't you tell me if it's men in the race, the tallest guy wins?"

"Usually." I scanned all the short people walking along the street in front of the pub.

"I just read about that mayor of New York back in the twenties who played the piano when campaigning. How about adding some music to your campaign. You sing a little, and didn't you tell me you once wanted be a piano player?"

"Still do, but I realized my tongue was better-suited to speaking, and my fingers ... you know about my talent there."

Her eyes brightened, and she wore a lascivious grin.

"If you win, do you think you can get Congress to sing your song and hum your tune?"

"When I win, I want to be more than simply a pianist in a bordello."

"Even if I sat on your piano and sang your song, Dickie?" Her grin became even sexier. "So you want to be the conductor of the orchestra, right?" she said.

"Before leaving Congress, I want to become the ... musical soul of a pitch-perfect symphony."

"Have I ever told you how much I love you for your modesty?"

Although my staff had planted the tiniest seed of doubt, my optimism remained more or less unscathed.

"One is a majority if he is right," President Lincoln said after overruling the wishes of his close advisors. Come Election Day, I'd be putting that to the test.

—Richard Milhous Nixon Youngblood
October 15, 2010

CHAPTER 1

The first duty of a revolutionary is to get away with it.

—Abbie Hoffman

I WAS BORN IN THE TEPEE MY FATHER BUILT, though I'm not sure that was intentional. Said tepee was located in the Red Fog commune in a remote forest in Mendocino County, California. Here, Yuri Yablonsky Youngblood and Rita Mae, who preferred to be called Infinity Blossom, lived for several months before my birth. In truth, Rita Mae lived in the commune while Tri-Y spent most of his time on political pilgrimages that sometimes took him across the nation but mainly to the University of California at Berkeley, which he often referred to as the Center. Berkeley was his uncompleted alma mater and his bastion of revolutionary thought, social idealism, and controlled substances.

As the date of my impending birth drew close, Rita Mae became a bit more conservative. Having read some of my father's correspondence to her during this time, I can't say I blame her:

> Lenin and Mao, Castro and Me.
> We'll bring this country to its knee.
> After a sojourn to the Center to see what's true,
> I'll be at Red Fog in a day or two.

Apparently, my father often wrote and spoke in rhymes during this phase of his life, an eccentricity no one regarded with any particular alarm. After consultation with the only commune member experienced in giving birth, my mother decided that the increasing frequency of her contractions made a VW bus ride over the hills to the nearest hospital impractical. I was born on Election Day, but it wasn't until the following day—November 6, 1968—that I was a given medical visa to enter the world at a hospital in Ukiah, California.

Tri-Y apparently returned three days later, nearly exploding with contrition. My mom exacted retribution by framing and hanging my birth certificate in the tepee. Realizing he was in deep matrimonial and communal doo-doo, Try-Y behaved—for a few months, at least.

Tri-Y called me Little Che, but Rita Mae always called me Dickie. Maybe she thought Dickie was cute, or maybe it was a "get tough or die" choice, like naming me Sue would have been.

A few months later, two dark suits in a dark sedan arrived at the commune. The residents stashed all their little baggies of what Rita Mae calls herbs while Tri-Y took off into the redwoods to stash himself.

Dating back to a 1935 movie, the commune mates referred to the agents as G-men. The G-men flashed their badges and wore well-practiced stone faces. They tried for a loud authoritative voice as their noses twitched and their eyes darted about.

"Where is Yuri Yablonsky Youngblood?"

"Maybe in Ireland."

"North to Canada?"

"No, he's with the pig farmers in Ecuador."

This sent the G-men off in a controlled huff to Rita Mae's tepee. In a lapse of legal protocol as well as good manners, they walked in unannounced. Rita Mae continued meditating.

"Are you the wife of Yuri Yablonsky Youngblood?" G-man #1 asked.

"Ooooommmm ..."

G-man #1 noticed the framed birth certificate on the wall.

"So your son is named after our commander in chief?"

"Or maybe our commander and chief is the father," she said. "Oooommm ..."

After searching the area and finding nothing of interest, they departed, but not before they were invited to "crash" there for a while and "mellow out." No one around Northern California laid eyes on Tri-Y for a couple of years after that, but my mom and her comrades certainly heard about him. Apparently, the FBI wanted him for questioning regarding bombs planted by the Weathermen faction of the Students for a Democratic Society. They also believed he could provide information about the Black Panthers' campaign to arm the black community.

All of which confirmed that in certain circles, my pops was becoming "the" radical icon of the sixties and early seventies.

Tri-Y's original sin was dodging the draft. When student deferment was no longer an option, he bought himself time by seducing the draft board secretary. When that liaison came to an acrimonious end, his file suddenly reappeared at the top of the stack.

For his next scheme, he began to construct an undesirable psychological profile. He visited any professional who would listen to him for free or cheap, often delivering his eccentric diatribes in rhyme. I know this because I found one in my mom's study, a verse probably inspired by Arlo Guthrie.

> It will be such a thrill
> As soon as I get to kill
> Rifle, bayonet, grenade
> Send me to the crusade.

When Tri-Y finally realized the draft was imminent, he did what every well-connected kid and professional athlete had already done: he tried to join the National Guard. Unfortunately, the psychological profile he'd developed made that impossible. The Guard was pickier than the regular army.

Later the same year, he joined the Native Americans who took over Alcatraz. Although Tri-Y looked about as Native American as Richard Nixon, he trotted out his last name as proof of his connection to the Cherokees. It wasn't until I was a grad student at UCLA that I discovered that his *Youngblood* was actually a bastardization of my pop's middle name, Yablonsky. I never did tell him—it would have been a shame to burst his bubble.

In May of 1970, Tri-Y's comrades on the West Coast spotted his picture on the cover of *Time* magazine among the protesters at Kent State, where the National Guard killed four unarmed students and wounded nine others.

It wasn't long after Tri-Y's disappearance that my mom took me out of Red Fog and returned to the upper-middle class community of her birth in Marin County.

"We'd love to have you back," my grandmother told her. "And we can't wait to see our sweet grandson."

Even though my mom had left her radical picket sign back in the Mendocino forest, she wasn't ready for a big group hug with her Republican parents. Congressman and Mrs. Stapleton Lambright agreed to take care of me during the day—or, more precisely, hire a nanny who would double as their housekeeper— while Rita Mae attended classes at Berkeley.

The situation suited me just fine. I loved Carlotta, my Guatemalan nanny— until one day she simply wasn't there anymore. I later found out she'd been deported. Even now I'm amazed at how many citizens welcome paperless immigrants into their homes yet do nothing to stop their sudden departure.

Now equipped with a degree in psychology, Rita Mae opened a yoga studio in Marin County. We lived on a houseboat in Sausalito among a flotilla of similar residences. These decrepit watercraft were a source of consternation for the authorities until, after a series of legal battles in the seventies, the houseboats were gradually reborn as semi-palatial residences subject to building regulations— and, most important, property taxes.

One of my earliest memories of this era was my mother's gentle tone as she commanded me to "mellow out, sweetie." Occasionally, we harmonized to a few "Oooommms," a fun game for a toddler. We'd also stretch out and listen to our breathing. To this day my bond with my mom is spiritual, loving, and maybe psychic.

One day when I was almost four years old, a man ambled onto the mini-pier of our floating home. He smiled, he laughed, and he exploded with charisma.

"Hey, Little Che," he said. "What's happening?"

This is my first real memory of my father.

Whenever Tri-Y was around, I was the center of attention. He taught me to "do the Nixon," which included raising my short arms in double victory signs. As Watergate unfolded, he taught me to say, "I'm not a crook," which I'd do on cue for just about anyone.

CHAPTER 2

When the president does it, that means it is not illegal.

—President Richard M. Nixon

DURING THE WATERGATE AFFAIR, my pops was in and out of my life, though mostly out. His visits made my mom increasingly anxious. She realized it would be the height of New Age consciousness to have Tri-Y around, but when his abrupt departures were followed by visits from dark-suited G-men, she told him he'd overstayed his welcome. When I was five or six, my mom and I were at a music festival near the Sonoma coast. As we were sitting on large logs in an audience of maybe a thousand people, I could have sworn I saw Tri-Y.

"Mom, isn't that Pops?"

"No, sweetie, that's just a tall guy with long hair."

A few minutes later, I swear I heard someone yelling, "Little Che, Little Che!"

I took off and circled the audience. I heard Rita Mae yell, but she didn't follow, convinced I'd be safe among the "kind and gentle" folk in the audience.

I was soon lost in the sea of people, and my pops was nowhere to be found.

"What'd you learn from this experience?" Rita Mae asked when I finally wandered back.

"I should've brought a tall person with me."

* * *

I remember cheering alongside my family at my grandfather's home on what I now know was Election Day, 1972—the day Nixon trounced the senator from South Dakota. That was also the day my grandfather, Congressman Lambright, became Senator Lambright. In spite of my grandfather's conservative nature, we shared a close bond, and I always suspected him of being a closet liberal. Maybe that's why, despite my father's eccentricities, I never felt torn between Tri-Y and the senator. As I grew older and began to develop my own political opinions, there were times when I could agree with both of them.

In the 1972 presidential campaign, the Nixon administration's paranoiac fear of losing ushered in the Watergate affair. So politically minded was our commander in chief that he actually wrote a memo to his daughters about the importance of personal anecdotes that they could "use" if the press queried them during the campaign.

He signed this note, "The President."

The more I study history, the more I realize that Nixon's problems date back much, much earlier than Watergate, probably all the way back to his role as an interrogator on the House Un-American Activities Committee in the late 1940s—a performance that made Joe McCarthy seem restrained. Nixon's statement to the press after his loss to Pat Brown for California governor in 1962 says quite a lot about how he saw himself: "You won't have Nixon to kick around anymore, because, gentlemen, this is my last press conference."

Psychiatrists say that some people with delusions of grandeur often refer to themselves in the third person. So, citizens and future constituents, if any of you ever hear me say, "Youngblood believes, supports, dislikes, or is in favor of *anything*," I hope you'll have me impeached—or, failing that, assassinated.

CHAPTER 3

If Lincoln were alive today, he would be turning over in his grave.

—President Gerald Ford

MANY WOULD SAY GERALD FORD DESERVES to be remembered for pardoning the draft dodgers seeking asylum in Canada and other places around the globe. Although I have vague recollections of him as president and his ability to pardon my father, it was Chevy Chase's *Saturday Night Live* impersonations of him that left an indelible mark on my memory. On occasion, I stayed up this late because an errant baby-sitter was more involved with her boyfriend than with her duties. From what I recall, his routine consisted almost entirely of falling down and tripping over everything in the Oval Office.

It wasn't long after the pardons that Tri-Y made a reappearance in the Bay Area to take partial credit for ending the war, the draft, and Nixon's presidency. Around the time of the inauguration of Jimmy Carter, Tri-Y dropped out of sight again.

"Why did Pops go away?" I asked.

I was sitting outside with Rita Mae, drinking in the sunset over the top of the Golden Gate.

"He thinks the FBI will arrest him," she said. "Or maybe he's just being mysterious."

"So he's a criminal?"

"This is the part where I'm supposed to say you'll understand when you're older." She sighed and smiled. "What I want you to remember about your father is that he strongly believes he's doing good things for the world."

When I was nine, in 1977, I became aware that my name was, if not a cross to bear, at least a heavy lunch pail to carry. While nicknames like Dickhead and Dick-for-brains never brought me to tears, they at least sharpened my tongue for the rigors of verbal combat.

"Hey, Dickie," a classmate said, "you ever play with your dick?"

Though I wasn't exactly sure what they found so funny, I managed a riposte.

"At least I have one to play with."

One Saturday morning I was contemplating the fog swirling over the San Francisco skyline and enjoying that sense of supreme optimism that comes naturally with youth. This is probably why I wasn't worried when three bedraggled creatures in a decrepit skiff cruised up to our dock.

"Hey, little man, you Dickie Youngblood?" This was from the biggest and hairiest of the trio.

"Maybe," I said.

"Name's Orca. Want to trip on our boat?"

"No thanks—"

He and another one grabbed me and forced me, kicking and flailing, onto their boat. We were halfway across the bay before one of them spoke.

"We need you, Dickie," he said. "We need your grandpa to help us bring down the capitalist pigs that run this country."

"The what?"

"The pigs, man—the people that oppress us!"

His cohorts—Kimwabe and Cousin Clean, I later

learned—grinned and raised their fists in the air. Even though I was more terrified than I'd ever been in my life, as we passed a myriad of fishing boats it occurred to me that my captors weren't the shiniest lures in the tackle box.

We headed east toward the Oakland Inner Harbor, which also serves as the demarcation line between Alameda and Oakland. We went past the Naval Air Station, past the huge commercial ships unloading hefty cargo with giant cranes, past yachts and smaller skiffs, until we finally pulled up to a sagging half-rotten pier.

I was even more scared when I was dragged out of the boat and up the dock toward an abandoned warehouse—a dark, dank warehouse, as I found out the minute we were inside it. We passed a couple of small boats and a beat-up truck on the way into a grungy office at the far end of the building. Sitting in a big chair was a supersized Janis Joplin. I realize I was evaluating her through nine-year-old eyes, and most likely I've been exaggerating with each retelling of this story over the years, but I'd still peg her at twice the size of the real Janis Joplin. Her raspy voice did nothing to dispel the impression.

"This the fascist senator's grandkid?" she said.

"Yep," Orca said.

Janis squinted at me through rainbow shades.

"You want to help us bring justice and peace to the planet and give the working people of the world their just rewards?"

Everyone looked at me. I blinked back tears. "I wanna go home."

There was a flicker of compassion in her eyes. "Sorry, kid. We can't let you go just yet."

"Red Emma, what do you want us to do with him?" Orca asked.

"Lock him in the storeroom for now." I later learned Red Emma had named herself after Red Emma Goldman, the famous radical anarchist deported to Russia in 1919 for speaking out against conscription and WWI.

"Let me go," I said, "or my grandpa will send out the army."

She frowned. "Your grandpa can do that?"

"Yep, and my dad will rescue me."

Now they chuckled.

"Tri-Y hasn't been seen in years, kid."

"He'll find me." I believed it, too. "He's magic."

After a few days in captivity in my ten-by-ten storeroom, I learned that Red Emma's assortment of malcontents had a name: the Lennarchist Mutinous Militia, which I couldn't begin to pronounce even if I wanted to. Written on a kind of plaque in the Revolutionary Quarters of the LMM was its credo, a twisted abbreviation of John Lennon's song:

> Imagine Anarchy where there is....
> No heaven
> No countries
> Nothing to kill or die for
> No religion too
> No possessions
> No greed or hunger
> A peaceful brotherhood of man and woman

After a few days of reading this, by now more bored than scared, I asked myself: what would Tri-Y do? So I stole a pen and added a line: "No kidnapping either."

Red Emma spotted it a few hours later.

"Dickie, did you do that?"

"I did, and my only regret is that I have no more words for kids everywhere."

I didn't know it at the time, but ransom notes had been sent to both Rita Mae and my grandpa. For my safe return, they demanded that Buley Bickford, whom they described as a "political prisoner," be released from incarceration at Folsom Prison. Bickford had been convicted of armed robbery, repeated exhibitionism, narcotic trafficking, and threatening President Ford with dismemberment. He was also Red Emma's revolutionary brother and old man. Later ransom notes demanded that the senator also provide a private jet and a million dollars.

Once the senator was apprised of my kidnapping, he immediately contacted the FBI, over the objection of Rita Mae, and a strategizing powwow was held at the Lambrights' mini-mansion in Marin County. The feds wanted to keep the kidnapping from the press for the time being, reasoning that the perpetrators' secondary objective was notoriety. Rita Mae thought the best chance of recovering her only son was to get as much publicity as possible, in hopes of alerting Tri-Y.

The issue became moot when the next ransom note was sent directly to the main San Francisco newspaper.

Meanwhile, back at the ancient nautical warehouse, my daily routine included long periods in the storeroom with breaks in the kitchen for mini-lectures from Red Emma about the glories of the class struggle.

One day Orca came into my storeroom.

"Hey, little man, you want to go on a fund-raiser with me and Kimwabe?"

"Groovy," I said, excited about the prospect of leaving the warehouse (and yes, I now realize that by 1977, *groovy* was already on display in the museum of passé slang).

As we were preparing to leave, Red Emma stopped us.

"The little comrade is not ready to take such a big step," she said, and I was again locked in the storeroom along with several volumes of revolutionary literature, including Mao's *Little Red Book*—part of Red Emma's crude attempts at brainwashing.

I flipped through the text and saw there was nothing there of interest to me. As a graduate student, I would later revisit this so-called earth-shaking text that was pounded into the brains of the

Chinese proletariat, and I found little to change my nine-year-old perceptions. Perhaps something was lost in translation.

I later found out "fund-raising missions" meant armed robbery of convenience stores. In the spirit of supporting the downtrodden, they primarily targeted 7-Elevens, which at the time were owned by an immoral corporation. After a week or so of captivity, Red Cliff and Kimwabe failed to return from a fund-raising mission. Orca and Cousin Clean disappeared soon after that.

Local law enforcement found Kimwabe duct-taped to a mural in Coit Tower atop Telegraph Hill in San Francisco. The mural of which he'd become a 3-D appendage was an illustration of a shipyard and railroad workers—the silver duct tape fit right into the color scheme.

Orca was found attached with Velcro bands to the former cell of Al Capone at Alcatraz. Since the Native Americans had left in 1971, the "Rock" had come under control of the National Parks Service and had been open to the public since 1973. The park rangers discovered Orca early one morning in a delirious state while "That's the Way I Like It" blared from a nearby boom box. He was charged with burglary, armed robbery, and drug trafficking.

An early-morning commuter on the Golden Gate Bridge spotted Cousin Clean hanging by his feet from the upper structure. Cousin Clean apparently suffered from severe acrophobia, and although he survived, he was comatose for hours after his arrest.

That same morning, which was after a major concert, custodians at San Francisco's Winterland found Red Cliff passed out with a bong still in his mouth.

Each of the gang members claimed a deranged hippie and a gang of black-clad Aussies had kidnapped them. The police were much more interested in their roles in the robbery of twelve 7-Elevens in the Bay Area.

The following evening, Red Emma and the three remaining militia members, distraught over their missing comrades, sat drinking Southern Comfort. Maybe they overdid it or, more likely, whiskey wasn't the only component of their beverages, but either way it sent them to early dreamland.

In the dead-silent storeroom, I stared at the dim cracks of light around the door. It occurred to me that the gang hadn't locked me in.

I was about to try the door when someone outside cracked it open.

"Shussssh."

The door swung open, and there in all his glory stood Tri-Y. He took my hand and together we tiptoed past the office filled with slumbering militia members. Just as we were about to make our final escape, we heard someone move.

"Who's there?"

We ducked behind an old dinghy. I held my breath as footsteps emerged from the office and moved toward us.

Just as he passed the dinghy, Tri-Y tackled the militia member from behind, wrestled him to the ground, and pinched a point in his neck.

The militia member slumped back into dreamland. My dad grabbed my hand and we ran out the door, down a boardwalk, through an open chain-link gate, and down several steps to the deck of a ship—well, kind of.

My pops rapped on the hatch of the yellow deck. It opened, and I descended a minuscule stairway into a submarine.

"Hey, mate," a funny-sounding sailor said.

"Got away, did ya?" said another. "Good onya."

Every one of them was fit, dressed completely in black, and spoke with an Aussie accent, with the exception of an Asian man who said mainly "ye."

Quiet orders were issued. The engine started with a bang and a swish, and we were off. As we proceeded out of Oakland Harbor and past a U.S. Coast Guard ship, they let me look out the periscope.

In the bay, the noise and the pressure changed as we dived under the water.

"Are we going to Australia?" I asked.

"Australia's pretty cool," Tri-Y said, "but we need to get you back to your mom."

As much as I enjoyed seeing my pops, the thought of being back in the warm security of our floating home in Sausalito was very appealing.

I was beginning to doze when the submarine surfaced. Tri-Y and I climbed the ladder to the deck, where a skiff was waiting. Less than three minutes later, my pops and I were on the front porch of our floating home.

We knocked on the door. Rita Mae was there in seconds, greeting me with hugs and sobs. When our embrace ended, we looked around. Tri-Y had vanished, presumably into the bay.

"He'll be back," she said.

I told Rita Mae the whole story, and early the next morning she reported my return to the authorities. They were on the porch of our floating palace within the hour, along with several members of the press.

"The police want to hear about your adventure, Dickie," Rita Mae said.

"What should I tell them?"

"The truth, sweetie."

"Even about Pops?"

"Don't worry about your father," she said. "He's pretty much omnipotent."

"What does that mean?"

She smiled. "As you know, he has magical powers."

"Do I have powers?"

"What would you do if you did?"

"I'd save kids all over the world."

With that resolved, my mom ushered in the police, two other men and a woman—all smiles but still businesslike.

"So, Richard," one guy in a suit said, "can you tell us about your ordeal?"

"My what?"

"Can you tell us who kidnapped you and where they kept you?"

"It was Red Emma—she's a gigantic Janis Joplin. She's the boss of the gang."

"And what did you do all day?"

"They made me spend hours in the storeroom with the Lennarchy Creed. Orca and the guys went out a lot on missions."

"What kind of missions?"

"They called them fund-raising missions." I thought about this. "And they took guns with them."

"And how did you manage to get away?"

I summarized my "rescue" by Tri-Y. As the story progressed, their smiles turned skeptical.

"So, Dickie," one said, "your father took you across the bay in a yellow submarine?"

"Uh-huh."

"Have you ever heard the Beatles' song about the yellow submarine?"

"Yeah, my mom used to play it all the time."

They exchanged smiles. "So maybe it was just an imaginary yellow submarine?"

Clearly I hadn't explained things right.

"No," I said, "it was a real submarine with a hatch and a periscope."

"Why do you think the men on the ship were Australian?"

"Their accents, and they called each other 'mate' and 'bloke.' Mom has a friend who talks like them. Oh, and there was one guy who mostly said 'ye.'"

"So where'd your dad go after he brought you home?"

I shrugged. "He disappeared."

"Did he say where he was going?"

I shook my head.

Next they questioned my mom, who related the whole thing from her perspective. When they asked about Tri-Y, she shrugged. "I have no idea," she said. "He was only here for a second, then he was gone."

The police were looking less smiley than when they'd come in. Rita Mae walked them to the door. When the press started shouting from the end of the boardwalk, she told them the police could answer all their questions.

One reporter saw me standing in the doorway and yelled out. "Happy to be home, Dickie?"

I couldn't resist—I raised my arms in double victory signs.

Next morning, a picture of me "doing the Nixon" was seen in several California newspapers. In the *Chronicle* and the *Examiner*, it was accompanied by the headline "Youngblood Escapes Kidnappers in Yellow Sub." The article went on to question the veracity of my story but gave me credit for my "bravery in surviving the ordeal." For weeks, local TV stations, comedians, and even a weather reporter made acerbic references to "yellow submarine sightings" in the bay.

Senator Stapleton Lambright was unavoidably detained in the nation's capital but issued a statement reiterating his grandson's bravery and his hopes that the criminals who did this would be brought to justice. He even implied having had a hand in my escape, though he went nowhere near the subjects of yellow submarines or Tri-Y. I think he wanted to believe me, but as a government official he could hardly admit the security implications of having an unidentified submarine nosing around San Francisco Bay.

My captors couldn't wait to implicate each other and they all ended up confessing. I was a bit disappointed that I didn't get to float my story in public again, since nobody seemed to believe me. Still, it was my submarine and I sailed on it.

CHAPTER 4

When I was a kid, I used to pray every night for a new bike. Then I realized, the Lord doesn't work that way. So I just stole one and asked Him for forgiveness.

—Emo Philips

As an aspiring politician who's unlikely to net a majority of evangelical Christian votes, I've been advised by historical precedent—as well as my staff—to attend a Christian service, profess a belief in God, and otherwise avoid the subject. However, such obfuscation would sabotage the purpose of this work.

I wasn't brought up in a particular faith, but I enjoyed a variety of religious experiences, from chanting with the Hari Krishnas to singing at a synagogue. At a Presbyterian church, which I attended with my grandmother, the minister said faith got you a first-class airfare to eternal life. Being age twelve, I already knew I was immortal.

Somewhere in this pre-Ronald Reagan era, my mom and I spent a long two days with the super-smiley members of the Unification Church—also known as the Moonies—at a "retreat" near Napa Valley. Apparently, some of the recruiters had spotted Rita Mae looking forlorn near the fountain in downtown Sausalito.

The post-dinner festivities for us kids involved a few semi-fun games followed by standing in a big circle and holding hands.

"Feel the spirit."

"Can you feel the spirit?"

"Jesus is with us."

"Reverend Moon is with us."

The longer it went on, the more this experience began to feel like my incarceration with Red Emma.

"I'm really tired," I said. "Are you about finished?"

I was ignored.

By early afternoon the next day, my mom was also feeling like a less-than-happy camper and decided to go for a walk down the lane, off the retreat property. Two shiny, happy people quickly flanked her. I was following close enough to hear them, giving her space but wanting to get away myself.

"Where are you going?" the happy man said.

"For a walk. This place is making me sort of uptight."

"You should stay inside with all your new friends."

"You mean I can't go for a walk?"

"Of course you can!" the happy woman said. "We'll go with you."

"What if I want to go by myself?"

"Why would you want to be by yourself?" they said in unison.

"Look, could you please just leave me alone!"

"We can't do that."

"Then take us back to Sausalito." My mom collected me and we headed toward the drop-off area.

The group leader arrived on the scene, along with several happy people.

"Good, you're here," Rita Mae said. "We're leaving, and we expect transportation back to Sausalito."

"No, no, you and your son need to experience the entire spiritual journey," the group leader said. "That takes at least two more days."

"Did you happen to notice my last name when I signed in?" she said.

His smile wilted a bit. "Lambright."

"I assume you also noticed my son's last name is Youngblood— as in Yuri Yablonski, as in Tri-Y? That's Dickie's father, and he always seems to know when his son isn't happy." She turned to me, arms folded. "Are you happy, Dickie?"

I gave my most convincing scowl. "No."

By now the Moonies were using every facial muscle they possessed to maintain those smiles.

"So," my mom said, "I expect the white van over there will be here soon, as in twenty minutes, to take us back to Marin County."

We were on our way home within the half-hour.

To this day, when I encounter extraordinarily happy people, I'm never sure which is worse: that they might be insincere or that their sincerity is absolute. In either case, they're generally devoid of humor—apparently, their God doesn't giggle.

CHAPTER 5

Without education we are in horrible and deadly danger of taking educated people seriously.

—G.K. Chesterton

I SPENT MUCH OF MY EARLY EDUCATION in and out of all sorts of "alternative" schools, including a brief stint in a Montessori school and an even shorter one in a Swiss boarding school while Rita Mae went to study meditation in Nepal. When I finally entered mainstream education at Rio de Mañana High School at the age of fourteen, I quickly became friends with two other students who, like me, had enjoyed a less-than-conventional education.

Lily Livinski, although Jewish, had done time in Christian and Buddhist schools, with a few brief intervals of home schooling. At Rio de Mañana we shared two classes: biology and geometry. Our geometry teacher was Mr. Tavish, a man with long graying hair tied back in a ponytail, a pocket protector, and an infectious passion for his subject. He spent the first few days impressing upon us the breadth and depth of his field, from geometry in nature (snowflakes and rainbows) to the golden formula and the Fibonacci sequence. He showed us pictures of colorful fractals, Egyptian pyramids, sacred *and* unsacred symbols with geometric origins.

"Youngblood!"

"Yes, sir!"

"Your grandfather's a senator, isn't he?"

"Yeah."

"Imagine a geometry of politics, of elections, of checks and balances, even hereditary leaders. Maybe there's a formula for becoming the next president!" He pointed at me. "Think about it."

"Do you think we're ever going to learn any actual geometry?" I asked as Lily was leaving class that day.

"I kind of hope not. Math isn't my best."

"Maybe tomorrow he'll get into the geometry of food."

"Or the geometry of all these school rules," she said.

I felt the first tingling of inspiration. "Math classes are supposed to have a lot of homework, right?" I said. "The way I see it, as long we let him know we're interested, he'll never make it to problems or homework."

"Not bad," she said. "Tomorrow I'll ask him about the geometry of sex."

I laughed, but in the hormonally piqued state of early adolescence, her casual use of the word sex was very titillating.

Walking right behind us was Adolphus, who'd been following our repartee. I later discovered that his early education in Christian fundamentalist schools had not only perfected his sense of humor but had also sharpened his skepticism considerably.

"Rad." He giggled. "I'll ask him about the geometry of Jesus. I can tell my dad God is still in the public schools."

Adolphus became the final member of our freshmen trio. The three of us spent lunches together and eventually invaded each other's home nests and refrigerators. We were still friends even after I joined the Neanderthals, as Lily referred to the school jocks.

When I first entered the classroom of my world history teacher, Ms. Helen Hanal, I was greeted with a stack of worksheets and an exhaustive list of class rules (which she recited daily). Ms. Hanal was a stylish blonde, probably in her late thirties and trying desperately to look younger. My classmates were unmerciful, behind her back, of course. Her name was the easiest target—even the least creative of her charges could simply forget the "H." My problems with Ms. Helen Hanal were her toneless lectures and colorless worksheets, which I thought I was adapting fairly well to until the day she started in on life in Tsarist Russia.

"Ms. Hanal, do you think life was worse under the tsar or under the Communists?" I asked.

She looked up at the map of the world and then back at her thirty-one students, who were actually showing signs of interest for the first time that day.

"Maybe by the end of year we'll have enough information to discuss questions like these. For now, let's just stick to the facts."

"Couldn't we at least speculate?" I asked. "And why aren't their lives part of the facts?"

"It's a good question, a complex question. But for now I think you'd all better stick to the worksheets."

"I just thought we could talk about something important," I said, "instead of filling in the blanks from a textbook."

"Richard," she said with a faint quiver in her voice, "you're very close to earning a trip to the vice principal's office."

"I apologize for wanting an education, Ms. Hanal."

She'd certainly have carried out her threat if the bell hadn't rung just then. Instead I let myself be swept into the hall, where Lily Livinsky congratulated me on my small rebellion.

Just a few days later, President Reagan announced he was sending Marines to the minuscule Caribbean nation of Grenada to liberate them from the Communist regime that had recently seized power.

The next morning, Lily handed me a large button with a very unflattering picture of our commander in chief giving his thumb-in ear response to the press. Superimposed over this were the words "Grenada: Let's call the whole thing off."

"Ready to stand up for what's right?" she said.

"What if someone tells us to take them off?"

"It's our right to freedom of speech. Are you with me or what?"

All told, seven students sported these badges in Ms. Hanal's second-period world history class. Since the day's lesson had to do with the indigenous people of the Americas prior to European invasion, I thought it appropriate to bring up the events in Grenada. Emboldened by my badge and my desire to impress Lily, I raised my hand.

Ms. Hanal glared at me. "Yes, Richard?"

"Ms. Hanal," I said in my most earnest voice, "could we discuss the Marines waging war in Grenada today?"

"This is not a current events class, Richard."

"But this is history in the making, right? Isn't that why we take history?"

She drew herself up to her full and not remotely imposing height. "We study history to appreciate our heritage."

"So, what if our heritage made a big mistake?"

"Richard, the class does not possess the knowledge or context to discuss this event meaningfully, and we have work to do here today." For the first time she seemed to notice the symbols of our anti-war sentiments. "And take off those silly badges, all of you."

"Ms. Hanal, are you afraid of our opinions?" I said.

"I'm afraid you can go discuss your insolence with our vice principal." She folded her arms. "Please leave, Richard."

This was the first disciplinary action in my school career. I felt a twinge of guilt for provoking her, immediately eclipsed by an exhilarating sense of validation for standing up for my beliefs.

I entered the administrative offices and showed my pass to the woman at the desk.

"Sit down, Richard. Our substitute vice principal, Mr. Yablonsky, will be with you soon."

Five minutes later I was ushered into the office—where, in a dark blazer, white shirt, and rep tie, sat my pops.

With great relish, he hugged me tight.

"So, Dickie. You having problems with the man?"

My radical father had, to my knowledge, never held a real job in his adult life. Nor had I ever seen him wear anything but jeans before. At least his hair was still long, though tied back fairly neatly.

There was only so much cognitive dissonance I could take. "What are you doing here?" I asked.

"Checking on the quality of your education," he said, trying not to laugh. "What's with the cool badge?"

I gave him a brief synopsis while he leaned back in his temporary seat of authority and loosened his tie.

"Really, Pops," I said when I'd wrapped up the story of my most recent misdeeds, "why're you here?

"I'm here to get you out of trouble or, better still, get you into more," he said. "You ready to take it to the wall, get the Marines out of Grenada?"

"Depends. How long are you going to be here?"

"Until they figure out I'm not who they think I am—so probably a couple of hours." He flipped through a dark red folder. "Man, look at all the rules. They should call it Rio de Reglamento. Ever feel like you're just a spoke in the wheel of the capitalist machine?"

"Sometimes, but I don't think I'm ready for the life of a radical," I said. "Unless you wanted to take me on a quick field trip to check it out?"

"No, Dickie, one of the few things I'm afraid of, other than foreign agents, is the quiet wrath of your mother." He paused for a moment. "Your teacher, Ms. Hanal—does her first name happen to be Helen?"

"Yeah, why?"

"I'm pretty sure I knew her—a long time ago. So when I send you back to class, maybe I'll send her a little note." He chuckled.

"Why don't you stick around for a while?"

"Sorry, Dickie. They're still after me."

"Who?"

"Maybe the CIA, FBI, or foreign agents." He squinted and looked toward the window. "And soon I'm off to Cambodia."

"People still think I'm wacko when I tell them about the yellow submarine."

"I read your version in the *Chronicle*," he said. "You got the story right. Besides, would you rather be a little loony or boring?"

He wrote a longish note for me to take back to Ms. Hanal. He folded it in two, winked, and—just in case my genetic rebelliousness wasn't sufficient—told me *not* to read the note.

As I walked back to class, I unfolded the paper.

Ms. Hanal,

Richard agreed to cease and desist his disrespectful behavior. Like you, the administration believes that one of the most disquieting trends in modern education is allowing or in some cases actually encouraging students to express ungrounded questions or opinions in the classroom. If Richard continues to disrupt your class with these radical demands, we will have to take the next step and consider him for temporary suspension.

In regard to his wearing that offensive badge, I'm afraid the U.S. Supreme Court seems to think students have some sort of rights regarding free speech. Hopefully, we will one day be free of those liberal judges who proclaimed, "Students don't shed their rights at the schoolhouse door."

Mr. Yablonsky, Acting Vice Principal

PS: Helen, I remember how we reached our "human potential" together at Esalen in Big Sur. I'll never forget how close we came to nirvana in the hot baths that evening.

Love and peace, Tri-Y

When I handed the note to Ms. Hanal, her face registered confusion—followed by the most sincere smile she'd ever exhibited as her mind connected the Ys. She then blushed and shooed me back to my seat.

"Sit down, Richard."

Soon Reagan declared victory and installed a "friendly" government in one of the smallest nations in the world. The subject of the badges and my behavior never surfaced again in Ms. Hanal's class.

During my freshman and sophomore years at Rio de Mañana High School, I not only became aware of politics and girls, but I also grew into a spindly tower. At six feet two-plus inches, I was a giant, especially standing next to Lily Livinsky.

My initial attraction to Lily had as much to do with her razor wit as her cute curviness. But as our relationship matured and her wit was increasingly sharpened at my expense, my romantic interest couldn't help wilting. Our bond was downgraded to friendship, where it remains to this day.

The story of my life at Rio de Mañana wouldn't be complete without an account of my athletic endeavors. By the third basketball game of my junior year, anything I launched into the air was magically sucked into the basket. I was rapidly becoming the star of the team.

Two weeks later, my rising star plummeted. In the closing seconds of a tied game, I was knocked down to the hardwood near mid-court. I was still a little dazed when I saw the ball rolling toward me, but I grabbed it, got to my feet, and made the longest mid-court shot of the season.

Unfortunately, the shot was into the opposing team's basket, which resulted in our third loss of the season.

For the rest of the year, I had to weather the mockery and outright hostility of close to half the student body. In a rare moment of research and creative aplomb, the student newspaper unearthed one of the first incidents of a player's scoring for the opposing team. At the Rose Bowl in 1929, Roy Riegals of the

Cal Bears heroically ran an interception to the wrong end zone. He was known forever as "Wrong Way Riegals," and thanks to the school paper, I became "Wrong Way Richard." Or sometimes it was simplified to two-dub. Still, it was a welcome respite from odious variations on "Dick."

In the spirit of full disclosure, my original reason for trying out for the basketball team was a future teammate's assertion that it was a great way to "get girls." So I waited patiently, and once memories of my mid-court gaffe faded, I noticed bigger smiles and friendlier hellos in the hall. But no smile across the hardwood was brighter than that of the head cheerleader, Judy LaTrudy, my coach's daughter. When she was in her cheerleader regalia or 1985 Madonna fashion, Judy sported them with more style than anyone in the school.

One of the perks of being an athlete was being kept apprised of the party locations. I showed up at them all, and eventually one Saturday evening I was actually sipping out of the same beer can as Judy.

"We finally get to talk," she said. "Have you noticed me smiling at you a lot, Dick?"

"I've noticed all your attributes."

"Attributes?" She giggled. "You really are a nerd—but a cute nerd."

This conversation was followed by making out on the back patio. We continued our "conversation" over the course of several dates, until about three weeks later when we found ourselves in her best friend's bedroom while a party carried on downstairs.

When Judy jumped off the bed, I assumed it was time to stop. Instead, she locked the door and slowly returned, unbuttoning her blouse as she walked. What followed was amazing, and amazingly not awkward.

Of course, there was still the matter of getting Judy home—and it was now well past curfew. Panties in pocket, she tried to open the front door, only then realizing she'd left her keys at the party. Convinced her father would appear at any moment, I made a hasty retreat to my car, faster than any fast break I'd ever executed on the court.

The more I came to understand the rapport of Judy LaTrudy and her dad, the less I worried. Judy was clearly way downcourt, while her father had yet to get the rebound. I think the coach would subscribe to Teddy Roosevelt's tenets on parenting: "I can either control Alice or be president of the United States. I can't possibly do both." Judy was a year my senior, and she soon left Rio de Mañana for the land of the Trojans at the University of Southern California. I missed her dearly. As I began writing this book, I sent her the following e-mail, along with the pages pertaining to our relationship.

> Hi Judy, do you find any part of my written history to be offensive? If so, I'm happy to delete these passages or change names to protect the guilty as well as the innocent.

Her response?

> Hey, Dickie. As you un-pad your resume, you're only padding mine. You may or may not know that I'm the sex editor of the women's health and fitness magazine, _Erofit_. Actually, after my recent promotion, my official title is 'Editor of Intimacy Issues.' Best of luck in the upcoming election. Love and Democracy, Judy.

My senior year at Rio was filled with sporadic basketball performances and a just-less-than-stellar academic performance but a dazzling SAT score. I got into the University of Washington as well as a few UC campuses. I even received an invitation to join the freshman class at Stanford University, along with Lily Livinsky. She made it in on merit, but SAT scores notwithstanding, I was pretty sure I'd been drawn from the category of applicants related to outstanding major contributors to the university—namely, my grandfather.

CHAPTER 6

Madaming is the sort of thing that happens to you—like getting a battlefield commission or becoming the dean of women at Stanford University.

—Sally Stanford, former San Francisco madam and mayor of Sausalito, California

I WAS IN AWE OF THE STANFORD CAMPUS: Romanesque buildings tempered with a hint of California cool, surrounded by indigenous oaks and Aussie eucalyptus.

When I first entered my dorm room, I found a large, disheveled Asian standing at the window. He was almost as tall as me, sporting a sunny smile and that just-rolled-out- of-bed look that wouldn't become fashionable for at least another decade.

"Hi, you must be the Dickster. I'm Sacatchy."

"Hey, Sacatchy, what's up?" He seemed to have dismembered the phone and scattered the parts across one of the beds.

"Making sure the phone isn't bugged." He laughed.

As I scanned our room, I saw two personal computers hooked up to a lot of peripheral gadgets. On the walls over Sacatchy's bunk was a poster commemorating Woz the Oz, inventor of the first Apple computer, a large black-and-white poster of the anarchy symbol, and a smaller picture of Red Emma Goldman.

"You really named after Tricky Dick?" Sacatchy asked.

"My claim to fame," I said. "How do you know so much about me?"

"Information is my avocation. I can hardly wait to meet Tri-Y, by the way."

"Somehow I don't see him dropping in for parents weekend," I said.

"Too bad. Anyway, I think we'll make an awesome team."

"Wait, what?"

A few days later, I came back from class and picked up the phone to call Lily to regale her with the intellectuality I'd gained after just five days at Stanford. There was no dial tone—just some clicks, swishes, and buzzing, interspersed with a cheery voice from someone's answering machine.

"What the hell?" I asked Sacatchy when he came in.

"War dialing." By this he meant using his computer to call sequential numbers in the same area code to determine which had modem connections.

"So who has a modem?" I asked.

"Some of the offices on campus—Engineering, Computer Science, Admissions and Records. Oh, and the Apple and Intel offices down the road."

"Could you actually see their records?"

"Interesting question." He looked up at his posters and seemed to drift into thought.

A couple of weeks later, Sacatchy burst into the room. "Hey Dick, let's go get a burger."

"I'm supposed to meet Lily Livinsky and her roommate for dinner," I said. "Care to join us?"

"Do they like burgers?"

"I think they may be vegetarians, actually."

We all met up at El Camino. On the door to this non-corporate eatery was a sign that read, "We've Beefed Up Our Vegan Menu."

Lily and Amber scrutinized their menus, printed on simulated grape leaves.

"How are the soy burgers prepared?" Amber asked.

"Broiled on our vegan-only open flame with just a smidgen of organically grown macadamia oil, which has been certified by the Vegetarian Society of America and by the Makini Organic Farms in Hilo, Hawaii."

"Do the same chefs who prepare the vegan entrées also sear the flesh of animals?"

"Yes, but they wash their hands thoroughly in our special decontamination machine."

I shot Sacatchy a quick glance. He raised an eyebrow.

"What fuels the flame of your broiler?" Amber said.

"Natural gas."

"We prefer wood flames," she said. "Natural gas is a product of dead animals from the past."

The waiter looked down at his pad so he couldn't see him roll his eyes.

Amber and Lily ended up ordering vegan salads and soy burgers while Sacatchy and I each got the equivalent of a half-pounder with double cheese.

As conversation ensued, we discovered that Lily was merely flirting with veganism. Amber Green, however, was an okra-nibbling fundamentalist.

"You should come to Union Square on Saturday," she said. "We're holding a demonstration against the fur trade."

"Sorry," Sacatchy said. "I'm going hunting with my uncle on Saturday."

Amber's eyes widened. "You go kill defenseless animals for fun?"

"That and food," Sacatchy said.

"There are plenty of things to eat besides animal flesh," Amber said. "An animal's life and soul are as just as important as ours."

"Does that include rats?" Sacatchy said.

"Of course," Amber said.

"How about insects?" I asked.

"We don't even eat honey," she said. "It's exploitative. If everyone was vegan, our aggressive impulses would eventually become extinct and we'd enter a new
era of—"

"Hitler was a vegetarian, wasn't he?" I asked.

"A *vegetarian*." She sniffed. "Not vegan. And he wasn't even a *real* vegetarian."

"What about societies where hunting has been part of their culture for centuries?" Sacatchy said. "You'd just steamroll right over that?"

"Of course we'll need to make a giant paradigm shift," Amber said. "But this is a moral imperative."

"And how many vegetables died for your greener-than-thou salad?" I asked.

She sniffed. "Your hostility only proves my point."

"Look at the time," I said. "Lily, I left that book I promised you on my desk—care to walk me back to my room?"

We were on our way back to campus when she brought up the issue I was trying to get away from.

"Dickie, don't you care about the animals?"

"You know I volunteered at the SPCA in high school. I'm still a card-carrying member."

"And I thought you just did that to pad your college apps."

"Look, I like animals, but you've got to admit Amber's a little over the top." I did a pretty good imitation of her saying, "Honey is exploitative."

Lily suppressed a giggle. "She *is* a bit intense."

The next day, Sacatchy made another energetic entrance into our quarters.

"There's a meeting Thursday of Students for the Ethical

Treatment of Animals," he said. "Want to help me put up these fliers?"

I looked at one.

"This says Students for the Ethical Treatment of Insects."

"I know," Sacatchy said. "Don't you just love it?"

The original flier before it was modified by Sacatchy, was a notice of the monthly meeting of Students for the Ethical Treatment of Animals and ARF (Animal Rights on the Farm) that promised new vegan recipes. Sacatchy's flier, printed in the same font and style, offered free samples of "inspired vegan cuisine" from the Students for the Ethical Treatment of Insects.

The gathering took place on folding chairs outside another dorm. Sacatchy and I observed from a small hill just behind the meeting area.

"Until two years ago," the head vegan said, "I ate out of necessity rather than for pleasure. I now realize I was consumed with the subconscious guilt of the murder that preceded my salmon, tenderloin, or Big Mac. Vegan sisters and brothers, we need to spread the message of health and nonviolence."

Amber Greene began reading a manifesto.

"We hold these truths to be self-evident: that all living creatures are created equal and endowed by our creator with certain unalienable rights, and among these are life, liberty, as well as the absolute right not to end up cooked and eaten—"

Audience members shrieked, jumped up, and ran for higher ground, leaping over two folding chairs in the process. General panic ensued for a few seconds as they were consumed by the cognitive dissonance of wanting to love all creatures and simultaneously wanting to stomp the life out of these insects.

"Do I even want to know what kind of bugs they are?" I asked.

"Spiders," Sacatchy said. "Specifically, black widow look-alikes. Got 'em from a friend in the entomology department who owes me a favor."

It wasn't long before a green van showed up from Bug Genocide.

Men in zip suits carrying tanks and spray guns descended on the scene to exorcise the scourge of spiders.

This was just the first of several Sacatchy-sponsored events in which I was increasingly a participant.

At the end of the first quarter, grades were posted near the professors' offices. I was pleased with mine except for the C in math. There was a definite whine in my voice as I explained this injustice to Sacatchy.

"Would you say you deserve a B?" Sacatchy said.

"At least!"

A week or so later, I received my transcribed grades by way of campus mail. I now had a B in math.

Later that evening, after more than a few beers and a bit of medicinal marijuana, I asked Sacatchy about it.

"Let's just say good things happen to good people," he said.

The next quarter I received an unusually high grade in my ethics class. Coincidentally, that was a class I shared with Amber Greene, who claimed she'd received the lowest grade in her educational life. This time I said nothing despite the sensation of sliding down a slippery slope and into a slightly polluted pond.

CHAPTER 7

I thought using the Ayatollah's money to support the Nicaraguan resistance was a neat idea.

—Lieutenant Colonel Oliver North

I SPENT THE SUMMER AFTER MY FRESHMAN year as an intern in my grandfather's San Francisco office, sorting files and answering phones. By July of 1987, those calls increasingly dealt with the Iran-Contra Affair. To refresh your memory, Oliver North and certain members of the CIA hatched a secret plan to sell arms to moderate elements in Iran, which was then engaged in a war with Iraq. The proceeds from these sales were used to fund the Contras in Nicaragua. Naturally they were caught. But even after committing perjury, violating the Boland Amendment, and shredding top-secret documents, Ollie stared down the senators investigating the incident and insisted he acted out of patriotism.

I was alone in the office when a reporter from the *San Francisco Chronicle* called.

"Does the senator agree with his colleague Jesse Helms about Oliver North being a genuine American hero?"

I thought fast. "Senator Lambright cannot call Ollie North a hero, as it appears he violated an act of Congress and was less than truthful in his testimony before Congress."

The next morning, the *Chronicle's* headline read: "Senator Lambright Says North Is No Hero." As I was reading this—with a mix of trepidation and a small nugget of pride—the office phone rang.

"Dickie, you trying out to be my new press spokesman?"

"Really, really sorry, Senator," I said.

"Not to worry. Even though it is almost three years until the election, it's time to start replenishing the campaign coffer."

I'd already observed that almost every staff discussion—at least, the ones I'd been in on—involved the subject of fund-raising.

I skimmed the rest of the article. "There's a charge of nepotism here at the end," I said. "Guess that means me."

"You're not getting paid enough to make nepotism sound that sinister."

The next day Lily called from New Mexico, where she was prospecting for old bones at an archaeological dig.

"Dickie, you have a knack for publicity."

"But not good publicity."

"There's no such thing as bad publicity, or so they tell me," she said. "I see Senator Youngblood in your future."

Later that summer I picked up the phone and gave the prescribed greeting.

"Good afternoon, this is the San Francisco office of Senator Stapleton Lambright. I'm Richard Youngblood. How may I be of service?"

"This is the international operator. We have a call from the foreign minister of Nicaragua. Please stay on the line."

I didn't have time to respond before I was put on hold.

"*Buenos dias,*" I heard after a moment. "Is this the *oficina* of Senator Lambright?"

"This is his San Francisco home office," I said.

"Does the senator dislike democracy?"

"No," I said in my most neutral voice. "The senator is an elected official."

"Then why does not he talk loud against the Contras? We, the Sandinistas, we're elected!"

I really hoped an international incident wasn't in the offing.

"Even though the senator did not vote for the Boland Amendment," I said, "he does not support breaking laws."

"So he would be OK with sending money to the Contras if the Boland Amendment didn't pass? He is OK with using blood money from Iran to help the Contras?"

"Sir, I suggest you contact the senator directly at his Washington office," I said. "I'm sure he'd be most pleased to give you his views on the situation."

"Please inform the senator that I am holding a press conference tomorrow in Managua to name the Americans who do not support democracy in Nicaragua."

Uh-oh.

"Mr. Minister, I urge you not to do that until you've talked with Senator Lambright directly—"

"Time is of the essence!" Then I heard a chuckle. "Gotcha, Dickie."

"Pops!" I let out a long sigh. "You had me going for a minute."

"Very political of you, Dickie. So you're a Republican now?"

"Not really. Are you in Nicaragua?"

"Somewhere in Central America."

"When are you going to drop by? My roommate's dying to meet you."

"I'd like him?"

"He's a radical technocrat with a perverse sense of humor."

"Sounds like my kind of guy," Tri-Y said.

CHAPTER 8

The people have spoken, the bastards.

—Political trickster Dick Tuck

ONE WEEK INTO MY SOPHOMORE YEAR, Lily and I were in my room discussing matriarchy in primitive societies when Sacatchy barged in.

"Hey, you guys aren't pro-life, are you?"

"I definitely support life over its alternative," I said.

"You know what I mean, smart-ass."

"I'm not fond of abortion—"

"Is anyone *fond* of abortion?" Lily said.

"I assume you're asking if the woman or the government should decide?" I shrugged. "I vote for the woman."

"There's no way in hell I'd let some feeble old white guy make that decision for me," Lily said.

"I'm so glad to hear you say that," Sacatchy said.

Several days later, regular attendees of a pro-life group were puzzled to find themselves at a meeting to "support life and oppose capital punishment."

As the year progressed, we added Sheils to our inner circle—Sheila Tomko, tall and a bit gangly with frizzy blond hair and a criminal mind to rival Sacatchy's. She also had a unique sexiness, which I explored further over coffee.

"So, Sheils, why'd you come to Stanford?'

"Maybe I came to meet you."

I rolled my eyes. "Sure."

"OK, my parents and grandfather are alumni and my SAT score was awesome for an underachiever. Plus I think the Farm needs someone like me to loosen the place up."

"Any interest in loosening me up?"

"A cheesy question, but I'll think about it." She glanced up and then back at me. "I should go to class for a change. See you soon." Then she was off—but not before giving my shoulders a quick massage and a kiss on the ear.

Sheils and I found a way to sneak up to the top of Hoover Tower at dusk to watch the sunset. The Hoover Tower was normally locked, so we had the place to ourselves. It was a spectacular sunset, followed by a more-than-spectacular amorous tribute to it.

For the next few months we were in a passionate-political union. Sheils played my heartstrings like a violin, my previous liaisons at best well-strummed banjos in comparison. But I soon began to sense it was only a fling for Sheils. My first clue was that she talked incessantly during sex.

"Do you think the real Nixon ever had this much fun making love?"

"He probably did it with his tie on."

"You're not serious?"

"He had a bowling alley installed in the White House. He used to go bowling alone while wearing a tie."

Which is better: laughter or sex? I suppose it depends on the intensity of each, but I soon found out it was difficult to pursue both at the same time without losing some enthusiasm for one or the other.

During our sophomore year, Sacatchy, Lily, myself, and sometimes Sheils became pranksters of increasing infamy. We mostly targeted conservative causes whose hypocrisies we thought needed to be exposed.

One fine spring day, Sacatchy, Lily and I were out on one of Stanford's large lawns throwing the Frisbee when a student who looked like a young Michael Dukakis approached us.

"So y'all are the famous trio?"

"I hope we're not that famous," Sacatchy said.

"I heard about y'all," he said. "I'm from the Beth Zablonsky campaign. We were hoping you could help us out." Beth Zablonsky, a candidate for student-body president, had a commanding presence reminiscent of Barbara Jordan. She stood for Stanford's complete divestment from any company doing business with the apartheid regime of South Africa and wanted more student control over curriculum.

"And we want to do this because?" Lily said.

"Because we're dead meat unless we get some new ideas," he said. "We need literature, slogans, anything you guys can come up with—anything lawful, that is."

"What's your name?"

"Mike Due."

"Really?"

"My great-grandfather picked it out at Ellis Island when he saw a sign that said 'payment due here.'"

Initially we limited our creative energies to developing slogans such as, "Zablonsky: A Fresh Voice on the Farm" and "Stanford Students, Not Stanford Serfs." We also wrote and distributed brochures. It wasn't long before the novelty wore off and these responsible activities chafed at our seditious nature. But it was Robert J. Banks who ultimately forced our hands.

Everything about Rob screamed hypocrisy, from his name to his WASPish demeanor. Even Lily, who relished her role as the group's moral compass, agreed that stronger measures were called for.

"How about I attend some of Rob's meetings?" she asked.

"I like it, but what about our moral compass?" Sacatchy said.

"I'm starting to sense that might be a lost cause."

We were soon the proud possessors of an audio recording from one of Rob's meetings, in which he wondered aloud if the Gay and Lesbian Alliance at Stanford (GLAS) "would ever be completely successful in achieving equal rights because, unlike women and minorities, their status involves aberrant behavior." In the same discussion, he said, "the status of women won't advance much further at Stanford" because of their "special role in society."

"Lily, didn't they ask who you were when you walked into a Banks meeting?" I asked.

"I told them I was the president of the newly formed campus organization Jews for Jesus and Banks."

"And they bought that?"

"They're not the sharpest knives in Stanford's kitchen drawer," she said, "maybe because most of them were men."

Rob's most vitriolic statements, however, were directed toward the animal rights groups. Because Sacatchy was partially in harmony with Rob on that one, some persuasion was in order. We finally convinced Sacatchy on the grounds that more issues meant more targets for creative mischief.

For inspiration we researched the great political dirty tricks of our nation's past. Along the way we stumbled on Dick Tuck, who'd infiltrated Nixon's 1950 campaign for senator.

"So who wants to be a double agent?" Sacatchy said.

"Isn't Lily already doing that?"

"We need to get into his inner circle," Sacatchy said. "It's got to be a guy."

"I can do it," Mike Due said.

When accused of being sexist and supporting cruelty toward animals, Rob responded with, "I love women and animals." Later, in a small gathering of his ardent male supporters, he qualified the statement: "I love women in bikinis and animals sautéed." Michael Due brought us a recording, which we sent to several organizations around campus.

A poll taken by the student newspaper ten days before the election indicated that the Zablonsky slate trailed Banks by seven points.

"We're in trouble," I said.

"Nah, it just means they haven't heard of us yet," Sacatchy said. "We're going to fix that."

"Fellow tricksters," Sacatchy said at one of our late-night gatherings over pizza, "are you ready to launch the final volley in this battle?"

"Depends," I said. "How many rules will the final volley break?"

"It's no fun unless you break a few senseless rules."

"I think I need to grab that moral compass again," Lily said.

"You haven't even heard the details yet," Sacatchy said.

The details were as follows: at lunchtime on the Friday before the student-body election, there'd be tables set up all over White Plaza, representing groups as diverse as the Women's Community Center and Sigma Chi. There would also be tables for Beth Zablonsky and Rob Banks.

We were forced to expand our nefarious committee—some were zealots, some were just there for laughs. We were tasked with procuring various animals (selected personally by Sacatchy for humor or controversy). My partner, Hayden Hasper, and I were assigned turkeys.

"So, Hayden," I asked, "where we going to get some turkeys?"

"Hills," he said, "there's plenty in the hills. They can walk fast and fly a little, but we shouldn't have a problem getting them in the truck."

The day before the big event, we motored out to the hills of western Santa Clara County. After capturing eight ugly birds, we returned to the Stanford campus, arriving at the parking lot closest to White Plaza at noon on the dot.

We'd decided on the drive back that trying to herd turkeys would be like herding cats, so we threw some grain at their feet and ran ahead, laying a trail to the plaza.

"What are you doing?" a Stanford cop asked us.

"An experiment for our psychology/biology seminar," I said.

"And where'll the birds go after your experiment?"

"Back to nature," Hayden said.

At that moment he received an urgent call on his walkie-talkie, leaving us (and the turkeys) free to continue on our way.

At White Plaza, we saw that the rest of the team had arrived. There were several piglets (some with signs that said "Carnitas for Roberto"), jackrabbits, a donkey (with a sign that said "Democrats for Banks"), and at least fifty gerbils surreptitiously liberated from the Stanford science labs.

Between the surprise guests and the several hundred students milling around, it was pandemonium. As Lily held down the Zablonsky table with rehearsed obliviousness, the animals began to congregate around Rob's table.

At this point I observed Michael Due in conversation with Rob. To my surprise, they laughed and shook hands.

Rob and his supporters tried to shoo the animals away while a photographer from *The Stanford Daily* recorded the event. As more students gathered, five women in bikinis and ski masks began sauntering past the area with sashes that said "Rob's Girls" or "Rob's Ideal Woman." One parading girl's only complement to her ski mask was a monokini. As she paraded by, another girl shook her head.

"Where does she think she is, Berkeley?"

Having eaten most of the feed on the ground, the turkeys began cleaning up some of the students' unattended lunches. Somehow a few got through the doors of the Tresidder Union building, where they flapped, pooped, and squawked.

We made the front page of *The Stanford Daily,* along with pictures of the melee and the headline "Banks Gets Animal Vote."

"So what happened to all the animals?" Lily asked over coffee afterward.

"The hamsters and gerbils are enjoying the sunshine as they munch on wild acorns on the fringes of the Farm," I said.

"And the rest?"

"Well, the jackrabbits are probably hopping in the hills, munching and procreating. Some of the turkeys might end up as road-kill, but they'll be forever remembered in the annals of turkey martyrdom as being sacrificed for the noblest of causes."

"How'd you like to be sacrificed for the noblest of causes?" Lily said.

"I'd do it in a second," Sheils said, "if you weren't such a hunky sexpot."

"Are we talking about the same Dick?" Lily asked.

The following Tuesday, students turned out to vote. We circulated around campus with maps of polling places and a few Z-slate fliers.

"Do you know where to vote tomorrow?" I asked a huge athletic guy.

"Sure." He took the map. "Sorry I missed the fun on Friday. That Banks guy must be pretty creative."

A cute girl who was probably a freshman was passing the other way. I thrust a flier at her.

"Beth Zablonsky and the Zablonsky slate would really appreciate your vote tomorrow."

"Did you guys make the big mess at White Plaza on Friday?"

"I wouldn't exactly call it a mess—"

"And what happened to all those animals?"

I'm not sure what I told her, but she took my map.

Two days later, the results were announced: after a record-breaking turnout of student voters, Rob Banks and the Contra Slate had 54 percent of the vote.

The political lesson? Never campaign for your opponent.

Unfortunately, the Stanford Judicial Council didn't see the humor in this event. We're still not sure if Michael Due was a double agent, but someone must have been. Sheils and Lily remained unscathed in the ensuing investigation. Mike probably forgot to mention their roles in a last-minute attempt to curry favor with the fairer sex.

When I was called before the dean and the Judicial Council, I looked to my namesake for inspiration. I didn't have a dog, but I did have a gerbil I'd rescued from the event. Sacatchy and I named it Alan because it bore a vague resemblance to California Senator Alan Cranston.

I carried Alan's cage into the hearing and set it on a side table.

They began questioning me about the "ruckus at White Plaza." I admitted to helping plan the event but maintained that it was all in good fun. Then I picked up the cage.

"One thing I got from the event last Friday was our pet gerbil." I let him out for a quick cuddle. "My roommate and I named him Alan. And I just want to say right now that regardless of what you say, we're keeping it."

Alan ran up my arm and nibbled on my ear. A professor on the committee peered over her bifocals.

"The Checkers Speech," she said. "I could charge you with plagiarism, but I suppose your given name provides you some sort of vague ownership. Nice try, Richard."

So much for the gerbil defense.

"Mr. Youngblood, two of your grades during your freshman year were illegally altered. Were you aware of this?"

"I was aware some grades were higher than I thought they would be."

"Can you tell us if your roommate, Mr. Sacatchy Sun, had anything to do with that?"

Uh-oh. "I don't have the answer to that question."

"Mr. Youngblood," he said, "your cooperation could be very helpful to us."

"I'm sorry," I said. "That's all I have to say."

After being released, I ran back to our abode. Within the hour, Stanford police arrived with the equivalent of a search warrant. In the act of seizing Sacatchy's computer, they discovered a long-forgotten and partially smoked joint of marijuana.

That night Sacatchy and I did what any young men in our situation would—we got drunk and tried to sort out where things had gone wrong. Our best guess was that Mike Due had sold us out.

"We might get kicked out," Sacatchy said, "but we had some laughs. And we forced people to think."

"About what?"

"We got the vegans good."

"What's this *we* shit? All I did was laugh. And I don't have anything against vegans—just fanatics."

"We shed light on the inconsistencies of the pro-life crowd," Sacatchy said.

"There is that."

"And as part of our crusade against Banks, we supported women's rights."

"I'm pretty sure our lofty ideals got lost in the shuffle," I said. "Maybe next time we can do more than just make people think."

"Next time?"

Even though Stanford is famous for keeping students in the "family," in our case the verdict was swift and uncompromising: I was suspended for two quarters and would have to reapply to the Judicial Counsel for readmission. Sacatchy was suspended for one academic year and would have to reapply, too. We were both allowed to finish our classes.

After procrastinating for several days, I finally called Rita Mae.

"Dickie, failure is part of life." I thought I detected a hint of disappointment. "I hope it was a learning experience."

"If nothing else, it was that."

"My business is doing well," she said. "So wherever you want to go to college now, I can help."

"Thanks, Mom." I paused. "But I think it's time I did something on my own."

CHAPTER 9

What is deferred is not avoided.

—Thomas Moore

To my surprise, Sheils agreed to accompany me for at least part of my journey. We packed up our things, including Alan the gerbil, and headed down the fast route of I-5. Sheils chatted about everything from rhinoceroses to Reagan, and her delightful conversation kept me north of depression on the drive.

Nearing her parents' home in the Valley, I asked—not for the first time—if she wanted to accompany me the rest of the way south.

"Dick, even you don't know where you're going."

"I was thinking Mexico." I hadn't been, but the idea had a certain appeal.

She shook her head. "I need to check in with my parental unit."

Their house was a menagerie filled with ferns on steroids, ten birdcages in the living room alone, and a gigantic aquarium crammed with tropical fish (including the semi-official Hawaiian state fish, humuhumunukunukuapua'a). Inside the aquarium, paddling among the guppies, was Sheils's twelve-year- old brother, Seneca.

"He thinks he was meant to be a fish," she said. "It's kind of like people who discover they're the wrong gender."

"Seriously?"

"Is there such huge difference between a yuppie and guppy?"

In addition to the fish, there were a half-dozen or so arrogant cats, three or four bouncy miniature poodles, and a golden Lab who seemed to be in charge.

"Are you sure there's room for Alan in here?"

She laughed. "Are you kidding?"

I shook hands with Sheils's father, a scruffy-looking professor in safari shorts, and accepted her mother's invitation to stay the night. The next morning I hugged Sheila, cuddled Alan, and got back into my Volvo. From there I headed straight south on I-5 and didn't stop until I reached the Mexican border.

For the next two weeks or so I practiced my Spanish. By the time my sojourn was over, I was just two mezcal shots short of fluency.

Unfortunately, I still had no idea what to do with the rest of my life. I knew I wanted to make a difference, maybe as a teacher, but for that I needed a degree. And since I didn't feel like sitting out the next two academic quarters, I'd have to find somewhere other than Stanford—somewhere, preferably, that I could afford without dipping into my mom's or the senator's pockets.

Eventually I turned north and set out once again toward the Southern California sprawl. I found a microscopic apartment not too far from Los Angeles Valley College, where I enrolled for the fall of 1988.

Now I needed a job, and as fortune would have it, the local office of the nearest congressperson was nearby. I marched in and asked if there were any positions available.

"Sure, we love volunteers," the assistant said.

"I'm looking for a paid position," I said. "Preferably something part-time."

"Do you have any experience?"

"Last summer I worked in the home office of Senator Lambright in San Francisco."

"Hmmm. Let's go talk with Renee Luducci, the congressman's chief local assistant in her office, if she's available."

After a powerful handshake from Renee, I filled her in on my summer.

"As the summer progressed I dealt with the press, wrote memos, and occasionally sat in on policy committees. I became intrigued with the process."

"So after working for a Republican senator, why come to work for a Democrat?"

"The senator's my grandfather, but my heart is in the Democratic Party."

She grinned. "Does the senator know you're applying here?"

"I'm not sure he could handle any more unpleasant news on top of my dismissal from Stanford."

"You got kicked out?"

"Suspended for two quarters, officially."

"Why?"

"I was involved in some political pranks to defeat a Republican right-winger during a student-body campaign. They didn't quite work."

"So let me see if I've got this straight, Dickie—you don't mind if I call you that?"

"I answer to just about anything."

"Your main political qualifications," she said as she ticked them off on her fingers, "are that you worked for a Republican, got kicked out of Stanford for interfering in an election, and you're named after the only president ever forced to resign?"

"Sounds about right."

"You're hired."

CHAPTER 10

Poor George, he can't help it. He was born with a silver foot in his mouth.

—Texas Governor Ann Richards

MY PART-TIME POSITION WITH REPRESENTATIVE Silvia Santos consisted mostly of fund-raising and event organizing. Silvia was a third-term congresswoman in a relatively safe district, but no one considered her victory a done deal.

Her opponent was a young attorney named David J. Banks. His brochures said he was a graduate of Stanford and the Gould School of Law at the University of Southern California and that he supported "maintaining a strong defense." And who ever lost an election by advocating more guns and bombs?

Even though I'd never met the man, his photo looked familiar. I called Banks's local campaign office.

"This is the office of David Banks for Congress," came a cheery—also familiar—voice. "My name is Rob. How can I be of assistance?"

Rob Banks—well, that explained why David's photo rang a bell.

"Hi, my name is Tom Ganity," I said. "We're new to the area and I'm interested in your candidate's positions and experience."

"Could I send you a brochure?" Rob asked.

"I have one of your brochures, but I have a few questions."

"I can help you. I'm not only a campaign worker, I'm also the candidate's brother."

"So how old is the candidate?"

"Twenty-nine, but he already has substantial experience in local politics."

"It says here he was student-body president at Stanford University. What does that have to do with the real world?"

"Last spring I was also elected student-body president at Stanford, and I can assure you it was a challenging campaign," he said. "I think it's excellent training for the real world."

"What about this Silvia Santos? She has three terms and I hear she's favored, right?"

"Do you know about Silvia's ... ah ... family?"

"Nope, not a thing."

"She's a single parent who lives with her son and another woman."

"So why is that important?"

He cleared his throat. "It's not exactly the all-American family. You can draw your own conclusions, but my brother and I believe traditional families should be considered sacrosanct."

"Well, I think that answers all my questions," I said. "Thank you very much for your time."

The Banks campaign sent out a mailer with three pictures: one of Silvia Santos hugging a woman, another of her standing in the audience at a Gay Pride parade, and the third showing her son in his soccer uniform as Silvia and another woman looked on with pride. A large caption at the bottom of the page said: "Are these the kind of family values you want from your congressperson? VOTE DAVID BANKS FOR CONGRESS."

The growls of disapproval came mainly from the so-called evangelicals outside Silvia's district. Within her district, there were mostly happy yaps of support.

* * *

After doing some campaigning at Valley Community College, I was encouraged to take my game to UCLA. Even though I wasn't a Bruin, the Young Democrats were more than happy to have me man the midday table a couple times a week and distribute my "Santos for Congress" pamphlets.

I was stationed along the walkway near the Bruin Plaza on one of those perfect Southern California mornings. The fog had dissipated, the sky was blue, and the temperature was an even seventy degrees. Directly across from my table was a station offering "free makeovers" where I spotted the most magnificent creature I'd ever seen.

Her hair was the gold of a California hill in September, and her smile had a better chance of making the world safe for democracy than the rhetoric of Woodrow Wilson. During a slow period, I sauntered across the sidewalk.

"Excuse me," I said, "are these makeovers only for women?"

She looked me up and down.

"The last thing you need is a makeover."

Before I could offer a flirtatious retort, I noticed a small group of students at my table. I smiled and returned to hawking my political wares.

Later, as the midday crowd subsided, she walked over to my table.

"So, Young Democrat, will I see you here again?"

"Only if you give me a makeover," I said.

"Even though you don't need one?"

"Especially if I don't need one."

She smiled and then she disappeared.

Two days later, I was back. The makeover booth was gone, but my golden girl was still there—as the noontime spokesperson for the Young Republicans.

I ambled over.

"So are you a capitalist offering makeovers or a Republican offering George Bush?"

"Why can't I be both?" she said.

"Depends," I said. "How do young Republicans feel about Young Democrats?"

"Are they all as cute as you?"

Glancing toward my table, I saw a mob of potential Democrats clustered around it.

"Duty calls," I said.

I was sitting outside my pre-Starbucks coffee spot when out of the corner of my eye I saw a familiar silhouette: Sacatchy Sun.

"Hey, Dickster, how's it going'?"

We hugged.

"It's great to see you," I said. "What are you doing here?"

"I'm about to enroll in Cal State Northridge. I heard you had coffee here, so I dropped by to say hi."

"*I* barely know I have coffee here," I said. "But it's still great to see you ... I think."

"I hear you're involved in the Santos campaign."

"Against none other than Rob's big brother, Dave," I said. "But our campaign is better-funded, so we're not worried."

"Dickster!" He looked wounded. "Shouldn't character count more than dollars?"

"McCain and Feingold are going to introduce a bill controlling big money and issue-advocacy organizations," I said. "I think we need to go further, but until then, *c'est la vie.*"

"I have a way to affect an election on the cheap." He held up one of Banks's fliers. "How about we make a flier of our own?"

"We?"

"We'll dig up every distasteful remark Banks has ever made and put them all in a mailer. Better still, I've got some new photo-editing software. How about we superimpose his picture out drinking and clubbing with marginally clad women?"

"Sacatchy, this is the new me—with ethics."

"You mean the bland, boring you?"

"So far I've been kicked out of a hundred percent fewer schools."

"What would Tri-Y say?"

I rolled my eyes. "Not exactly a role model for those of us trying to work within the system."

Sacatchy pulled up a chair.

"David Banks recently gave a speech to some conclave of the moral majority in which he said some truly horrible things. Apparently there were no mainstream reporters present." He paused. "You really don't think people ought to know?"

I sighed. "You make a compelling case." I finished my coffee. "Do you think you can find a copy of his speech?"

He smiled. "How do you think I found out about this in the first place?"

The Santos campaign needed sincere deniability, so I breathed not a word of our plan to anyone at the office. The next day I met Sacatchy at our new coffee spot to cherry-pick the most appalling statements from Banks's speech.

We headlined the flier "Can David Banks Represent the People of This Congressional District?" We listed five of the best quotes—or worst, depending on your perspective.

1. "Only Christians understand true American values. As your congressman, I will work to bring back these values to our cherished institutions. It has to start with the family where mothers are in the home teaching those values."

2. "Where are we as a society if a woman's right to choose includes murdering her unborn child? We not only need a constitutional amendment banning abortion, we need to also define it as murder on the part of the mother as well as the person performing the abortion."

3. "Every day, immigrants are charging over our borders to sign up for welfare, enter our overcrowded schools, and clog services in our hospital emergency rooms to give birth

in the United States. As your representative in Congress, I'll make sure to seal our borders, with a shoot-to-kill policy when necessary."

4. "The environmentalists are killing American capitalism with their socialistic agenda. Let's leave the flora and the fauna alone to compete for nature's bounty."

5. "To maintain the absolute sanctity of marriage between one woman and one man, we should institute a tax-significant surcharge to two adults cohabitating without the blessing of marriage."

Sacatchy got the fliers printed at a suspiciously low cost, and we distributed them to businesses and civic organizations. Somehow he actually got Girl Scouts to include them with boxes of cookies, though the Jehovah's Witnesses turned him down.

The following Monday morning, the calls began to come in.

"No," Rondo said, "I don't know anything about an anti-Banks flier."

A few minutes later, Renee answered the phone. "We don't have any knowledge of that," she said. "We're committed to positive campaigning."

The following day, I was surprised to be invited to a major strategizing session with Renee Luducci, Silvia, and campaign manager Joe Vasquez.

"What do we think?" Renee asked. "Act of desperation on Banks's part?"

I struggled to keep a somber face.

"I doubt it," Joe said. "But it's a working theory. Question is, what do we do?"

Silvia turned to me. "Dick, you've worked with Republicans. Any thoughts?"

"How about a one-sentence statement to the press?" I said.

"Something like, 'These fliers seem to be an act of desperation intended to discredit the excellent record of Congresswoman Santos.'"

"Why not make a more pointed comment against Banks?" Silvia asked.

"As much as I'd love to stick it to a bigot like him, I think you need to look like the front-runner who's barely affected by criticism," I said. "You don't want to get in the 'gutter with that guy,' as Eisenhower once said about Joe McCarthy."

Silvia nodded and glanced around the table. "What do any of you think about me coming out at this time?"

"Voters aren't ready," Renee said.

"When *will* they be ready?" Joe asked.

"Doesn't matter," Renee said. "You can't drop a statement like that eight days before the election."

"At this point," Silvia said, "I think we should go with Dick's idea. Dick, why don't you work with Joe on the wording."

She would breeze to reelection with 59 percent of the vote.

A few months later, in a speech at UCLA, Congresswoman Santos solved the problem of her sexual orientation. Tall, resolute, and with her black hair blowing in the Pacific breeze, Silvia's words brought shivers to my soul.

"Over the course of my seven years serving as your congressional representative, some emissaries of intolerance who claim to have a monopoly on morality have cast doubt on my lack of family values. I can assure my constituents that I value my family more than anything in my life. My family consists of my son and my lifelong partner, and I look forward to the day when we can legally marry. I assure you, that day is not that far away. Although some very intelligent people have advised me that admitting to be gay would end my political career, I can assure you my political career is not over, and I've faith the voters will help me continue to fight for their interests and oppose intolerance in any form."

Silvia's coming-out party was noted in most of the national media, but the story didn't have legs. Within her congressional district, the news was met with a big sunny California "ho-hum." The most miasmic comments were from a few evangelical ministers who apparently had long since neglected New Testament warm fuzzies like compassion and "love thy neighbor" in favor of "God is pissed" and "the devil is turning up the gas on the hellfire." As the Reverend Nat Lomberson preached, "Apparently, Congressperson Santos wasn't sufficiently awed by God's wrath against the sinful state of California by the recent Loma Prieta earthquake. I pray for the dwindling flock of God-fearing people in the Golden State when California slips into the ocean."

CHAPTER 11

Education: the path from cocky ignorance to miserable uncertainty.

—Mark Twain

DURING THE FALL OF 1988, I continued my studies at Valley Community College and applied to UCLA. My only misgiving? The question: "Have you ever been the subject of disciplinary action at another college or university?"

The truth, I realized, was my only option. A "yes" was supposed to be followed by a written explanation. I did my best to put a positive spin on things.

About three weeks later, I received a letter from the Admissions Office:

> We regret to inform you that your admission request as
> a transfer student for the spring semester for 1989 has
> been denied, but we welcome you to reapply for the fall
> semester. However, you may appeal this decision if you
> wish to appear before an admissions committee.

Of course I appealed, so two weeks after the election I was invited to a small conference room on the periphery of Bruinland to present my case. I walked into the room wearing a tweed sports coat, tan khakis, and as much confidence as I could muster.

Inside, I stopped short to take a good look at one of the four panelists. Tri-Y's hair and beard were trimmed, but his professorial sport coat was rumpled and I detected a few new lines on his face.

"Mr. Youngblood," a woman said, "I'm Dr. Lacey Sahar, deputy assistant vice chancellor of student affairs. To my left is Dr. Dylan McAdam, the official second assistant officer in the admissions office, and to my right is Dr. Fisher Bailey, assistant to the assistant to the dean of the College of Social Sciences. To his right, representing the history department, is Dr. Yule Yablonsky, temporary assistant lecturer."

I nodded.

"So, Mr. Youngblood," Dr. Sahar said, "please tell us more about why you were asked to leave Stanford University."

"I'd love to tell you I was a victim of circumstances, but that wouldn't be the truth." I did my best to keep my gaze on Dr. Sahar and off Tri-Y. "I was a participant in and helped plan several political dirty tricks during the student government elections. My roommate changed two of my grades, one from a C to a B and one from a B to an A. All I knew was that the grades were higher than I'd expected, but I turned a blind eye and was thus tacitly complicit."

Dr. Yablonsky's baritone voice filled the silence that followed.

"Mr. Youngblood," he said, "can you elaborate on some of these so-called dirty tricks?"

"We secretly recorded our opponent making outlandish statements, then sent those recordings to various groups on campus. To illustrate our opponent's antipathy to animal rights, we unleashed several species of animals at Stanford's main plaza."

Tri-Y swallowed a smile.

"Mr. Youngblood, what did you learn from this experience?" Dr. Bailey asked.

"My maturity level has made a quantum leap," I said. "I've done a lot of soul-searching since then—uncomfortable but important."

"What are your aspirations?" Tri-Y asked.

"Above all, I want to make a difference—preferably in education or government service."

After a few more innocuous questions, Dr. Sahar turned to me.

"Richard, you'll receive a letter within a week informing you of your admission status. You may go. Now, will the members of the committee please remain for a few minutes? It shouldn't take long."

Tri-Y gave me a wink. I decided to linger outside.

In less than ten minutes, he walked out of the building sporting a big smile.

"Hey, Dickie, looks like you're in. Let's do lunch."

"How did you get a job as temporary assistant lecturer in the history department?" I asked as we walked downhill to Westwood Village.

"Emphasis on *temporary*." He seemed to be searching the sky toward the Pacific.

"As temporary as your stint as vice principal of Rio de Mañana?"

"Something like that."

Just as we were leaving campus, an unmarked helicopter hovered at two o'clock and a black sedan cruised slowly by. Inside I spotted two guys in dark suits and glasses. I'd have thought they were FBI if not for the "Nicaragua is for Lovers" bumper sticker.

When I looked back, Tri-Y was gone.

A week later, I was admitted to UCLA with probationary status for the spring semester beginning in January of 1989. During the next year, which I spent specializing in history, I could never find anyone who remembered a temporary assistant lecturer named Yablonsky.

CHAPTER 12

Stalking is such a strong word. I prefer intense research of an individual.

——anonymous

My favorite class during my first semester at UCLA was American History From Ike to the Gipper.

"I understand we have someone actually named after Richard Nixon in the class," the professor said after delivering his analysis of the Watergate affair. "Mr. Youngblood, where are you?"

"Over here, Dr. Bensky." I threw up a quick double-victory sign.

As I left the classroom, a short but cute brunette followed me out.

"Hi, Dick," she said. "Has anyone ever told you you've got a Nixon nose?'

"My nose is infamous," I said. "What's your name?"

"Amanda Patricia Nixon," she said. "Call me Pat. We should get together sometime."

We went for coffee.

"Where do you live?" I asked.

"Apartment off campus with a bunch of roommates. How about you?"

"Studio on the far side of Westwood."

"By yourself?" she said. "Don't you get lonely?"

"Not so far. Why, you want to help me out with that?"

"What if I come by tonight with food and drinks?"

She came by with Chinese takeout, two bottles of wine, and music. Halfway through the second bottle of wine, she started massaging my thigh. Halfway through the second playing of *She Drives Me Crazy*, we were in bed.

Amada Patricia was nothing if not enthusiastic. In my limited sexual history expressions of ecstasy involved loud sounds, from *mm mm, yesssss* to *ommmigod!* Amanda Patricia's vocalizations were much more specific.

"God, yes, Nixon, *more!* Ohhh, Nixon—*yes!*"

Nor did she stop when it was over.

"You really are Tricky Dick," she said, which made me wince. "Just think, you and me, Dick and Pat, eternal bliss."

"Um ... what?"

"It's meant to be," she said. "Just like Richard and Pat Nixon."

Apparently I'd missed something. "What is?"

"Us, silly. Fate brought us together."

"I thought it was wine and hormones."

"Our connection is so much deeper. Can't you feel it?"

"Amanda, we had a nice evening. Let's not get carried away."

"We don't have to force it." She gave me a big weird smile. "It's fate."

When she left in the morning, I said, "See you around."

"How about tonight?" she said.

"Can't. I've got a lot of studying."

"OK," she said and then attached herself to my neck and stuck her tongue down my throat.

The next day in class, Amanda Patricia sat next to me. As Professor Bensky finished his analysis of Watergate, her hand started creeping up my thigh. Even though I found this titillating, I took the high road and moved her hand. Within a minute it was back, but this time I removed it with a frown. It wasn't so much about propriety as taking a stand against weirdness. The minute that class was over, I sprinted out and didn't slow down until I was safely hidden in the social sciences section of the library.

After browsing through an evaluation of the successes and failures of the Carter administration, I began searching the stacks for works by or about Jimmy. As I pulled out a copy of *Why Not the Best*, I peered through the gap.

Two wide eyes and a weird smile peered back.

I ran up two floors to the back of the physics section.

As soon as I took my seat in Dr. Bensky's class the next day, there she was. I ran out as soon as class was over and jogged all the way to a coffee shop in Westwood, where I pondered my problem over a bagel and a cappuccino.

The following day as I headed to the bookstore adjacent to Bruin Plaza, I thought I saw a pair of eyes peek out at me from a nearby hedge. I sped up, and by the time I reached the bookstore and shoved my bag into one of the cubicles near the entrance, I'd convinced myself the eyes were just a product of my overactive imagination.

When I went to grab my bag on the way out, I could have sworn it wasn't in the same cubicle I'd put it in. I didn't think much of it until later that evening when I was reading my textbook for American history. There, taped over a picture of Richard and Pat Nixon, were the faces of Amanda and me.

The next afternoon as I entered my building, the superintendent waved me down.

"Mr. Youngblood, your girlfriend was here today."

"Sorry, Abraham, don't have a girlfriend."

He looked confused. "You better tell her that. She said it was your birthday and wanted to surprise you. Cute girl. Short brown hair, big eyes. Looks like a cross between Meg Ryan and a young Pat Nixon."

A feeling of dread crept over me.

"You let her in?"

"I hope that's OK."

"Me, too," I said.

In the elevator, on an advertisement for a nearby Mexican restaurant, the face of a comely senorita had been replaced with the face of Amanda Patricia Nixon. I was torn between worry and perplexity. Long before Facebook stalking, this was the time when real stalking entered the common lexicon. I realized it would be impossible for Glenn Close to surge out of the bathtub with a giant knife as she did in *Fatal Attraction*, mainly because I didn't have a bathtub. I did, however, have a shower, and I suffered with a brief image of Janet Leigh's classic black blood dribbling down the gray drain.

I cracked open the door to my apartment. Everything seemed to be in order.

I breathed a sigh of relief and decided I was hungry. I grabbed a half-empty box of leftover pizza, shoved it into the microwave without looking, set it for sixty seconds, and walked to the refrigerator.

Thirty seconds later, the microwave started spitting mini lightning bolts, and then it began to wheeze.

I opened it and yanked out the box, and there underneath the pizza was a stainless steel spoon still glowing with the smiling face of Richard M. Nixon. I still ate the pizza.

Later that night, as I reached to turn off the light on my nightstand, I noticed that the drawer was slightly ajar. Like many an optimistic young student, I kept a packet of condoms there—but on opening the drawer, I saw that it was empty. On the box was a Post-it Note: tiny stick-figure drawings of a two-parent two-kid family over the tiny printed words "We won't need these, Dickie."

A quick investigation of the wastebasket revealed the four condoms blown up like balloons. By the time I spotted them, probably because of their advanced age, they'd lost most of their air and now looked more like defeated marbles. On top of them was a vintage bumper sticker: "President Nixon: Now more than ever."

Apparently, hiding out in the library and coffee shops wasn't going to cut it. The next day as we walked out of class, I steered Amanda Patricia toward a bench in a nearby shaded garden. We sat down side by side.

"Amanda, I'm so sorry I led you to believe there was anything between us besides a fun evening," I said. "I can't see you again."

"What do you mean?"

"You have to leave me alone. This Dick-and-Pat thing is cute, but I prefer to live in the real world. I'm not Richard Nixon and you're not Pat Nixon, and—"

"Yes, you are. You have his nose and I have her chin."

I closed my eyes for a minute.

"Amanda, the Nixons are still alive," I said when I opened them.

"We're their new incarnations. They'll never die."

I'd figured I was opening a can of crazy. I hadn't counted on opening a whole barrel.

"Amanda … have you ever talked with anyone else about this?"

This got me a wide, disconnected smile.

"You haven't accepted it yet, Dickie, but you will—you have no choice."

"I've got a choice about everything, except maybe dying."

"And when we die we'll be together for eternity."

I watched the windows break and the flames grow higher in Amanda Patricia's house of reality. Still, I readied the fire hose of sanity and did my best.

"Amanda, you need help. I can't be your boyfriend, husband, significant other, or friend—not now, not ever."

"Now *more* than ever."

I stood up.

"I'm leaving now. I hope I've made myself clear. If you ever break into my apartment again, I'm calling the police."

"You'll be very, very sorry, Dickie."

I walked away. For almost a month after that, I didn't lay eyes on Amanda Patricia. Life was good—sort of.

CHAPTER 13

Love is what happens to a man and woman who don't know
each other.

—W. Somerset Maugham

DURING THIS TIME, I AGAIN RAN into the tantalizing Young
Republican from the makeover booth.

"Hi, Democrat!" she said.

Her hair sparkled in the sun as she walked by the Shapiro
Fountain on the UCLA campus.

"You still a Republican?"

"Yes, and I'm pretty sure we won the presidency."

I stuck out my hand. "So what's your name?"

"Amanda Kristina."

"I'm Dick."

She paused. "And what's the rest of your name?"

"Well, if you want the long version, it's Richard Milhous Nixon
Youngblood."

"You're kidding."

"Afraid not."

"No wonder you became a Democrat."

"My grandfather is a rather prominent Republican."

Her eyes flickered as she processed the facts and reached a
conclusion. "Your grandfather is Senator Lambright?"

"Yep."

"And isn't your father some sort of enigmatic radical?"

I grinned. "You're pretty well-informed for a Republican."

"So I'm in the presence of celebrity."

"Will you have coffee with a celebrity?" I asked.

She gave me a glorious, sexy smile. "Love to, Richard."

From that day forward, Amanda Kristina never called or referred to me by any name other than Richard, God bless her.

Two weeks and several coffee dates later, I was holding a meeting of the Young Democrats in a small classroom on the edge of campus when Amanda Kristina walked in, wearing tasteful heels and a dress that showed off her delightful curves.

I paused my condemnation of the so-called Moral Majority in midsentence.

"I'd like to introduce an officer of the campus Young Republicans, Amanda Kristina," I said. "Are you here because you've finally seen the light?"

"I'm just looking for a bleeding-heart liberal." Three guys raised their hands. She rewarded them all with a dazzling smile and then turned to me. "If you don't mind, I'll just stay until the end of the meeting—unless you think I'm here to spy."

I decided to wrap up my speech with a bumper sticker saying:

"The Moral Majority is neither moral nor a majority." I glanced at Amanda Kristina. "Meeting adjourned."

The twenty or so Young Democrats filed out, leaving me alone with Amanda.

"So am I your bleeding heart?" I said.

"How do you feel about going on a real date?"

"As long as you don't spend the evening trying to tell me how the Moral Majority is saving the nation."

She practically purred. "I doubt we'll have much time to talk politics."

* * *

On Friday night we arrived at the park above the Santa Monica Pier just as the sun set. We ogled the view and kissed with an intensity that rivaled the orange glare on the western horizon. We then sampled the cuisine at a nearby Asian fusion restaurant, along with a bottle of pinot grigio—purchased by Amanda Kristina. As we ate, our eyes locked and our free hands entwined beneath the table.

"So what do you want to do with your life?" I asked

"I hope to be an attorney," she said. "How about you?"

"Maybe teaching or politics. Wherever I can do the most good."

"So you don't care about making money?"

"Only so I could take you to places like this."

"Richard, I've thought of a night like this since the third time I saw you."

"Why not the first time?"

She laughed. "The first time, I thought you were just some gorgeous guy who happened by to harass me."

"And the second time?"

"I thought you were just a gorgeous guy I'd like to seduce," she said. "If I were a loose woman, that is."

"So you're not a loose woman?"

She lifted her glass. "Maybe if wined and dined properly."

As we walked out of the restaurant toward my Volvo, she said, "Would you like me to drive?"

In short order we were parked in front of my apartment.

"This must not be goodnight, unless you planned on driving my car home," I said.

"I hope not."

Because my building's minuscule five stories featured one of slowest elevators in La La Land, the ride up gave us ample opportunity to explore each other's mouths as our bodies quivered in expectation. By the time we were inside my studio, snaps were unsnapped and belts unbuckled.

More study dates, coffee dates, and bedroom dates followed.

Our conversations covered everything from history to Hollywood, but every time we neared the subject of politics, one of us always steered the conversation out of those troubled waters.

Several days later, in American History, I felt a prickling at the back of my neck. I glanced over my shoulder, and there in the back row sat Amanda Patricia.

After class I ran past her and down the hall and darted into a stall in the men's room. I was still in there five minutes later, waiting till I was sure the coast would be clear, when I heard someone enter the stall next to mine.

"Hi, Dick. I knew you are in here."

I bolted from the restroom and ran all the way to the center of Westwood.

Early the next morning, I went straight to the UCLA counseling center and asked to see one of the psychologists. A half-hour later I was ushered into the office of Dr. Margaret Klosky. She was about forty, tall, and had a definite glint in her eyes.

"So how can I help you?"

"I'm concerned about one of my fellow students."

"Let me guess. A female student?"

"Very perceptive."

"Is she a girlfriend, ex-girlfriend, lab partner, or what?"

"None of the above, though she might say otherwise."

"So why are you here?'

"She's mentally unstable."

Dr. Klosky sighed.

"That could include a significant swatch of the population of Southern California. Could you be a bit more specific?"

"How about pathologically obsessive?"

"One psych class and you just toss the terms around?"

"You asked for it."

"And I take it you're the object of her obsession."

I nodded.

She didn't look particularly impressed.

"So tell me about this young woman's behavior."

"You're going to have a hard time believing it."

"I've heard everything."

I took a deep breath. "I was named after Richard Nixon and her name is Amanda Patricia Nixon and she thinks we're the modern incarnation of the real Nixons and that we're destined to be together for eternity."

She blinked. "Aren't the real Nixons still alive?"

"I know." I fleshed out the details of our brief but deeply weird relationship. "I think she could benefit from your wise counsel."

"Before I use up my daily quota of wise counsel on you, let me see if we can even contact her."

She left the office and returned about ten minutes later.

"Dick," she said, "we have five Nixons currently enrolled and they're all males."

"But she's a student in my history class."

"I assure you she's not. So either she's sneaking into classes—it happens more than you'd think—or the name she gave you isn't her real one." She paused. "Or both. You sure know how to pick them, don't you?"

CHAPTER 14

Paranoid? Probably. But just because you're paranoid doesn't mean there isn't an invisible demon about to eat your face.

—Jim Butcher in *Storm Front*

OVER THE NEXT FEW DAYS, I SEARCHED Los Angeles County records, the phone book, and what passed for the Internet in 1989. I couldn't find anything on Amanda Patricia Nixon, so I phoned an expert.

"Sacatchy, I need your unparalleled expertise."

"Love the way you say that."

"I'm trying to find a girl—"

"Who isn't?"

"Except this one's certifiably nuts and she's making my life miserable."

"What's her name?"

"She said it's Amanda Patricia Nixon, but that may be bogus." I filled him in. "This is serious, Sacatchy—if Amanda Kristina finds out about crazy Amanda Patricia, I'm thinking the fire of our new romance goes ice cold."

"So you're hot for the new Amanda and the old Amanda is hot for you?"

"In a nutshell."

"OK," he said. "I'll see what I can dig up on the mysterious Miss Nixon."

"Thanks, Sacatchy."

"You want to go to a hip-hop concert Saturday night? Me and Roc Cindy have an extra ticket. I could probably rustle up one more if you wanted to bring Amanda Kristina."

"I hope you take this in the best way possible, but I don't think she's quite ready to meet you."

"I'm sensing that 'she's not ready' is code for you're not ready."

"Pretty much. Who's Roc-Cindy?"

"New girlfriend. She's an art and design major at USC. She's really cool, at least I think so. So, you coming to the concert?"

"Do I have a choice?" I asked.

"Not really."

In truth, I didn't mind—I was newly fascinated by the raw poetry of rap. And I found Roc-Cindy delightful—she was big, charismatic, and beautiful.

"Big Daddy Dick!" She gave me a hug. "Good to see Sacatchy's numero uno homey in the flesh. Those stories from Stanford, they just Sacatchy hyperbole or the real deal?"

"As Sacatchy once told me, who needs the truth if it's boring?"

Over pre-concert snacks and drinks, I asked him if he'd made any progress on our research project.

"My search for Amanda Patricia Nixon led me to an eighty-one-year-old former stripper in Trenton, New Jersey, and a forty-four-year-old minister's wife in rural Iowa."

"And your search ended there?"

"You're kidding, right?"

I glanced at Roc Cindy. "How do you put up with this egomaniac?"

"My sharp tongue can puncture even his bloated ego," she said.

Sacatchy folded his arms. "Lucky for Dick, my ego's reputation is well-deserved. She did give you the right name. There is an Amanda Patricia Nixon who graduated from Whittier High

School in 1984, which as you probably know is the alma mater of Richard Nixon."

"She's the right age."

"If it's her, she's got a pretty dicey academic record—suspended from high school at least four times, enrolled at Cal State Fullerton but asked to leave after her first semester."

"For what?" I asked.

"Threatening a professor with dismemberment. For the next year she worked at Disneyland."

"Seriously?"

"Yep—wore a Mickey Mouse suit, greeted kids at the entrance, photo ops, that kind of thing. She was fired when she told a six-year-old boy Goofy would strangle him if he didn't shut the fuck up."

"Sounds like my girl at her barmy best."

"Her official dismissal cited 'profoundly unhappy behavior that undermined the spirit of the Happiest Place on Earth, therefore causing Walt Disney's erratic rotation in his grave to temporarily shut down Tomorrowland.'"

"I'm guessing the last part is your own addition."

"I speak nothing but the truth."

"And her next career move?"

"She worked for B-1 Bob—briefly."

"Who's B-1 Bob?" Roc-Cindy asked.

"Bob Dorman, a conservative U.S. congressman from Orange County," I said. "He loves B-1 bombers, but that's the least colorful part of the story."

"Give me the highlights," Roc-Cindy said.

"He was an Air Force pilot who crashed at least two planes. He also got into a scuffle on the floor of the House of Representatives after calling a fellow congressman a "draft-dodging wimp." And he once referred to the "screaming transvestites and lesbian spearchuckers who were hoping for his defeat."

"Now, are you the one embellishing?" Roc-Cindy said.

"How do you know all this?" Sacatchy asked.

"I'm a history major. So what's B-1 got to do with Amanda?"

"She worked in his local office. Apparently, when journalists called to straighten out the inconsistencies in Dornan's military background, she called them pinkos and Communist sympathizers. I lost her for a while after that, until she enrolled in four classes at Valley Community College last September, including two classes with you. She got two Cs and two Fs."

"You mean she was following me around even before UCLA?" I shuddered. "What about her family?"

"Her father died of a self-inflicted gunshot wound when she was eight. August 8, 1974. That date swirl the dust in the library of your history brain?"

"The day of Nixon's resignation speech." I sighed. "And her mother?"

"In Oxnard for the past ten years, a resident of Cloud Nine Gardens."

"What goes on there?" I asked.

"A locked mental illness facility."

I stared at the garish Caribbean prints on the wall behind Roc-Cindy and tried to visualize a middle-aged progenitor nuttier than Amanda Patricia.

"So if you didn't detect any recent employment, what does she live on?" I asked.

"Apparently she's a minor-league 'trust-fundian' courtesy of her grandparents, who died in a small aircraft that crashed into the Salton Sea."

"She lives *where?*"

"Last September she signed a six-month lease on an apartment in West Hollywood, but the building recently burned down. No idea where she's keeping herself these days."

Roc-Cindy checked her watch. "I hate to interrupt such a fascinating story, but we better hit the bricks."

After the concert, I bade farewell to Sacatchy and Roc-Cindy with *ba-boom, ba-boom, ba-boom* still reverberating through every cell of my body. I fell asleep the minute my head hit the pillow, but I woke two hours later in a cold sweat from a nightmare in which a gang of white rappers with Amanda Patricia's face were chasing me down a dark alley that dead-ended in a brick wall.

CHAPTER 15

I'm not afraid of dying; I just don't want to be there when it happens.

—Woody Allen

TOWARD THE END OF THE SPRING semester of 1989, I received a letter from the Richard Nixon Library and Birthplace Foundation inviting me to attend a "meeting of interested and informed citizens to discuss final plans for the Richard Nixon Library being constructed in Yorba Linda, California." I suspected my grandfather had a hand in this invitation and was sufficiently intrigued to head southeast to Yorba Linda in my Volvo on the evening in question.

I arrived just as the sun dipped below the Southern California smog. I parked parallel to the construction site and walked toward a small house that I assumed was the birthplace of Richard Nixon. The newly laid foundation was surrounded by bright yellow keep-out tape, and I was the only person here, or so I thought.

"Hi, Dickie."

I turned to see Amanda Patricia Nixon in all her demented glory.

I closed my eyes, but when I opened them she was still standing there. Her demented glory was even enhanced.

"It's meant to be," she said. "You and me, together forever."

"Amanda, you need help—"

She pulled out a pistol—what I assumed, with my limited knowledge, was what gun-control advocates call a Saturday-night special.

"Why are you pointing that at me?" I kept my voice as even as possible—no easy matter when you know you may be speaking your last words.

"I love you so much." Her aim drifted from my torso to various limbs. "Soon we'll start our journey through eternity."

"Amanda." I kept my hands up and resisted the urge to wipe the sweat off my brow. "Put the gun down and we'll go have coffee, talk things over—"

"Shut up and move over to the foundation."

I ducked under the tape and backed up to where construction crews had apparently just laid a new section of the foundation for the Richard Nixon Library.

"We'll be part of history." She sighed. "I thought you'd like that."

I stopped about five feet from the wet concrete behind me.

"Keep going."

"No!" I raised my palms in a "stop" motion and, in my best Diana Ross, began to sing: "Stop! In the name of love."

I thought I saw flicker of a smile.

"Very cute, Dickie, but keep moving or I *will* shoot."

"You know I'm a Democrat, right? My mom is a New Age yoga instructor—my dad's a radical hippie icon, for God's sake!"

"But you're named after one of the greatest Americans of all time."

"I guess it's more entertaining than being named after Eisenhower—usually, anyway."

She lowered her gun a bit. I actually considered making a run for it, but if she pulled the trigger at that angle, my DNA would never dive into the American gene pool. My whole body began to shake.

"How could anyone named after a man like Nixon act like he doesn't give a shit?"

"Maybe because he was the only president to ever resign?"

"Everyone knows he was hounded out of office by the radical liberals." She raised the pistol to my chest and then lowered it back to groin level. "Back up."

"Stop, in the—"

Bang! She raised the gun and fired four shots into the air. I slowly backed up against the wet foundation.

"Amanda, you don't want to do this."

"Don't think I'm not serious."

With her double-negative warning, she fired double shots down in front of me. One ricocheted off something hard and struck my inner thigh.

I screamed and fell into the wet concrete, except it wasn't all that wet. I sank about an inch and lay as still as I could while in excruciating pain.

Amanda stood on the edge of the foundation and put the gun to her temple. I heard a click, and then she threw the pistol aside and fell back into the wet concrete next to me.

I struggled to get up. Amanda lay on her back, seemingly in a state of nutty nirvana, as she stared up at what passed for stars in the Southern California sky. I struggled to my knees and crawled out of the concrete. I heard footsteps and moments later found myself blinded by a flashlight.

"What the hell's going on here?"

I squinted past the glare—a security guard.

"She tried to kill me," I said.

As it happened, the security guards had just returned from a lengthy coffee break—which Amanda Patricia (with the assistance of Ben Franklin) had encouraged them to take.

One of the guards was trying to coax Amanda out of her concrete bed when I heard sirens. I was soon whisked off by ambulance, but not before the press managed to snap a photo of me, half-caked in concrete with blood dripping down my leg while the dreamy-eyed Amanda was strapped to a gurney behind me.

* * *

I was dozing peacefully after my surgery when a young man walked into my room.

"Are you Richard Youngblood?"

I gave a slower-than-usual nod, thanks to the delightful narcotics I'd been given. "Who are you?"

"I'm Detective Diaz. Can you tell me what happened at the site of the Richard Nixon Library?"

"You're not going to believe it."

"Try me."

I took a deep breath.

"Amanda Nixon thinks that she and I are the next incarnations of Richard and Pat Nixon and that if she killed me and then herself we could spend eternity together under the foundation of the Richard Nixon Library."

He stared at me. "What say we take this from the top?" I provided him with a moderately detailed account of my relationship with Amanda Nixon. Detective Diaz shook his head as he took notes.

"Assuming your version of this event is mostly correct," he said when I was finished, "she might not be sane enough to stand trial."

"I've got a feeling she'll rise to the peak of mental health after she's arrested. By the way, I don't suppose there's any chance of keeping this out of the news?"

"Too late." He produced a copy of *The Orange County Register*. The headline read: "Senator's Grandson Shot as He and Girlfriend Fail to Cement Relationship."

Two days later, *The Orange County Register* and the *Los Angeles Times* ran my account of events. The follow-up in the *Register* said Amanda Patricia Nixon was being charged with attempted murder.

The following morning I was deluged with visitors.

"Richard, what in the world happened?" Amanda Kristina said

as she swept into my room. "Did some deranged woman really shoot you?"

This was a moment I'd been dreading. "She did."

She stood up taller and crossed her arms. "And how did you know this ... person?"

I told her the truth—that my one-night fling with Amanda Patricia predated Amanda Kristina by at least a month. That she'd stalked me before she shot me.

"And you didn't tell me because?"

"I had no idea she'd take it so far," I said. "And I didn't want you to think I make a habit of associating with deranged women."

She smiled and came over to my bed and kissed me passionately. I wondered if there was any chance of locking a hospital door from the inside. She lightly touched my knee and massaged my lower thigh.

"When do I get to see your scar?" She winced. "I trust the shot missed ... my second-favorite part of your body?"

"An inch higher and there would be no heirs to my throne."

Her next kiss gave me an erotic charge so strong it temporarily overrode the dulling effects of my morphine drip.

"So what's your favorite part of my body?" I said when she pulled back.

"Your mind, of course."

Our reunion was put on hold when Rita Mae swept into the room.

"Dickie dear, who's that woman who tried to kill you?"

"Amanda Patricia Nixon," I said. "And, Mom, this is my girl-friend, the lovely Amanda Kristina"

"I've heard so much about you," she said as they shook hands. Then she looked back at me. "All these Amandas ... Maybe it's a karmic inheritance from a past life."

"Just how many Amandas do you know, Richard?" Amanda Kristina said.

"Only a few, but you're the only one who calls me Richard."

"They just don't know you like I do."

The phone rang. Rita Mae picked it up and handed it to me.

"Hi, Dick. This is your grandpa. How are you?"

"I'm feeling fine. Mom is here, and so is my girlfriend."

"You've got impeccable timing," he said. "My name was nowhere in the California news, and now I'm the talk of the town."

"Happy to be of help," I said.

"What do you have planned for the summer?"

I glanced at Amanda Kristina. "Nothing yet."

"Want to go China with me and some of my colleagues?"

"A real junket?"

"Democrats have junkets, we have fact-finding missions."

"Either way, I'm there."

"Actually, Dick, this is a bipartisan mission. Your recent employer, Congresswoman Santos, should be coming along as well."

"Was that your grandfather?" Amanda asked when I hung up the phone.

"Yep," I said. "I'm going to China."

I spent six days on our "fact-finding mission." Ostensibly, we were there to study China's progress toward increased trade and capitalism. Unofficially, we were there to discern just how nefarious the Chinese regime had become after the Tiananmen Square protest and whether the United States should consider diplomatic or trade sanctions.

At the time, I thought the information we gathered would serve as the basis for a more enlightened foreign policy. I soon realized we saw only what those in power wanted us to see.

All twelve of us had the opportunity to bow and shake hands with Deng Xiaoping and his successor, Jiang Zemin—who, I soon discerned, understood most of the English words swirling about the room. Since I was one of four who weren't elected representatives, I figured I could afford to be a little less diplomatic.

"What happened to the man who stood in front of the tank?" I asked when someone skirted the issue of Tiananmen Square.

At least five members of our delegation, including the senator, cringed.

"He is in ... good hands," Jiang said with feeling and compassion. He may have been the best Chinese politician ever.

That evening as we feasted on Mandarin cuisine at the Beijing restaurant selected by our hosts, I found myself seated within a loud whisper of both Congresswoman Santos and Senator Lambright.

"I hope you're not considering a career in the diplomatic corps, Dick," my grandfather said.

"I know it was presumptuous," I said, "but it needed to be asked and I thought it would be better coming from someone like me rather than an official like you or Congresswoman Santos."

"You know you're always welcome in my Washington, D.C., office," Silvia said. "We need articulate young people with courage."

My grandfather smiled. "Maybe, but I can pay more than you."

"Why do Republicans always seem to have more money?" Silvia said.

My senior year at UCLA was a rousing academic success, surpassed only by my arousing romantic success with Amanda Kristina. From the sparkle of her strawberry-blond hair to a smile that could blind, I was enthralled.

In November of 1989, Amanda Kristina decided it was time for me to meet her parents.

"How much do they know about me?" I have to confess, this was something I'd been dreading. I gathered that Amanda Kristina's parents were even more politically conservative than she was.

"They know you're the senator's grandson and you don't see a lot of your father. I told them you aren't that political."

I raised an eyebrow. "Anything else, or should I just stick to the weather and everybody's health?"

"Just don't mention Oliver North as anything less than a true American hero or Michael Dukakis as anything but a friend of rapists."

Amanda's family lorded over a porta-potty empire that financed things like their daughter's education and their mini-mansion with a dramatic view of the Pacific in Orange County's Laguna Beach. Rachel Kristina met us at the door.

"Richard, it's great to meet you. You're so cute I'd jump your bones myself, even if you are a Democrat."

"Mother!" Amanda glared. "He can't be embarrassed, trust me. Where's Dad?"

"Back in his study. He's recently concluded that the military might be more efficient if it were privatized."

"We already have that," I said. "They're called mercenaries."

She laughed. "Why don't you kids go back and say hi? Ask him about dinner tonight."

Amanda Kristina's father, Eugene, was a barrel-chested man with a bone-crushing handshake.

"I hear you went to China with your grandfather," he said. "Guess the Commies will go capitalist before we turn Communist."

I glanced at Amanda Kristina, who shook her head. "Mr. Kristina," I said, "I'd love to hear about your foundation."

"Privatize Our World?" He beamed. "We're based on the idea that private enterprise is the only viable system. So we're raising money to tell the world about the facts, set up think tanks, maybe even start a university."

"You want to make all schools private?"

"It's the only way to make them competitive."

"What about those who can't afford the tuition?" In my peripheral vision I saw Amanda shake her head a touch more vigorously this time.

"More folks need to learn to haul themselves up by the boot straps." He clapped a hand on my shoulder. "That's how I built my business. If we can bring the motivation of private enterprise to all of our public institutions, we can shrink the government, increase efficiency—"

"Private schools, private army ... Sounds a lot like a third-world country, doesn't it?"

Amanda Kristina dragged a finger across her neck.

"Not much of a big-picture thinker, are you, son?"

I cast around for a topic change. "Amanda tells me you served during the Vietnam War, sir?"

"Volunteered in 1966," he said. "Every man should serve his country."

"I agree." Finally, some common ground—or close enough. "Where were you stationed?"

"Bein Hoa." His pronunciation was certainly creative.

I nodded and bit my tongue. There followed a deep but brief pregnant pause in the room.

"So, Dad," Amanda Kristina said, "where are you taking us to dinner tonight?"

The next day I called Sacatchy. "Got a challenge for you."

"I doubt that, but you've piqued my curiosity. What's up?"

"What can you find out about the military career of Eugene Kristina in the sixties?"

"Amanda Kristina's father?"

"The same."

"Why do you want to know?"

"I suspect you'll tell me."

A week later, over coffee, Sacatchy provided me with Eugene Kristina's complete résumé.

"He was commissioned through ROTC after graduating

toward the bottom of his class at Texas A&M in1966. The most notable thing about his three years of active duty was that he started and ended as a second lieutenant—never promoted. The closest he came to Vietnam was a honeymoon in Waikiki Beach in 1968." He paused. "Just to impress you, I did a little more digging. Seems Mrs. Kristina inherited the porta-potty business from her father, who died of a heart attack at age fifty-five."

That confirmed my suspicions, but what could I do? I wasn't about to tell Amanda Kristina her father was a liar. I decided to just file it away in the bulging container of right-wing hypocrisies.

During this delightful autumn, which was amazingly like summer in Southern California, I was contacted by reporters to comment on the upcoming trial of Amanda Patricia Nixon.

"Will you be attending the trial?"

"I don't think so," I said.

"But she tried to kill you."

"I trust the judicial system, and unless I'm called to testify, my deposition will suffice."

"Don't you want closure?"

"Is closure kind of like revenge?"

In the end, Amanda Patricia copped a plea and was sentenced to six years for attempted murder.

I was more or less content. As Buddha once said, "Holding on to anger is like grasping a hot coal with the intent of throwing it at someone else; you are the one who gets burned."

CHAPTER 16

I can tell you this: If I'm ever in a position to call the shots, I'm not going to rush to send somebody else's kids into a war.

—George Herbert Walker Bush

As I NEARED THE END OF MY COLLEGE career, my credit cards were maxed out, my student loan payment plan was brutal, and I still had no idea what I wanted to do with my life.

Over a long weekend, I pointed my Volvo north up Highway 1 and periodically pulled over to walk on the beach. The Pacific seemed to go on forever, pounding swells under a deep blue horizon.

I continued north. By the time I saw the San Francisco skyline, I knew where this journey would end.

"The Army?" Rita Mae said. "With the guns and the tanks?"

"I'm graduating next month," I said. "I need a plan."

"How about we have a meditation marathon." She tucked her long nimble legs into the lotus position as she sat on her couch. "I'll have you feeling so peaceful you won't even know what the word *army* means."

"I'm not sure that's how meditation works."

"Then you haven't meditated with me lately." She was starting to look concerned. "Dickie, you need to rediscover your inner beauty."

"I'm already a believer in America the peaceful." I sat down in an antique wooden chair opposite her.

"Peace only comes from within, sweetie. What if there's a war?"

"Not likely." I paused and smiled. "I promise I'm not turning into a right-wing nut. I just want my country to help me with student loans, that's all."

She moved over behind me and began to gently massage my shoulders and neck. At 41, she was ageless, standing straight and strong and tall, with wavy brown shoulder-length hair. She was a floating advertisement for yoga and meditation.

"Dickie, between me and your grandfather, we can bring your accounts into Zen-like balance. You know we'd love to help you."

"This debt's between me and Uncle Sam."

She moved around to face me, hands on her hips.

"What does Amanda Kristina think?"

"She's not happy I may be leaving, but I'm sure her parents will love it."

"And what are *her* plans after she graduates?"

"Law school." I looked away. "I think she'll wait for me. We're not ready for marriage."

"How about you get a big backpack and go explore the globe?" She looked hopeful. "I'll make payments on your loans until you get back—you'll just owe me instead of the government."

It was a tempting prospect until I pictured Amanda Kristina bidding adieu to her neo-hippie boyfriend with a pack on his back.

"That sounds great, but I feel like this is something I have to do. I wish I could explain it better—I know you and Pops hated the whole thing."

Rita Mae sighed and went to the refrigerator. When she emerged she held up a beer. I nodded. She poured herself a glass of wine and we went to enjoy the view from her newly enlarged deck. Evening was coming on and the lights across the water were just beginning to glisten.

"Remember when you were a kid and you asked me about your other grandparents?"

"I think you told me they died long ago." I wondered where this was going. "Is this one of your cosmic connections?" I glanced at the Buddha at the end of the deck. I'm pretty sure he winked at me.

She shook her head. "How did I raise such a cynic?"

"Not a cynic, just a skeptic."

"Anyway, your grandmother Nancy Trabor was a college instructor near Boston in the late 1940s, probably part-time. Your father was the result of a one-night amorous encounter between Nancy and Army Sergeant Nathan Yablonsky Youngblood."

"So Grandma Nancy got around, huh?"

"She and the sergeant lived in relative bliss until your grandfather was shipped off to Korea." She took a sip of wine. "When the war was almost over, the sergeant wanted to surprise his family. Nancy claimed she heard noises outside her locked door about three in the morning, so she grabbed the bottle of Champagne she'd been saving for a possible reunion, stood behind the door, and when a dark figure walked in she brought the bottle right down on your grandfather's skull."

"Knock him out?"

"He was in a coma for the rest of his short life."

"Uh-oh. So what happened to Grandma Nancy and Little Yuri?"

"Journeyed around the country for a while, then landed in Greenwich Village about 1958, where they lived in a communal family."

"A free spirit long before it was fashionable, I see."

She smiled. "Nancy left Yuri with this family and hit the road with two guys. Yuri got cards and letters from New Orleans, San Francisco, and finally Hawaii. A few months later, your father got the news that Nancy had drowned somewhere off the big island of Hawaii."

"So what happened to Tri-Y?"

"He was sent to live with a well-heeled uncle and aunt on the peninsula in Burlingame." She pointed south toward the city.

I watched the water from the bay lap onto the deck as I digested this tale. "So you think I have genetic proclivity towards militarism?"

She sighed. "It's your story now. You can make it into whatever you want it to be."

As I drove back south the next day, I felt an unexpected sense of well-being—and amazingly, the feeling remained intact even after a conversation with Amanda Kristina.

"Don't get me wrong," she said, "I'm certainly proud, but … why serve as an enlisted man? Why not Officer Candidate School?"

"I'd have a longer period of enlistment."

"Are you sure the senator won't pay off your student loans?"

"Of course he would," I said. "But after I was kicked out of Stanford, I promised myself I wouldn't ask for his help, and I haven't."

"You're not only a Democrat, you're a … a *democrat!*" She seethed for a second and then turned serious. "So what about us?"

"Just don't marry a Young Republican before I get back."

"And what are you going to do after the Army—besides marry me?"

"I was thinking about a master's in history."

"Great, you'll have two useless degrees."

The rest of my friends had similar responses.

"You're shittin' me," Sacatchy said.

"Why now?" the senator asked.

"Did going to UCLA make you nuts?" Lily Livinsky wrote from Stanford.

CHAPTER 17

The trouble with learning from experience is that you never graduate.

—Doug Larson

My commencement ceremony was held at UCLA's Pauley Pavilion. In retrospect, I should have been suspicious when Sacatchy and Roc-Cindy insisted on a front-row seat.

As the dean challenged the thousands of graduates "not to rely on the past way of thinking but to soar like birds to new dreams and make those dreams a reality," a wild turkey waddled out in front of the podium.

Security guards herded the bird off the stage. When the laughter died down, the dean resumed.

"Perhaps Ben Franklin was right," he said. "The turkey should have been our national bird." This elicited muffled laughter. "I'd like to thank the friends and relatives who have flown here from all over the country—"

A couple of more turkeys waddled over to the podium. It took two additional security guards to remove them, and the laughter didn't die down for a good five minutes. It took me only a moment to spot Sacatchy and Roc-Cindy shaking with laughter.

The ceremony proceeded without incident until it was time to receive our diplomas. Just as I began my hasty walk across the stage, I saw the first of five turkeys appear at the edge. As I shook hands with the dean, a sixth turkey flapped its way down from the rafters above.

The dean ducked. I looked toward the stands and did the Nixon. Not only did the turkeys and I get the biggest laugh, but we also got thunderous applause. As I was stepping off stage I heard a very familiar, amplified voice.

"Way to go, Dickie, you're my hero."

I looked everywhere, but I couldn't spot Tri-Y.

After the ceremony, we all met up at Bruin Plaza for congratulatory hugs.

"Thanks for the graduation present, Sacatchy," I said.

"If you mean the turkeys, I admit nothing—at least, not in front of the senator." He shook hands with my grandfather. "But it was easily the highlight of the ceremony."

"What do you think, Mom?" I turned to Rita Mae. "Was that Pops?"

"It was his voice, but for all I know he has a telepathic connection from the rain forest in Borneo."

"I'd really like to meet that guy," Sacatchy said.

"If you two got together, it might be a peril to western civilization," the senator said. He had met Sacatchy back during our days at Stanford when he was invited to give a speech.

Although I assumed I could escape from UCLA and into the Army with relative anonymity, I had no such luck. The next day as I was crossing the UCLA campus, I noticed a copy of the *L.A. Times* folded back to the entertainment section. There was a picture of me surrounded by turkeys, doing the Nixon. The caption read: "Turkeys gobble up honors at UCLA graduation as Richard Youngblood, grandson of Senator Lambright, receives his diploma."

CHAPTER 18

In war, you can only be killed once, but in politics, many times.

—Winston Churchill

As I was on my way to Saudi Arabia aboard a military charter, I questioned—for the umpteenth time—why I'd signed up for the infantry.

Of course, as I'd told Amanda Kristina, the more technical or academic military occupational specialties (MOS) required a longer enlistment. But the closer I got to my new desert home, the more I realized you can be shot during a short enlistment just as easily as during a long enlistment.

As General George Patton said, "The purpose of war is not to die for your country, it's to make the other bastard die for his." During my sixteen weeks of basic training at Fort Benning, I'd presumably learned exactly how to accomplish that, but more important as a prerequisite for politics, I was now unflappable. No matter how loud the bellow of the drill sergeant, I could control my anger, as well as an irresistible urge to giggle. After training, I was assigned to a light infantry unit quartered in the Schofield Barracks, on the Hawaiian island of Oahu. I used that brief yet glorious time to sample the many fruits of Hawaiian life, but just as I was getting into the aloha spirit, we received orders to report to Saudi Arabia for Operation Desert Shield. There were a lot of things about Saudi Arabia I'd rather not have known, but I also knew it was a major source of crude oil and thus remained our friend.

We landed in late November of 1990, and I was ordered to report to a Captain Murphy at headquarters company, which turned out to be a makeshift office.

"So, Youngblood, you have a degree from UCLA?" The captain was a tall intense-looking man whose accent placed him as being from the outer boroughs of New York City, perhaps Brooklyn or the Bronx.

"Yes, sir."

"Do you know what we do here?"

"Not really."

"We're G-2—that's intelligence for the division. If you're going to serve here, we'll need to up your security clearance."

My new assignment had me reporting for duty at 0430 hours to condense all overnight intelligence into a succinct statement for the division commander's briefing at 0630 hours. One morning I wrote something to this effect: "Overnight reports by aircraft, infrared, and ground sensors indicate increased activity near the intersection of the Saudi Arabia, Kuwait, and Iraq borders. Though it does not appear to be a major force, this may be some sort of probe to detect the vulnerability of the multinational force at that point."

At 0655 hours, the division commander himself arrived. General Crane was tall and lanky—I always thought I detected a hint of stork in his profile. I jumped from the comfortable chair in my palatial trailer.

"Good morning, sir."

"Relax, son," he said. "Tell me about this possible probe of the border."

Knowledge is only powerful in proportion to who wants it and how fast. A general wanted knowledge and he wanted it now—and I was the only soldier in Saudi Arabia who could give it to him. Heady stuff.

"Sir!" I held up several pieces of paper. "Out of seven sources during the last twelve hours, six indicate increased movement by the Iraqis at this juncture." I marked the precise spot on the wall map.

"You're sure about this, Youngblood?"

"Sir, in my brief tenure with Army intelligence, it seems to be both an art and a science. These reports have elements of both."

He shook his head. "Where'd you learn to talk like that?"

He left before I could answer.

Not long after that, the captain came to fetch me.

"Youngblood! Let's take a little tour of Iraq, shall we?"

"Sure thing, sir, unless the general wants to talk with me again."

He laughed. "Right, I almost forgot you're the general's best buddy."

An hour later we were in a light observation helicopter headed toward the Iraq-Saudi Arabia border to observe, photograph, and take notes on anything we saw. We didn't see the alleged Iraqi force on the border, but as we changed directions toward the Kuwait-Saudi Arabia border, we spotted a small tank unit. Further along we saw a company-size makeshift fire-support base—with its AK-47s pointed at us.

The pilot made a diversionary move, but not before a bullet struck the rotor. We managed to maintain erratic flight. When a second bullet hit the helicopter, we hit the Saudi Arabian sand with a jolt. As we ran from the aircraft, we saw two or three Iraqi soldiers moving in.

We dropped to the sand and readied our weapons. As the Iraqis got closer, they dropped down and opened fire.

Before infantry training, I honestly believed I could never shoot to kill. My dedication to nonviolence vanished the second I heard the shots coming my way.

We were too far out of range for either side to be accurate, so I informed the pilot and the captain that I was going to move up to the next sand hill. The captain followed, and we peeked over the crest.

Another aircraft approached, one of ours. The Iraqis withdrew, and soon we were back to the safety of our base camp.

After this little adventure, I was recommended for my first medal: for "meritorious achievement against a hostile force during Operation Desert Shield." I was also recommended for the Combat Infantry Badge, which I soon learned was an honor important to anyone hoping for long-term career advancement in the Army. It was wasted on me.

I was one of seven proud enlisted types assigned to the Division G2. Most of us had spent time in college and shared a propensity for discovering the levity in military life. In addition to the captain, we were also commanded part time by Lieutenant Dulardo Ossius.

Lieutenant Ossius was an ideal commander: he was seldom there and never gave orders. He seemed to spend most of his time in his palatial tent, sleeping away the hours. If Captain Murphy were to find out about the lieutenant's incompetence, he might be sent away—and his replacement would probably demand more spit and polish than we enlisted folk thought healthy. So it was in our best interests to cover the lieutenant whenever the captain came looking for him.

"He just left to take some papers up to the intelligence tent, sir."

"He went to check on that equipment we ordered, sir."

"He took an early lunch so he could be here when the rest of go, sir."

Occasionally, the captain became suspicious, so we drew straws to see who'd have the honorable duty of waking Ossius up. This, I had to admit, was one of Lieutenant Ossius's greatest strengths:

he could roll directly out of bed and within ten minutes be fully alert in a crisp uniform with shiny boots. Once in a while, however, he appeared with a face so gray and eyes so bloodshot that his whole demeanor screamed "hangover." When this happened we'd prop him in front of a computer and pile lots of papers, charts, and graphs around him. He looked so busy the captain seldom stayed long.

"How can he have a hangover?" Operation Desert Shield may have been the largest alcohol-free operation in U.S. military history up to that time. "Where does he get the booze?"

"Officers got a secret supply," said Vaughnsky, a gregarious Texan sergeant who was always pointing out inequities in the army.

"Or they drive to Bahrain," Private Browne said. "It's not far once you make it to the gulf."

"Why can't we go to Bahrain?" I said. "Hell, even Lewis and Clark started off with whiskey rations, although when supplies were depleted they got real grouchy."

One morning at 1000 hours we were at our desks pretending to work when we heard the familiar bellow of the captain.

"Where's Lieutenant Ossius?"

"Better get him up," Vaughnsky said. "Captain sounds a little anxious today."

"Whose turn is it?"

"Mine," I said. "Back in a second."

I sprinted to the officer's tent. Unfortunately, Lieutenant Ossius wasn't there.

From the deep recesses of the structure, a lieutenant emerged.

"Can I help you, Private?"

"Yes, sir." I glanced at his name tag. "Lieutenant McClellan, I'm trying to locate Lieutenant Ossius. Do you happen to know where he is?"

"And why do you want to know?"

"Our captain's asking for him."

"Did your captain send you out to look for him?"

"Not exactly, sir."

He narrowed his eyes. "So you're one of the guys who covers his ass?"

There didn't seem to be much point in lying about it.

"Yes, sir."

"Well, Private, Lieutenant Ossius went to Bahrain last night with some Brits and I haven't seen him since."

"Officers can just go to Bahrain when they're not on duty?"

"Of course not, but apparently Ossius didn't get the memo." He shook his head. "I've known him since Officer Candidate School. He looks damn sharp in a uniform, but that's about it."

"Not a ringing endorsement for Officer Candidate School."

"Afraid not." He read my name tag. "Ever been to Bahrain, Youngblood?"

"No, sir. What's in Bahrain?"

"Booze and women, mainly. It's also where a lot of our 'supplies' are shipped through, so that's the main excuse when someone wants to visit." He started toward the exit. "Come on, let's see if we can find Ossius."

"How?" I asked.

"There's a Jeep parked outside. You have a military driver's license?"

"Yes, sir."

What could go wrong?

Less than an hour later, Lieutenant McClellan and I were leaving Saudi Arabia. At the U.S. military checkpoint, we were asked about our business in Bahrain.

"We're picking up supplies and equipment for my intelligence unit," I said.

"Do you have any written orders?"

"No, Sergeant, one of our major transmitters is down and we

need one in a hurry. The Navy base in Manama has what we need in storage."

We were waved through and we repeated the process at the Saudis' checkpoint thirty feet away. It was just past noon when we motored onto the Bahrain Causeway with the Persian Gulf on either side. How many rules had I violated? Being with an officer gave our little venture some legitimacy—I hoped. Anyway, I was fairly sure the guys back at G-2 would cover for me.

We found Lieutenant Ossius in the second bar we checked. He was slumped in the back corner, mumbling the British national anthem. "Long live our noble queen ..."

"Lieutenant Ossius," I said, "the captain would like to see you immediately—and that was quite a while ago."

"Youngblood?" He looked around. "I barely know where I am. How'd you find me?"

"We were ... very concerned about you, sir."

He frowned. "You guys like me that much?"

"Sir, let's just say we like your leadership style."

"Or lack thereof?"

"That, too, sir."

Lieutenant McClellan and I decided to have a beer while Ossius sobered up. As we began to entertain the idea of leaving, three women who were most likely British strolled into the bar, along with a few local women who were most likely hookers. As the sunlight waned, Lieutenant Ossius suddenly disappeared, along with the most attractive woman.

Lieutenant McClellan and I passed the time with another round. It was near sunset when Lieutenant Ossius reappeared, standing upright and looking ready for inspection. The grease was back in his military bearing.

We started our journey back. As we drove across the causeway surrounded by the twilight beauty of the Persian Gulf, Lieutenant Ossius turned to me.

"So Youngblood, you have a vested interest in my dereliction of duty?"

"I wouldn't have put it quite like that, sir." I paused. "But why do you keep doing things that make us cover for you?"

There was a brief silence.

"Youngblood, I'll answer your question after you answer mine."

"What's your question, sir?"

"Why the hell are we here?"

"We're officially here as a show of force to get the Iraqis to leave Kuwait."

"You really believe that crap?

"It would make my life easier if I did, sir."

"We're here because our economy can't exist without Iraqi or Kuwait oil, and we're even addicted to thousands of gallons of it that lie under the Saudi sand."

"Why not just do your job and get it over with?"

"Because people will die while we get it over with. What's the point? Look at history—there'll always be another war. The whole thing makes me sick."

We left the causeway and approached the border checkpoints. The Saudis waved us through, but the Coalition checkpoint stopped us.

"Soldier, sir, and, uh, sir ..." He glanced at his clipboard. "Earlier today this vehicle cleared this checkpoint for the purpose of securing supply and ordnance. May I see your supplies, please?"

"Sergeant, the equipment we were sent to procure wasn't the proper ordnance, so we're returning to our unit for further explanation and orders." I was already fluent in military bureaucratese, but apparently not as fluent as I had imagined.

"Wait here, please."

He left and returned a few minutes later.

"It seems all three of you left your duty station without proper authorization. You're to report to your commanding officers immediately upon your return."

I spent the rest of the night weighing all possible scenarios—Captain Murphy wasn't available until 1100 hours. I decided the truth was my best bet, with just the slightest spin to subtly shift the blame to the officer corps.

I entered the office. "Good morning, sir."

"Nice trip to Bahrain, Youngblood?"

"Yes, sir, until the trip back."

"You lied to border security?"

"Yes, sir."

He leaned across his desk. "And what is it you hoped to find in Bahrain?"

"Lieutenant McClellan suggested we go in search of Lieutenant Ossius, sir."

"I get the impression you men spend a lot of time searching for Lieutenant Ossius, is that right, soldier?"

I paused. "Yes, sir."

I watched the captain lean back in his chair and hook his hands behind his head.

"Youngblood, here's the deal. I could charge you with being AWOL, but that is a court-martial offense. The colonel just finished reaming me out about those goddamn errant lieutenants, but he didn't mention you. So the least onerous punishment I can charge you with is Article Fifteen, non-judicial punishment for failure to be at the proper duty station at the proper time. You'll have ten extra hours of duty and we can all move on with our lives."

"Sir, I already work twelve to fourteen hours day. When could I do extra duty?"

"Let's see ... you're to be in the division formation at 0700 tomorrow to receive yet another medal. I'm prepared to count an hour or so of that as extra duty. And I'm sure you and your new commanding officer can work on some creative solutions for the rest."

"My new commanding officer?"

"The soon-to-be Captain Ossius."

I blinked. "You're kidding—right, sir?"

"Afraid not." He stood up. "Don't worry, he'll be fine so long as you guys keep covering his ass."

Our days of collecting data took on a more ominous tone when Desert Shield became Desert Storm on January 17, 1991.

On the ground and flying above, we in the field of intelligence were looking for troop movements and possible Scud sites. Scuds were point-and-shoot missiles, the Iraqis' low-tech answer to the overwhelming firepower of the United States and its allies. Unfortunately, the Iraqis had already shot several missiles into the urban areas of Israel—in spite of the fact that Israel was not an active participant in this conflict. The United States promised that if Israel did not retaliate, we would make an extra effort to root out the Scud emplacements.

My closest brush with danger took place on February 25, 1991, just days before the conflict was officially over. I was in a nearby tent when a Scud missile, probably by chance, hit American barracks in Al Khobar. I was hit with a tiny piece of shrapnel in my left calf but barely felt it—all I could feel was a massive rush of adrenaline.

I ran toward the barracks. By the time I reached the twenty-eight dead and ninety wounded soldiers, I was bleeding profusely. This resulted in my Purple Heart medal.

In late March, as the so-called war was winding down, Ossius strutted into our work area.

"Youngblood and Vaughnsky, we're going on a special mission."

"What type of mission, sir?"

"A ride in the desert towards Iraq." He gave me a curious look. "Apparently a Bedouin tribal leader has intelligence about the Iraqis, but he insists on passing it directly to you."

"Wait, what? Sir?"

"No idea, but the colonel's intrigued. I know I'm intrigued. Vaughnsky, are you intrigued?

"Yes, sir."

As we motored toward Iraq, a light breeze barely moderated the midday heat of Saudi's spring. In between reveling in the likelihood that I would be long gone before Saudi summer, I was racking my brain—why me?

"What do you know about the Bedouin, Youngblood?" Ossius asked.

"They're very tribal and live all over Arabia. They're now described as semi-nomadic, since a lot of them gave up their traveling ways and moved to the cities."

As we approached the Bedouin encampment, we saw a herd of sheep in the distance and a couple of camels resting on the ground. I wondered how the people or animals lived through the summer heat. When we reached what appeared to be the village center, we stopped.

A tall man with a long flowing robe, a long white beard, and a turban greeted us. He studied our name tags.

"Greetings and welcome to our humble village," he said. "Please, follow me."

Soon we were in a huge tent where we were invited to lay our M16s on a multicolored tapestry.

I glanced at Ossius. This was contrary to my training about the sacred "oneness" of the soldier and his weapon (never ever call it a gun). But in his ever more frequent leadership mode, the lieutenant nodded his assent.

I remembered the Bedouin were an honorable people. I hoped that was true.

Our guide then indicated that I was to follow him.

"Captain and Specialist, you must stay here until Youngblood returns."

So I followed him out of the relative cool of the large tent and back into the Saudi sun, through a building of sorts, and finally into another tent. Sitting cross-legged with his back to me was another man in white robes and a turban.

"Please sit," my guide said. He then exited the tent.

The man slowly lifted his head and smiled. "Hi, Dickie."

"Pops!" I took a minute to reconcile the scene. "Is there any point asking what you're doing here?"

"As always, I'm seeking the truth."

"So you're the one who sent for me?"

"I made a simple request to my Bedouin brothers."

I raised a brow.

"Don't they have a proverb—something like, brother against cousins and cousins against neighbors and neighbors against foreigners?"

"They think I'm their cousin." He reeled off a quick phrase in Arabic. "Anyway, I have some intel for you. You're in military intelligence, right?'

"Yes, I am."

"Here's the deal. I have two envelopes: the first one you turn over to your G-2 guys, the second one you only give to a CIA agent in Honolulu. You're going back there, right?"

"I have orders to go back to Schofield Barracks." My brain still hadn't fully adjusted to finding my father in a Bedouin tent in the middle of the desert. "So ... does this mean you're on our team now?"

"Let's say I'm trying out for your team. These envelopes might serve as my résumé."

"So what's in them?"

"The thinner one is information about Iraq's attempt to build a tunnel network near the border. Part of it is in Arabic, but I'm sure your guys can get it translated."

"And the other one?"

"Information about Iraqi weapons programs, but the details are all in code. Just turn it over to Big Kahuna in Honolulu." He glanced around the tent and handed me a card. "After you get to Hawaii, call this number and leave this message, word for word:

'The sand is soft on the Arabian desert.' Don't call until you're off the base. Wait a few minutes by the pay phone and you'll receive a call back. Got that, Dickie?"

"Sure thing, Pops."

"Oh, and don't try to look in the envelopes."

"Is that a 'don't look in the envelopes wink-nudge' or a 'seriously, don't look in the envelopes?'"

He grinned. "I have complete faith that you'll figure out the correct option. Now you'd better get out of here before they figure out I'm not really their cousin."

"Dick," Vaughnsky asked as we were driving back to the base, "why you? Why'd you get the envelope?"

"Family connection."

"You have Bedouin ancestors?"

"Not until today."

I turned the first envelope over to Captain Ossius, who presumably sent it further up the chain of command. When I got back to my quarters, I folded the second envelope into a military dress shirt and put it at the bottom of the bag I was packing in preparation to leave Saudi Arabia.

The next day I was asked to report to the colonel.

"Good morning, sir."

"Have a seat, Youngblood. So you received this envelope from your father at a Bedouin village? What was he doing there?"

"I'm not really sure, sir."

"Did he ask you to keep his identity a secret?"

"No, sir, I think he was on the verge of slipping away."

"Did he tell you what was in the envelope or why he gave it you?"

"He said it had something to do with an Iraqi tunnel system near the border."

The colonel gave me a thoughtful look. "Well, Youngblood,

this appears to be highly valuable intelligence. I'll recommend you for a medal."

And so, in April of 1991, I left the Middle East with a promotion, a Combat Infantry Badge, a Bronze Star of Service, a Bronze Star for Valor, and a Purple Heart—all for three days of not-that-dangerous combat.

I had lots of company. The U.S. military awarded a total of 117,235 medals during Operation Desert Shield and Operation Desert Storm, including hundreds of Combat Infantry badges. I was one of the thousands awarded Bronze Stars for service, and one of a few hundred recipients of the Purple Heart medal. All these decorations were given to combatants in a war that had 148 American combat deaths and lasted just under two months.

There were plenty of deserving recipients of these medals—I just wasn't among them.

CHAPTER 19

Hawaii is a unique state. It is a small state. It is a state that is by itself. It is a ... It is different from the other forty-nine states. Well, all states are different, but it's got a particularly unique situation.

—Vice President Dan Quayle

I FELT A TOUCH OF TREPIDATION WHENEVER I thought of the envelope tucked into the bottom of my suitcase, but I happily looked forward to going back to the United States and to Hawaii in particular. In addition to the spirit of aloha, I craved the signs and symbols of capitalism. I also missed Amanda Kristina, who surprised me by flying to Honolulu to greet me.

She was even more radiant in the trade winds of Oahu than in the Southern California sun. As I descended the stairs of the military charter, I beheld her in all her sexy glory, enhanced by a sheer Hawaiian wrap that covered only as much of her as island etiquette required. I'm reasonably sure that residents of the fiftieth state consume fewer bolts of cloth per capita than any of the other forty-nine.

When we embraced, the near bareness of her skin and the enthusiasm of her kiss left me shivering with delight.

"I've missed you so much," she said. "I'm so proud of you."

We spent four spectacular days together before she had to return to law school.

* * *

Now that I was a veteran, I had more freedom to come and go as I pleased, but I dithered a few days over my ... informal? secret? just plain weird? ... mission. What was in the envelope? Could I be court-martialed for not turning it over to the Army? Why the hell wasn't I reading it?

What stopped the dithering was a thought I couldn't shake: it would probably be a fun adventure if nothing else. And so, clad in my best Hawaiian uniform—shorts, hiking sandals, T-shirt—I took a bus to the center of Honolulu near the Aloha Tower and dialed the number supplied by Tri-Y from a phone booth. A toneless female voice invited me to leave a message.

"The sand is soft on the Arabian desert." I hung up.

Within seconds the phone rang.

"Aloha," I said.

"Please proceed to a phone booth near the corner of Kalakua and Kuhio in Waikiki. Ask where the surf's up."

I arrived at the second phone booth a few minutes later. The phone started ringing as soon as I closed the door.

"Where is the surf up?" I said.

"On the Persian Gulf," another female voice said. "Your instructions are taped beneath the booth's seat."

They read:

> Make sure the documents you have are out of sight and proceed toward the Pali Lookout before 4 p.m. today. Just before the actual lookout, find the trail to the Old Pali Lookout. Proceed down the windward side of the trail. After a few minutes of walking, the old road seems to stop. Here you will find a trail that enables you to hike under the new road. Then pick up the old road again. Proceed until you see a cement marker on your left that says, "EJL 1919." Force your way through the flora to immediate right of this marker and you will find a narrow dirt trail. Continue uphill. When you get to a clearing with a lookout, wait for a short woman named

Iwalani. Ask her, "Where are the rainbows?" She will respond, "Always Makai." She will then give you further instructions. Destroy this document after your mission is completed.

I checked that my packet of documents was still taped to my upper torso under my shirt (something I'd seen in a spy movie) and then added myself to a tour bus bound for the Pali Lookout. Once on the magnificent cliff where King Kamehameha drove thousands of his enemies to their deaths, I separated myself from the group.

I found the Old Pali Highway and was treated to an awe-inspiring view of the Pacific. Often the Pali featured gale-force winds, but today it was calm and shrouded in clouds. The clouds were parting when I reached the lookout where I'd get "new instructions." I sat and watched the rays of the sun brush the outer reaches of Kaneohe Bay. A misty rain began to fall. I was just considering leaving when I heard whispers, apparently coming from tropical flora.

I turned and there was the cutest wahine I had laid my eyes on during my brief tenure in Hawaii. She was gliding through the waist-high ferns—which, I realized as she got closer, would be knee-high to most of us. She had long black hair down to her tiny waist, red and white aloha shorts, bare feet, and a T-shirt that read, "Menehunes Make Better Lovers."

"Where are the rainbows?" I asked.

"Always Makai!"

And almost on cue, a small rainbow appeared on the horizon.

Iwalani beckoned me with a lovely smile. "Please."

I followed her as she moved effortlessly through the tropical maze of ferns and trees. As we approached a rock almost as tall I was, I contemplated giving her a leg up, but before I could move, she was at the top. Her bare feet seemed to be blessed with natural Velcro.

"Need some help, Dickie?"

I made it up the rock with much grunting and groaning. Sometimes size is not an advantage.

The forest thickened and night descended on Oahu's windward side. Finally we came to a camp of sorts: a shack, two small tents, kerosene lanterns, a small campfire, and the sweet smell of cannabis.

A man of about five foot three— towering over Iwalani— turned to me.

"Hey, brah, my name is Kekoa. I'm the brother of Iwalani." Kekoa's T-shirt read "Menehune Power."

"This is my cousin Makani and his brother Pika."

"You seem a bit taller than your cousins," I said.

"They got the most Menehune blood."

At that point a joint was passed to me. I had not indulged in weed since my days at Stanford, but with a nod and a smile from Iwalani, I took a shallow drag—ceremonial, you might say, a bit like toking on a Native American peace pipe.

"According to my contact, I'm to turn certain documents over to the CIA."

"You've found us."

"No offense, but you guys look more like vertically challenged marijuana farmers."

"Don't be fooled by appearances." Iwalani spoke with not a hint of the local pigeon that had colored her earlier speech,

"You went to Stanford, right? I'm Stanford '84. My brother here is USC, class of '86. The farmer getup is part of our cover for dealing with various Pacific and Asian cartels."

"Can you prove you're really CIA?"

"Didn't Tri-Y send you here?"

"You're seriously citing him as your credentials?"

All four of them produced IDs. They looked real, but my brief tenure in military intelligence hardly qualified me to tell the difference if they weren't. Still, how would they know about Tri-Y's sending me? I reached under my shirt and pulled out the envelope.

At that point, three guys rose out of the rain forest with guns drawn.

"FBI! Please give us the envelope," the most local-looking one said.

"CIA!" Iwalani said as she stood and held up her hands.

"Sure you are. Now hand the envelope—"

A coconut dropped. One of the FBI guys panicked and swung his gun toward Iwalani.

I dived at her, knocking her tiny body to the dirt as the bullet whizzed over our heads. She crawled out from under me, apparently unscathed.

"I think you saved my life."

Now we heard the buzz of two helicopters closing in above. One was clearly marked as Honolulu PD. From out of the forest, police emerged with guns drawn.

"Freeze!" they shouted.

"Hold on." The FBI guys held their IDs high in the air.

"And we're CIA!" The Menehune crowd lifted their badges.

"I'm Army intelligence." I held up nothing.

As the seven members of the Honolulu Police got closer, the rest of us raised our hands and dropped our weapons.

"Book 'em, Lano," someone yelled, "Book 'em all."

That was how I ended up in jail courtesy of the Honolulu Police Department, which turned out to have jurisdiction over the entire island.

"Youngblood," the police lieutenant said, "we understand you're in possession of an important envelope, is that correct?"

"Yes, sir."

"Could I see it, please?"

"If you're CIA, sure."

He left in a controlled huff but soon returned with a tall Polynesian-looking gentleman with silver hair and a crisp aloha shirt. He produced ID identifying him as George Paulani Aualoni, deputy director of central intelligence, Pacific/East Asia.

"Satisfied?"

"Where is the surf up?"

"On the Persian Gulf," he said.

I pulled the envelope back out.

"Here you go."

As I was released, I noticed the CIA "farmers" just ahead of me. I also noticed a colonel from Schofield, who I was quite sure was somewhere near the top of my new chain of command, and several Caucasian suits emerging from what appeared to be a major powwow.

The colonel offered me a ride back to Schofield.

"Sir, what's going to happen now?"

"Probably nothing." He glanced at me. "I hear you may have saved a CIA agent's life."

"It was a judgment call."

"I think I'll have to recommend you for promotion. How does Sergeant Youngblood sound?"

"Thank you, sir."

I scanned the Honolulu newspapers, but there was nothing for several days. Finally an enterprising reporter, a big-mouthed HPD detective, and a disgruntled FBI agent had a harmonic convergence that resulted in the headline "Spies and Sinsemilla: Confusion Near the Pali."

Details were sketchy in the initial article, but more emerged as each agency sought to paint its agents as being as low as possible on the wacko scale.

A few days later the headline read: "Decorated Gulf War Veteran Saves Spy Near the Pali." Every good story needs a hero, and I'd been cast as the quick-thinking sergeant who saved a noble CIA agent from the errant shot fired by an undisciplined FBI agent. About five days later an enterprising reporter for a San

Francisco newspaper put it all together, and what followed was a piece that canvassed everything from the yellow submarine to Amanda Patricia. I soon got a call from Amanda Kristina.

"Richard, I'm so proud of you. My father can't stop talking about you, hero."

I spent the next year in Hawaii. I split my leave time between Amanda Kristina in Southern California and Rita Mae in the Bay Area.

"I'm dying to hear the whole story behind the CIA fiasco," Mom said on my first trip home.

"Do you have security clearance?"

"Do you have a better place to stay tonight, Dickie dear?"

"Point taken," I said. "Well, right before I left Saudi Arabia, I was invited to visit a Bedouin village—and I ran into Pops."

"You're kidding."

"Nope. He said he had some information he wanted me to pass along."

"So he's in bed with *our* spies now?" She laughed. "Your grandfather will be so pleased."

CHAPTER 20

Political promises are much like marriage vows. They are made at the beginning of the relationship between candidate and voter, but are quickly forgotten.

—Dick Gregory

EVENTUALLY I RECEIVED AN HONORABLE discharge. I packed up my medals and my memories, flew back to California, and started graduate school at UCLA.

By the fall of 1993 I had my course work completed for my master's degree in history. Amanda Kristina and I were still going strong, and I decided it was time to grow up and offer her a formal engagement.

I reserved a table at the restaurant where we had our first real date, and again the sunset was spectacular. As we walked along the beach, we came to a spot where the waves were relatively calm.

"Look at those cool old bottles." I pointed at two antique bottles, one red and one blue, bobbing in the surf. I'd combed antique stores for days to find them. She waded into the ankle-deep water and picked them up. She handed them to me and I gave her back the red one.

"There's something inside." She held the reddish one up to the sunset. "Looks like paper." She removed the cork and managed to extract the scroll. "'It was love at first leer when I saw you selling makeovers and Republicans near Bruin Plaza,'" she read aloud. "'Now more than ever, you make my hormones dance and ego bulge. I always knew we were meant for each other in spite of our differences.'"

She giggled.

"What's in the blue bottle?" I asked.

With the same graceful dexterity, she extracted the second piece of paper. "'I believe our love will endure into old age. Even if our physical ardor wanes, it won't diminish my passion for you. I look forward to the day when we have a little Amanda or Richard running around the house.'"

I pulled a ring out of my pocket. Although I never considered myself a traditionalist, I found myself down on one knee.

"Amanda, I love you beyond reason. Please marry me."

"Oh, Richard, yes, yes, yes!"

Within seconds we were entangled. In the background, the western sky turned vibrant coral.

As we were dusting off the sand and preparing to walk back up the beach for our engagement dinner, Amanda Kristina noticed another bottle bobbing in the waves.

"More surprises?"

"Not from me," I said. "The only other person who knows about this is your father."

"You asked my father? How Republican of you."

She splashed into the water to retrieve the big amber bottle. Getting the message out of this one was more of a challenge.

"Richard, it's from *your* father. He says, 'Amanda and Richard, Big-time congratulations on your engagement, Love and Peace, Tri-Y.'"

I raised an eyebrow. "He actually said Richard?"

"OK, so I did a little translation. But how'd he know?"

I smiled. "Magic."

* * *

As the school year progressed, I concentrated on my thesis: one of the first research endeavors into the Gulf War. I kept it objective and withheld my personal account until the conclusion.

It was the conclusion that most interested my adviser. Dr. William Zachary had published several works for the general public—the "educated citizenry," to invoke a phrase from Jefferson. As we reached a first-name basis, Bill said my thesis had enormous commercial potential. He encouraged me to rewrite it, expand the personal narrative, and send it to publishing houses before the market became saturated with Gulf War books. I took his advice, and with his publishing contacts, *Was the Gulf War Really a War?* was published within six months. It didn't make me rich or famous, but it put some cash in my pocket. I loved seeing my name on the cover, and even more gratifying were the letters I received expressing how the book had changed readers' views on war.

"Richard," Dr. Zachary said, "you're an excellent researcher, and I assume you'd be good in the lecture hall. Why not pursue a doctorate?"

"I appreciate the compliment," I said, "but I think I need to find my niche in the real world."

"Isn't that why you joined the Army?" he said.

"The military is about as far from academia as you can get, but it's still not the real world."

"So what are you contemplating next?"

"Becoming a high school teacher."

"You're serious?"

"About as serious as I get."

A few days later I was sitting in a Bruin coffee spot when my fiancée made one of her famous entrances. I pulled out her chair and braced myself.

"I just signed a contract with the Los Angeles Unified School District," I said.

"You did *what?*"

"I took a job teaching high school."

She sat perfectly still—too still. Finally she spoke.

"And you didn't think you might want to run it by me first?"

"You know I've talked about becoming a teacher."

"Richard, we're getting married in a month."

"You still have a year left in law school," I said. "One of us needs to make some money."

"You think you're going to make money teaching *high school?*" She looked more upset than I'd ever seen her. "Richard, do you honestly think a teacher's salary can support us?"

"Plenty of people get by on less."

"So we're just going to 'get by'?" She folded her arms. "You're more than qualified to get a job in the private sector."

"Amanda—"

"You know why public school teachers are poor?" She glared at me. "Because there's no competition. They're not even part of the real economy!"

I took a deep, calming breath. "Everyone's part of the economy," I said. "There's no way to quantify the good that teachers do. Weren't you ever inspired by a teacher before you came to college?"

She frowned. "Maybe."

"So how do you measure that? How does that fit into your capitalist forces of supply and demand?"

She looked around the coffee shop and sighed. "Fine, but why not teach in West Los Angeles, or maybe a private school? Won't you be afraid to drive in and out of there every day?"

"It's on the edge of the Valley," I said. "There's very little violence."

"And aren't a lot of those students Hispanic? Should we really be educating illegals?"

"The kids didn't decide to immigrate." My turn to frown. "And didn't you tell me that both your nanny and housekeeper when you were growing up were probably undocumented?"

Her face became a bit red, but I doubt it was from embarrassment. "We never asked."

"So that makes it OK?"

A long silence—we were argued out. After a while she sighed, smiled and came around to my side of the table.

"OK," she said after a long tight hug. "Try the do-gooder thing for a year. I'll talk to my father—I'm sure he'll be happy to help keep us afloat until you can get a real job."

"I might be making a big mistake."

Sacatchy studied me over his cup of coffee.

"So call it off."

"In three days we say the vows," I said. "I can't back out now."

"Everybody gets scared before they tie the knot, right?" He shrugged. "It's a long proud tradition. Embrace it."

"She's 'letting' me get a job as a teacher—for one year."

"You bought a tux?"

"Sort of."

"I can hardly wait to see you stuffed into formal wear."

"If it doesn't work out, do what thousands of Californians do every day: get divorced. Just do it before you have kids or own a lot of stuff."

In August of 1994, we had a lavish wedding and reception that began at Laguna Presbyterian Church and ended at what I called the "Brahmin" Country Club.

"Richard, I hear you're going to teach high school," Eugene Kristina said at the rehearsal diner the night before.

"Yes, sir, American history and government."

"You learn any economics along with all that history at UCLA?"

"Yes, I think so."

"So what's your take on our recent economic problems?" he asked.

"It was probably caused over insecurities from the crash of 1987, tight monetary policy, and the end of the spike in oil prices caused by the Gulf War."

"They didn't teach you the real source."

"What's the real source?"

"It goes back to that pinko whiner Jimmy Carter."

"So tell me, how is Jimmy Carter responsible for our recent economic problems?" I couldn't seem to help myself, despite a distinctly un-amorous under-the-table thigh grab from Amanda Kristina.

"Carter always acted like he was holier than thou, a southerner teaching Sunday school and all, but he was really a radical social-ist. Carter brought us stagflation, and then he forced the Federal Reserve to raise interest rates, which created the recession of the early eighties. So they put more controls on banks and lenders. I can't believe you didn't learn this at UCLA. They must be all lefties in the history department."

"But the Federal Reserve is an independent agency. How could Carter control them?" I said. I registered thigh-grab number two.

"Sure, that's what they want us to believe. You see, Carter also started the Department of Energy and gave all those crybaby sermons about conserving oil. Carter also made Israel give back the Sinai to Egypt, and since then the Arabs think they can do anything they want."

"So what's the connection between these events and the recent economic downturn?" I asked, preparing myself for thigh-grab number three.

"They wanted us to believe that banks and financial institu-tions were underregulated so they'd have an excuse to institute their socialist agenda. Because Carter and his comrades forced the Federal Reserve to take action on stagflation, they instituted a lot of sneaky regulations that interfered with the natural market forces. Reagan tried to undo some of the overregulation, but they wouldn't let him. Now we have Clinton trying to get gays into the military and promoting Hillary's European-socialist plan for health care."

"You keep referring to 'they.' Who are *they*, sir?"

"The government, of course."

"Aren't we all part of the government?"

Only a masochist would have enjoyed Amanda Kristina's fourth warning clutch. That one was going to leave a bruise.

"Is that what they teach you at UCLA? Sure, that's what they want us to believe, but don't you think that's a bit naïve?"

I was ready to respond, but my marriage and maybe my thigh were saved when my grandfather came over from the next table.

"Eugene, it is a pleasure to see you again."

"Greetings, Senator. I've been trying to educate your grandson here about recent history."

"Have any success?" The senator asked.

"I was just clarifying how Jimmy Carter was mainly responsible for our recent economic problems."

"You really believe that crap?"

The senator was off glad-handing the people at the next table before Eugene could respond.

"I still have a laughing orgasm when I think about that shot you made in the wrong team's basket," Judy LaTrudy said.

"A laughing *what?*" Amanda Kristina asked.

When I invited all my old friends to the reception, I doubted that many would show. I was pleasantly surprised when nearly every one of them turned up.

"Sorry. I'm a writer for *Erofit Magazine,* and every sentence we write is supposed to include something sexy. It's started sliding into my everyday conversations."

"I'll play," Sheils said. "I'll always remember my titillating time with the Dickster."

Lily shook her head. "I swear, Dickie, when you left Stanford and enrolled at UCLA, you raised the average IQ of both institutions."

Amanda Kristina tried to smile, but I suspect the general laughter at the expense of her bridegroom may have embarrassed her.

"Ladies and gentlemen, if I could have your attention for a moment."

I looked up to the stage, where Sacatchy now stood ready to deliver his best-man toast. Though he was in formal wear and clean-shaven for maybe the first time since the early nineties, his hair was still disheveled.

"I wish I could say I was honored to serve as Richard's best man," he said. "I'd love to tell you he's been my best friend since we were at Stanford together." He paused. "Unfortunately, I barely knew the guy until he told me I could score a few free drinks if I'd put on a tux and give you this speech." He waited for the giggles to die down. "But before I continue, we have a special presentation via satellite from the continent of Antarctica."

The curtains behind Sacatchy were drawn back, revealing a huge screen. Aerial vistas of the Hawaiian islands filled the screen as the strains of "Aloha 'Oe" filled the room. The footage cut to a large computer-generated map of the Pacific, and then the view swept south past Tahiti. Within seconds we were nearing the continent of Antarctica.

Another cut and there, bundled up in a parka, was Tri-Y. He seemed to be standing on an endless slab of ice, but it was hard to tell. The area behind him was covered by hundreds of penguins.

"Congratulations, Dickie and Amanda. Sorry I couldn't be there, but my new friend Sacatchy tells me you think penguins are really cool, so we invited some to your reception."

Two actual penguins then waddled their way out to the podium. The audience went wild with cheers and laughter. Sacatchy finally recaptured the crowd and directed everyone's attention back to the screen.

"I'm currently very busy here in Hope's Bay," Tri-Y said,

"studying the changing environment of the Adélie penguins—and trying to increase their political consciousness, of course."

Six more penguins shuffled toward the podium.

"Dickie, you're my hero," Tri-Y said. "Someday I'll meet you and Amanda in some remote corner of the world. I want to extend a symbolic group hug to Rita Mae, the senator, Cicely, and Amanda's family. Party on, and don't stop until we have world peace. Bye for now and a big thanks to Sacatchy for pulling this off."

Just off stage, I saw what looked like local zoo personnel herding the penguins back into crates. Eventually the laughter died down and Sacatchy continued.

"These may be the most serious words I've uttered in recent memory, but when Dickie asked me to be best man, it was the greatest honor of my life," he said. "Even greater, I believe, than getting kicked out of Stanford University. Now, I lift my glass to Amanda and Richard."

Everyone lifted a glass and applauded. And calling me Richard definitely scored Sacatchy some points with my bride.

CHAPTER 21

There are advantages to being elected president. The day after I was elected, I had my high school grades classified top secret.

—Ronald Reagan

AT THE INSISTENCE OF MY IN-LAWS and over my mild objections, Amanda and I began married life in a semi-palatial apartment near Wilshire Boulevard in West Los Angeles—for which her father paid the rent. Amanda had a short commute to UCLA and I drove northeast to the outskirts of the Valley.

When I arrived at Millard Fillmore, Vice Principal Adrian Alverez met me in the parking lot.

"Mr. Youngblood, for today you're assigned to the front office. We have problems with personnel downtown and you may be going to a different school."

"But …" I said as Ms. Alverez quickly retreated to her office.

My front-office assignment lasted for two days, and I was assigned the unpleasant duties that no one else in the employment of Millard Fillmore wanted to do. I checked parking stickers for the staff lot, went on "sniff patrol" near the restrooms to detect whiffs of tobacco or marijuana, and delivered supplies to teacher's classrooms.

"Oh, and pick up any trash in the hallways. It sets a good example for the kids." Vice Principal Alex Bok said as I left the office on sniff patrol.

On the second day, I was able to make phone contact with the assistant personnel director at the central office, who remembered me from my interview. She told me, under promises of anonymity, that Dr. Conesto, my principal, had planned to place his nephew in my position at Millard Fillmore. She also said her boss was "in the process of educating Dr. Conesto as to the limits of his power."

On the third day, Ms. Alverez directed me to my classroom with the caveat: "Don't get too comfortable. You still might be reassigned to a different school."

The next day, the vice principal met with the new teachers. To use the latest educational parlance, the meeting was really a "training," and Ms. Alverez waxed, but far from eloquently, that everything was on the way up at Millard Fillmore: test scores, advanced classes, athletics, and pride in being a Fillmore Flying Fox. As I was soon to learn, Ms. Alverez's rosy view was not universally shared. Actually, the bell schedule at Fillmore was the main thing that was universally shared.

On my first day of teaching, students dribbled into the classroom, nearly all of them talking, the latecomers the loudest. Ethnically, my class was a microcosm of Southern California: about one-third Hispanic, one-fourth Caucasian, and the rest a mix of African-Americans, Asians, and Pacific Islanders. As I stood to my full height and stepped forward, their talk died to murmurs and mumbles.

"Good morning. My name is Mr. Youngblood. The class is U.S. History."

After thirty seconds, all eyes were on me. I later learned that this was strictly a first-day phenomenon.

"Why are you here?" I said.

No response. I scanned the class. Some appeared to be thinking, some looked bored, and others seemed uncomfortable with the silence.

"Really, why are you here?" Most of them were now trying to focus on anything but me. "I can wait as long you can."

Finally, a boy with sports logos covering his upper body raised his hand.

"We're here 'cause we have to be?"

"Who said you have to be here?"

"The law."

"So if you're not here, the police will hunt you down?"

"All right, my mom says so."

This was met with mild laughter—the first sign of life.

"Why are you taking U.S. History?" I asked.

"Because it's required," a cheerleader type in the third row said.

"Why is it required?" I asked.

"So we can be bored to death?"

"You think history is boring?"

"Oh, not *me*, I think it's freakin' fascinating." He waved a hand at the rest of the class. "It's all the other people out there."

"Anybody here ever watch *Saturday Night Live* and didn't get the jokes?" There were some scattered nods. "If you knew history and current events, you might."

"We study history so we can get the punch line?" asked a nerdy-looking girl toward the back.

"So you can get the punch line, get what's happening in the world, get the president, and get the ballot when you vote."

By the fifth day, I was deep into United States history. We were reading primary source documents to try to discern, as historians might, the answer to the question "Who fired the first shots in the Revolutionary War?"

147

"Mr. Youngblood, why do we care who fired the first shots?" Miguel asked.

"Bad guys start wars and good guys finish wars, right?"

By third period, the lesson war was losing traction. Heads nodded and yawns were pervasive. I looked out the window at the green grass and blue skies of a perfect Southern California day.

"Everybody up," I said. "Time to visit the village green at Lexington."

As my bemused students filed outside, I numbered off the class. The first eight were the minutemen, number one was Captain Parker, nine was Major Pitcairn, and the rest of the students were British soldiers. I told them to stand in lines, everyone armed with imaginary muskets. Just as in the source documents, the major was told to issue the command.

"Everybody get your muskets up," I said. "The British will say 'huzzah, huzzah, huzzah.' Ready?"

Just as we were about to simulate the battle, here came Vice Principal Bok, a short dark-haired man in an ill-fitting short-sleeve dress shirt with an ugly tie.

"Mr. Youngblood, what's going on here?"

"We're on the verge of starting the Revolutionary War."

"Are they holding pretend muskets?"

"Yes they are, Mr. Bok."

"Youngblood, how long have you been a teacher?" he asked.

"This is day five," I said.

"What if all those teachers," he said with a wave toward adjacent classrooms, "wanted to bring their classes out here?"

"Alex," I said, "so far, the green seems to be all mine—"

Bang!

One of my students had slammed a fat history textbook flat on the pavement.

"Who fired that shot?" I said.

The kids giggled but reformed the line and prepared to fire their muskets.

Mr. Bok walked away shaking his head.

Before I left on Friday afternoon, the social sciences chairwoman burst into my classroom. In the often-cynical atmosphere of a high school, she stuck out—even though she barely cleared five feet.

"How was your first week, Dick?"

"I loved most of it."

"We're happy to have you here. We really need young blood—no pun intended—and I've already heard a lot of positive feedback from the kids."

"Thanks—"

"And don't worry about that asshole Alex Bok. You want to teach on the beach, go for it—as long as they learn something."

"Speaking of administration, I haven't seen the principal. Is he on vacation or something?"

She rolled her eyes. "He'll make his 'fall splash' in a week or so, then he'll vanish."

"Where's he go?"

"I'm not sure anyone really knows," Janice said. "Donn Mueller—English department—has a pool you can buy into right after the fall splash. Whoever provides documentary evidence of Hamilton Conesto being on or near the campus at any time other than the splash collects the pot."

"I saw a Lexus in the principal's parking spot this morning."

She winked. "Things aren't always as they seem, Dick."

Indeed they weren't. The next time I walked by the principal's Lexus, it wasn't quite as shiny and seemed to have some creases in its sides—very odd. I wanted a closer look, but the parking space was fenced in. Even odder, the next morning it looked shiny with pride, crease-free, as though it had undergone a bit of bodywork overnight.

I picked up an acorn and lobbed it over the fence. It hit the hood of the Lexus with a soft thud and bounced off.

"So who blows it up?" I asked Janice the next time I saw her.

"Who blows what up?"

"The principal's Lexus."

"Most rookies don't figure out the mystery of the Lexus for a whole semester."

"I'm guessing it's one of the VPs. Maybe Adrian Alverez."

"Bingo," Janice said. "And no matter how early you get here, she's always here before you."

Monday morning, I happened by the desk of Ms. Tansy Toluma, assistant to the principal and vice principal.

"Hi, Ms. Toluma. How's it going?"

"Very well, and how was your first week in the classroom, Mr. Youngblood?"

"Everything's cool so far," I said. "Ms. Toluma, is it possible to talk with Dr. Conesto sometime this week?"

"You'll have to check with Ms. Alverez."

I noticed that the Lexus was absent the rest of the week, but the following Tuesday there it was, nearly bursting with air. I stuck my head in Ms. Alverez's office.

"It looks like Dr. Conesto is back," I said. "Any chance of having a brief word with him?"

"I'm afraid he's in a lengthy meeting, then he's off to another one off-campus."

As promised, Dr. Conesto made his annual "fall splash" during my third week. If I hadn't known better, I might have been impressed. He came by my classroom twice for about two minutes each time. The first time he left with a smirk on his face. The second time he walked into the classroom just as I was posing the question "Should the father have a say about the mother having an abortion?"

Hands shot up, but the bell rang before the discussion could ensue. As the students exited, Dr. Conesto made his way to the front of the room.

"Mr. Youngblood, what does abortion have to do with U.S. history?" the principal asked.

"Everything," I said.

"We'll see about that. I think I'll have to keep you under close scrutiny. When parents complain, the administration spends way too much time trying to make them happy. If you know what's good for you, you should steer clear of most controversial issues."

"So you mainly want me deal with the bland and boring?" I said.

"You're treading on the thinnest of ice, Youngblood. Also, I understand you had your whole class outside to play some sort of war game." And with that he exited my classroom. I was soon to discover he could hardly keep me under close scrutiny if he was seldom there.

That afternoon, he presided over a faculty meeting. He introduced all seven of the new teachers and was quite congratulatory toward all five of the vice principals. He praised Alex Bok for "keeping the ship of school on an even keel," and he was even more fawning toward Adrian Alverez for placing Millard Fillmore on "the cutting edge of innovation."

On Friday afternoon, to the delight of every student in the bleachers, Dr. Conesto donned a Fillmore letterman's jacket and rode his Harley into the first pep rally of the year. That evening, at the first home football game, he stood behind the team bench and high-fived every player who came off the field.

Sometime during October, I mentioned to Adrian Alverez (for the fifth time) that I'd like to meet with the principal.

"You really don't get it, do you?" she said.

"Get what?"

She waved me into a chair and shut the door. "Here's the deal," she said. "Nobody gets to see the principal. But the trade-off is he leaves you the fuck alone. *Do I make myself clear?*"

I hadn't realized it was possible to whisper a shriek.

"Why would I want the principal to leave me alone?" I said.

"Are you really that dense?" She leaned over the desk. "Do you have any idea how miserable your life would be if you had an asshole principal who was here all of the time?"

I left the office with my curiosity intact.

Shortly after my conversation with Sacatchy at Millard Fillmore, I was on campus later than usual one evening. Amanda Kristina was at a social event hosted by her new law firm, so I was in no rush to get home. By the time I finally made my way out to my car, it was dark—which is how I noticed the lights on in the administration building.

I could see right into the principal's window. There he was, Hamilton Conesto in the flesh, alongside oh-so-faithful Vice Principal Adrian Alverez.

Fortunately I had my new cutting-edge digital camera in my pocket.

I snapped a couple of zoom shots: Ham giving Adrian a little shoulder massage. I was shooting through a window, but the office was brightly lighted—there could be no doubt as to the identities of my subjects.

A day later I presented a five-by-seven glossy to English teacher Donn Mueller.

"How much do I win?" I asked.

He stared at the picture and let out a low whistle.

"I think it's up around $320," he said. "Nobody's won since the year before last."

"Just add it to the faculty sunshine fund," I said. "If anyone wants to see the picture, tell them to come by my classroom."

Over the next week, at least half the teachers dropped by for a peek. I was now a minor subterranean hero among the faculty at Millard Fillmore.

Later in my classroom, we discussed the post-Civil War era and Reconstruction, as well as the "equal protection clause" of the Fourteenth Amendment. Somehow the discussion turned to the recently passed California Proposition 209, which banned affirmative action in the state.

"I don't see the problem," a white student said. "It's not fair to hire people just because they're not white."

"It's not fair to only hire white guys, either," Melanie said. "That's why we had affirmative action in the first place."

"Who can tell me when and why affirmative action started?" I said.

"It started in the sixties to encourage recruitment of non-whites and women for jobs and admission," Robert said.

"Yeah, but it doesn't mean anything anymore," someone said. "Schools just gotta meet a quota for the year or whatever."

"That's not equal!" Gogia said.

I held up a hand.

"A hundred and thirty years after the Civil War and the Fourteenth Amendment, we still have discrimination," I said. "What *would* you do about it?"

"Isn't it against the law to discriminate?" Maria asked.

"Sure," I said. "But how do you prove you're being discriminated against?"

"That's so gay," Jackson said

"Do you mean happy or homosexual?" I asked.

Low giggles around the room.

"Well, like ... neither."

"Then what did you mean?"

"I meant I disagreed."

"If you just said you disagreed, you wouldn't have to risk offending homosexuals—or happy people," I said. "Tomorrow, I want everyone to tell the class where they stand on affirmative action."

"What if we're not sure?"

"Your homework is to think hard about it and decide."

The next day, every one of them declared a position with no interruption from their classmates. I then had them break up into five like-minded groups charged with writing a paragraph explaining their position and choosing one of their number to read it to the class.

After all five students had finished reading, I opened the topic to general discussion. The dialogue that ensued was among the most intelligent I'd ever heard from my class.

CHAPTER 22

When two people decide to get a divorce, it isn't a sign that they "don't understand" one another, but a sign that they have, at last, begun to.

—Helen Rowlands

WHATEVER I WAS DOING AT FILLMORE HIGH, it was working. Students started waving when they saw me cross campus, and in the classroom they were increasingly enthusiastic. I wouldn't deny that this attention was anything less than intoxicating.

"Are you planning on teaching again next year?" Amanda Kristina asked.

"Unless you want me to run for office." I was only half-joking.

She looked intrigued. "Which office?"

"There'll probably be some Assembly seats open in about a year."

"Fabulous." She flashed that perfect smile. "You can run as a moderate Republican."

I didn't like the sound of that. Nonetheless, I loved her dearly and lusted for her almost hourly. I decided to postpone any political plans until I could sort out my conflicting feelings.

A few months later, Amanda Kristina paced up and down our living room in full courtroom attire. Even with breasts tucked into a magenta blouse and hidden by a dark gray suit jacket, she had to be the sexiest woman admitted to the California Bar in decades.

"I supported your decision to join the Army," she said. "And I was proud of you for that. I'm even proud of you for being a teacher." She stopped and put her hands on her hips. "But do you really want to spend the rest of your life in a job where no one appreciates you?"

"Most of my students appreciate me," I said.

"I'll bet the girls do, but Richard, we both know you could be doing something that pays you what you're really worth." She swept her arm, encompassing our apartment. "Something more meaningful."

"Like bringing sweeter-smelling porta-potties to the masses?"

"Those porta-potties paid my way through college." Her voice had an edge.

"Actually, about 40 percent of your education was covered by the California taxpayer." I tried not to sound too self-righteous, but I think I failed. "Don't you think we should give something back?"

"Richard, what's wrong with making money?" She smiled. "What's wrong with wanting something more?"

"Nothing," I said. "But what I'm doing *is* meaningful, even if you don't see it."

"You're saying my job is meaningless?"

"Of course not."

"I guarantee I make a hell of lot more difference than you do," she said. "All the small businesses I represent? I make their livelihoods possible."

"How's that?"

"One of my clients owns a small inn right on the waterfront—it was built before that became illegal. He employs twenty people and he can't expand because of all the environmental restrictions and the Coastal Commission."

"How does he want to expand?"

"He wants to add rooms to his inn."

"How many?"

She shrugged. "About three hundred."

"Straight up?"

"Only ten stories." She held a hand above her head, revealing a bit more of her professional cleavage.

"What about all those people who may never see the ocean because his ten-story inn is blocking the view?" I asked. "You can't put a price tag on thousands of people who're inspired every day by the blue of the Pacific and the undulating waves."

"Can they eat the … undulating waves?"

"No," I said. "But I love the way you say *undulating.*"

She lowered her voice. "Like *un...du...lat...ing?*" This as she walked toward me and wrapped her arms around my neck.

Looking back, I suspect the reason our marriage lasted as long as it did was because our arguments, whether political, philosophical, or practical, tended to end with incredible makeup sex. Amanda could not only dance, but she could cha-cha, swing, and tango—so long as she was in charge.

During the last phase of our marriage, we became more vociferous in our arguments and less enthusiastic in the dance. Toward the end, Amanda wouldn't dance at all—not that I asked her.

While I was teaching, Sacatchy finally graduated from Cal State Northridge with a degree in computer science and information systems. A new company that dealt with the increasingly important issue of computer security hired him right out of the gate. Even though he was a bit vague about his actual duties, I had the impression he worked as a white-hat, testing the firewalls of corporations and government agencies and letting them know someone had broken in. His company's marketing staff would then contact the organization to sell it some security software. Essentially, he was being paid to do what he would have been doing for fun.

"Still like teaching?" Sacatchy asked over coffee in the middle of my third year of teaching.

"Love it," I said. "The kids are fun and even inspirational at times."

"How's the marriage?"

I sighed. A bit of unburdening seemed necessary.

"Sometimes I think we're on a slow boat towards the edge of the earth—back when the world was flat."

Shortly after my conversation with Sacatchy, I arrived at our apartment to find Amanda Kristina on the phone with her father.

"OK, Dad, I'll talk with him. Bye."

"What's up?"

"One of my father's supervisors resigned," she said. "He wants you to take his position."

"I know nothing about the porta-potty business and less about being a supervisor."

"My dad has faith in you. And he's willing to double whatever you make now."

"And if I'm not interested?"

"He's going to cut us off," she said. "No more free rent."

I paced, trying to bridge the gap between marital honesty and marital harmony.

"I never asked him to pay our rent. I'd be happy as a heifer in a Hindu village to be free of that albatross."

"He only wants to help—"

"It's not helping, it's controlling."

"You realize how paranoid that sounds?" She spread her hands. "Working for my father could be the opportunity of a lifetime ... *our* lifetime."

"I hope you take this in the most loving way, but how can you and your father even consider that I'd leave my job in the middle of a school year?"

"You're a *high school history teacher.*" She'd moved out of sarcasm into outright spite. "You're not irreplaceable."

I'd had enough.

"You know what? I wouldn't work for your father if he offered me a million dollars a year."

She stared. "Are you crazy?"

Maybe I was, but at the moment it felt fantastic.

"I could *almost* deal with his reactionary views—almost. But I'm not working for a liar and a hypocrite."

She flushed. "How dare you—"

"Amanda, he inherited the whole damn P-P business from your mom's family! I admire self-made people, but your father isn't one of them."

For a nanosecond her expression sank, and then she snapped back to boldface bravado.

"So? That doesn't make him a liar!"

"What about his service record?"

"What about it?" By now we were both shouting.

"The closest he ever came to Vietnam was the beach at Waikiki! Biên Hòa was an Air Force base, not an Army base ... And he doesn't even pronounce it right!"

If her jaw had gotten any tighter, she could have cracked a walnut with it.

"My father says he had a distinguished military career and I believe him."

I took a deep breath. It felt great to finally speak my mind, but I knew I'd crossed a line—right over a cliff.

"I know you love your father," I said, "but there's no way in hell I'm going to work for him!"

She crossed her arms over her chest. Her face was getting redder by the second. "Don't you want to be more than a teacher?"

"*More* than?" I took a deep breath. "I know you don't get it, but with every beat of my heart and every synapse firing in my brain, I believe teachers have one of the most important jobs in the world."

"What about politics?" she said. "What happened to that?"

"Amanda, the main reason I'd become a politician would be to help promote education and educators. And there is no way I can do that as a Republican."

"Richard, get the hell out of my house until you come to your senses!"

"Fine." At the door, I stopped and turned. "By the way, my name is Dick."

I rented a modest apartment near Millard Fillmore High. In my relatively small and initially depressing new digs, introspection was the order of the day. No running off to Mexico this time—I had classes to teach. And it was during this time that students and faculty of the Los Angeles Unified School District named me a teacher of the year. The only prize was recognition, which was why a local reporter from the *Los Angeles Times* came to interview me.

I waited until she'd exhausted all the standard questions.

"So, Karen," I said as I moved toward the white board, "do you have any interest in investigative journalism?"

"Sure, but it's tough to break into. All the big stories go to the main office downtown."

"Maybe you can find your own subject."

"Like?"

I wrote *Hamilton Conesto* on the board.

She raised a brow. "Not exactly a *Sixty Minutes* exposé."

"Might be if you can find him."

"How about his office?" She pointed toward the administration building next door.

"You'd have better odds winning the California lottery."

"Where does he spend his time?"

"That's what I want you to find out."

She pulled her notebook back out. "Is he ever here?"

"You might catch him next week for his annual 'fall splash.'"

"And then?"

"He disappears into the So-Cal smog," I said. "Though he's been observed in the office after hours with his vice principal Ms. Alverez."

"Working?"

"A little shoulder massage to relieve stress."

"Any evidence, or will I have to take your word on that?"

I opened my desk drawer, pulled out the photo, and handed it over.

She whistled. "Who took this?"

"That would be me."

"Maybe I should investigate you." Her expression changed to a salacious grin. "Who else knows about it?"

"Roughly half the faculty, but this is the only copy."

"Any chance I could borrow this one for a while?"

"Sure, as long as I remain your secret source."

She scribbled something in her notebook.

"And how much taxpayer money would you say he gets not to be here?"

"Probably about twice as much as teachers."

She slipped her notebook back into her purse.

"I'll be back next week to catch this guy in action," she said. "In the meantime, I'm pretty sure I saw a car in the principal's parking spot. I'll run his license, see what turns up."

"Get very close to the fence, study his car—it's a Lexus—and you'll uncover the first object of intrigue related to Dr. Hamilton Conesto."

Next week Karen Kracken was back with a photographer. Eager to present Millard Fillmore in the best light, Ham granted a brief interview in which he bragged about the staff and administrators, especially his vice principals.

The subsequent article included a brief profile of me as one of the teachers of the year and a few paragraphs about the positive atmosphere at Millard Fillmore High School.

I waited.

Two weeks later the paper published "Life and Times of Fillmore High's Principal Conesto."

Not only was Ham's salary well into the six figures, but it also turned out his doctorate had been awarded by mail from a now-defunct university in the Cayman Islands. His average week included two rounds of golf, a meeting at the LAUSD central office, and several sessions at the office of Green Pacific Investments, where he ran a small hedge fund under the name H. Hector Conesto. He also spent considerable time in a card room—right before a rendezvous with a starlet at the Beverly Hills Hotel.

The article also featured a copy of the photo I'd provided.

The district administration reacted by putting Hamilton Conesto on a "work plan," the first step being that he had to go to work every day. He wasn't just in his office, he was everywhere—but especially in my classroom. I suppose it hadn't been too hard to uncover the identity of Karen's "unnamed source."

As time passed, Conesto and I reached a separate and tentative peace: he had no way to fire me, and I'd already fired the only shot in my arsenal. Adrian Alverez, however, sneered at me every time I passed her office. I was forever to be the anti-Christ in her mini-parish.

CHAPTER 23

Coming back to where you started is not the same as never leaving.

—Terry Pratchett

ABOUT TWO MONTHS AFTER I SPLIT with Amanda Kristina, I was on the UCLA campus to touch base with some of my old professors when I happened by one of the large lecture halls. The sign outside indicated that a conference on southern Africa was in progress.

I walked in and stood at the back. At the podium, a professorial type was introducing the next speaker.

"In her brief career as an international reporter, she lists an astonishing body of work and has already received two of the most coveted awards in journalism. It is my pleasure to introduce Associated Press reporter and freelance writer Ms. Amanda Patina."

There was a smattering of applause as she stepped to the podium. She couldn't be much past her early twenties, but everything about her projected utter confidence.

"I won't pretend to be an authority on HIV/AIDS in Africa," she said, "but I've spent most of the past three months on the ground in Zimbabwe, South Africa, and Botswana, interviewing those stricken with illness as well as the medical professionals trying to cope with the impossible task of treatment. I've spoken with everyone from village chiefs to elected officials—who, for the most part, refuse to admit there's a problem."

She went on to cite statistics from which she ably extrapolated numbers to demonstrate the alarming upward trend of this epidemic. She was witty, poised, captivating. Oh, and unreasonably beautiful.

I had to meet her.

She finished to applause that bordered on thunderous. As the crowd filed out, I noticed that a card had fallen on the floor, no doubt from somebody's pocket: *Please join university administrators and faculty at a reception to meet and honor today's speakers from the Conference on Southern Africa.*

Sometimes luck just followed me.

As I walked into the reception, I spotted Amanda Patina at the far end of the room, surrounded by professors—including Dr. William Zachary, one of my major professors as a graduate student.

I swung by the catering table, grabbed a glass of wine, and sauntered over.

"Hi, Bill, how are you?"

"Youngblood! Ready to come back to graduate school?"

"Not yet," I said.

I waited for a break in the conversation surrounding Amanda Patina and then jumped in with both dimples and every ounce of charisma I possessed.

"My name is Dick Youngblood. I was intrigued by your presentation—do you think HIV victims in Africa will ever be treated in significant numbers while antiviral drugs remain so expensive?"

"Hi, Dick." Her sexy smile made my lips quiver. "There are actually some affordable drugs being produced in India, but if their use becomes widespread, American drug companies claim they'll lose incentives to produce better drugs."

"I have another question," I said. "How have you fit so many accomplishments into such a brief career?"

"I've always been a bit of an overachiever, but mainly I'm just lucky."

"And humble."

She smiled again. I probably grinned.

"So what do you do, Dick?"

"I teach high school history here in Los Angeles."

"That's a tough job," she said.

I studied her face, from her bright eyes to her smile. Sincerity radiated from every pore.

"It is, but mostly I love it."

"So what's your connection to UCLA?"

"I was a student here, BA and MA. I just happened by the lecture hall when you were being introduced and decided I had to meet you."

"So you crashed the reception?"

"I did," I said. "I know this is incredibly presumptuous, but how about you and I have dinner together in an hour or so?"

"I've been asked to dine with the dean."

"So ditch him."

"I'm an internationally acclaimed reporter," she said. "I can't just 'ditch' the dean."

"We're not talking Nelson Mandela," I said. "Take it from me, he's a boring old college administrator."

She raised an eyebrow. "And breaking bread with you will be nothing less than scintillating?"

"Relative to the dean, absolutely."

"Okay, tell me where to meet you."

I gave her the name and address of a well-known Westwood restaurant. I got there early, snagged a prime spot on the waiting list, and was sipping a beer at the bar when I heard an ethereal musical whisper.

"We all live in a yellow submarine."

I turned and found Amanda Patina singing in my ear.

"You found out about that in less than an hour?"

"I told you, I'm an award-winning reporter. Also, I had to make sure I wasn't dining with an ax murderer."

"So what else did you find out about me?"

"I tried to interview your grandfather about a year ago and was given the brush-off."

"Want me to give him a call?"

"Old issue, but I'll use your name next time." She grinned. "You didn't mention you were a decorated hero of the Gulf War."

"Are you done yet, award-winning reporter?"

"Has anyone ever mentioned you look like Conan O'Brien? Well, without the red hair. And that nose, definitely not Conan's."

"You ever see a profile of Richard Nixon?"

"Not that I remember."

"You have now."

"So you really are related?"

"God, I hope not."

We settled down to dinner, with which I ordered a bottle of chardonnay. We swapped family histories. I learned that her father was an Indonesian hotel manager and her mother an Australian diplomat. Her diversity manifested in dark blue eyes, bronze skin, and beautiful long black hair enhanced by lighter streaks.

By the time dessert and after-dinner liquors appeared, we still weren't even close to talked out.

"So what now?" she said.

"Let me walk you back to your hotel."

She studied me. "Is there anything else I should know about you?" she asked.

I guessed she'd discovered other things about me.

"I moved out of my wife's apartment about two months ago."

"Let me guess—she doesn't understand you."

My sunny demeanor suffered a momentary lapse. "Actually I think she was finally starting to."

"And what does she finally understand?"

"That I love being a teacher and there's no way in hell I'll ever join the family business."

"Which is?"

"Porta-potties."

She burst out laughing. "Seriously?"

"Capitalist porta-potties built on the wackiest ideals of the extreme right-wing, yes."

"I'm pretty sure that counts as irreconcilable differences."

As we walked, a tingly charge circulated around my body, apparently touched off by the simple gesture of her taking my hand. At that moment, she was the most alluring woman in Westwood or maybe in the whole Pacific Rim. We stopped in a dark corner of a park across from her hotel. We faced each other with her arms around my neck, and her expression quickly changed from sincere to sexy. She was almost as tall as me; we seemed to fit together as we indulged in a long, deep kiss.

"I really hope this isn't the wine talking, but the euphemistic phrase from very old movies seems apropos: Want to come up for a nightcap, Dickie?"

"Yes, yes, yes."

"Could your enthusiasm be the wine talking?" she said.

"I could be as sober as ... a Mormon missionary on a Sunday morning in Salt Lake City and wouldn't be able to say no."

After we closed the door to her room, within seconds we were dissolved into a haze of concupiscence. There were timeouts for giggles, timeouts for talk of relationships and even international politics, and at least in my case there were timeouts for falling in love. Our ardor was unabated until well past dawn.

The following evening we shared dinner and heartfelt goodbyes. Amanda Patina enthusiastically informed me she could be persuaded to repeat our assignation in some far corner of the globe. We exchanged e-mail addresses, but I suspected my best chance with her would be to keep e-mail contacts limited and judicious—for now.

Although I still loved teaching, Millard Fillmore was a bit too small for both Hamilton Conesto and me now that he showed up every day. Amanda Kristina and I had parted ways, and I looked forward to my unencumbered future stretching as far as my imagination could see.

At the end of the school year and three months after meeting Amanda Patina, I resigned from the school system, cashed in my retirement funds and the bonds the senator had given me as a graduation present, and flew to the Pacific.

I spent a few days in Hawaii before heading south to Tahiti and Tonga. In Fiji, over a cup of kava, I spoke with a few local radicals who remembered Tri-Y's passing through about two or three years back. I also found out Amanda Patina had left just two weeks before I arrived, having finished a story on Fiji's economic development.

At Internet cafes (now sprouting up on every corner of the globe), I stayed in touch with Rita Mae and kept tabs on Amanda Patina. Enamored as I was, I made sure to follow my own route—I didn't want her to think she had an international stalker.

In Australia I hiked up Ayers Rock with an aborigine who assured me I wasn't tromping on his ancestors. I loved the warmth and humor of the populace. In Asia I returned to Beijing to see if it had changed as a result of amazing economic growth. In Hong Kong, I observed the bustling business climate where you can allegedly start and end a business all in one day. In Tibet, Nepal, and part of India, I hiked up foothills of the Himalayas and tried to answer the question "What would Buddha do?"

In southern Africa I saw some of the dire conditions painted so vividly by Amanda Patina in her lecture at UCLA. In Egypt I stared in awe at the pyramids, trying with no success whatsoever to envision their being constructed without the assistance of giant cranes.

I was briefly detained in Iran and asked to leave when they discovered my grandfather's occupation. I moved on to Iraq, where I enjoyed viewing one of the cradles of civilization—until I saw the tenth huge photo and second statue of Saddam Hussein. I fought off the urge to revisit Saudi Arabia.

Moving on to Europe, I found Adriatic luxury at a minimal cost on the beaches of Croatia. I also received my fourth e-mail from Amanda Patina: "Hey, Dickie, are you following me around the world? If you are, I'm flattered."

I wrote back: "No, but I'm improving the odds that in some unsung corner of the globe, we may just happen to be walking down the same street or drinking in the same pub."

Her reply?

"If you happen to be near Budapest one week from today in the late afternoon, perhaps we can create a chance encounter. The clue to this rendezvous: 'Oh, Lord, won't you buy me a Mercedes Benz.'"

A week later I was combing the streets of Budapest near cocktail hour, desperately trying to find the Janis Pub. I finally located it, and there she was—Amanda Patina sitting at the bar, dark hair sparking. I sneaked up behind her and softly sang in my best raspy Janis Joplin: "Take a another little piece of my heart."

She turned and flashed a smile that illuminated the bar all the way to the back corners.

"Dick! Wow, it's amazing to run into you here—in this far corner of the globe. What are the odds of this happening purely by chance? It must be fate. Does that do it for you, sweetie?"

"Thanks for the clue," I said.

She looked confused. "I thought you sent *me* a clue."

"You sent me an e-mail that said if I happened to be in

Budapest today, we might meet in a pub with the clue 'Oh, Lord, won't you buy me a Mercedes Benz.'"

She shook her lovely head and stared at me.

"No, you sent me an e-mail that said if *I* was in Budapest today, we might meet in a pub with a blue door."

We couldn't figure it out. Her baffled expression evaporated, replaced by the sexiest smile in Eastern Europe.

"Somehow we're both here," I said. "And that makes me very happy."

"Truthfully and without sarcasm, I've missed you."

"So what do we do now?"

"You mean after we have another drink and go back to my room to unite Buda and Pest while barely getting wet in the Danube?"

Every time our glasses neared empty, they were immediately refilled. Snacks and *kolbasz* flowed freely and without our needing to order them. Eventually, though, the prospect of a more private rendezvous moved me to hail the Hungarian girl behind the bar.

"A check, please."

"Your bill is paid for." She pointed to a corner booth, but there was no one there. As we stared, a waiter held up a Janis Pub coaster.

"Are you Dickie?"

I nodded and he handed me the coaster. I flipped it over and saw something scribbled on the back:

> Hi Dickie! Congratulations on your world tour and
> Amanda upgrade. Sorry I can't stay and chat, but
> Budapest is still filled with spies. Toodles, Tri-Y.

"I think this explains the mystery of the e-mails." I handed the coaster to Amanda Patina.

"He was right here and you didn't see him?" She shook her head. "Does your dad show up often?"

"Not often enough, but his timing is almost supernatural."

* * *

We spent four wondrous days together in Budapest, immersing ourselves in the culture and our common desires.

"Amanda, do you ever want to stay in one place for a while?"

"Where?"

"How about somewhere in Northern California?"

"I'm happy to drop by, but I probably won't stay long," she said. "I love you *and* I love my job."

Then she was off to Krakow and I was off to Amsterdam to observe its experiment with drug legalization. From there I made my way to Northern Ireland, where I studied the fragile peace from my stool in a Belfast pub. Finally, after a few days in London, I spent most of my remaining pounds sterling on a plane ticket to San Francisco. It was almost five months since I had left, and if anyone asked, I could finally say I had been around the world.

Thanks to mechanical failure, I had a lengthy layover at JFK. I was sitting in the airport reading a novel when my new cell phone rang.

"Mr. Youngblood, this is Don Bonito of *The Dallas Morning News*. We've been trying to get hold of you. Amanda Nixon is holding a press conference in Dallas tomorrow."

"I haven't heard a thing about her since she was released from prison. Why would anyone come to her press conference?"

"She's a darling of Big D's extreme right wing. Until three days ago she had an AM radio talk show in Dallas and ten other stations in the South, *A New Dawn With Patty Dixon*. She said Governor Bush was too liberal with his compassionate conservatism."

"Yikes."

"In spite of her loyal fan base, her sponsors dropped her after an on-air comment about 'wetbacks, chinks, and towel heads' making 'all of the decisions from Austin to Washington, D.C.'"

"Pretty appalling, but what does that have to do with me?"

"She's calling the press conference to defend her rights to free speech, but an enterprising reporter—that would be me—uncovered her prior conviction. She claims she'll present information that sheds new light on it. The press conference is in downtown Dallas tomorrow at eleven in the morning. Interested?"

"I doubt if I'll be there, but thanks for the call."

An hour later, I headed to the Internet kiosk at the airport. The most enticing entry in my inbox came from Amanda Patina:

> Dickie dear, I miss you so much and my only chance of being in the US any time soon is this weekend in New Orleans. Any chance you could join me? We could make the Big Easy even easier. Love and jazz, Amanda (Patina— just in case you start to become Amanda-confused).

Within a minute, my fingers were clicking on the keyboard.

> Amanda P, I'll meet you in the French Quarter by Friday night. I'm making a brief stop in Dallas on the way. Je t'aime, Dickie.

As I approached the steps of the radio station, it appeared that the press conference had already started. In addition to onlookers (I counted ten), there seemed to be four representatives of the Dallas press, as well as a camera and a reporter sporting the new Fox News logo.

"We're becoming a nation of wimps!" There was Amanda Patricia, going strong. "I've received hundreds of messages from listeners that support my comments."

"Ms. Nixon, does your idea of freedom of speech involve using the most inflammatory words possible?" a reporter from a Dallas TV station asked.

"Free speech doesn't mean nice or politically correct speech," she said. "I'm just saying exactly what my listeners are thinking."

"Do your listeners know you were convicted of attempted murder and spent six years in prison?" Don Bonito asked.

"I only pled guilty because I'd been crucified by the liberal media." She pounded her podium for emphasis. "Dick Youngblood tried to kill me, but you try getting a fair trial when a senator's grandson is involved."

Just as she ended her sentence, she spotted me in the audience. Her face went ashen and her voice rose to a screech.

"He's right over there! Did you come to finish the job? You want to finish the job in front of all these people, Dickie? I hope you brought your gun—you'll need it! You'll be sorry, Dickie!"

After snapping a few photos of Amanda Patricia in meltdown mode, the press turned to me, with the Fox News reporter leading the pack.

"Mr. Youngblood, what is your reaction to these claims by Ms. Nixon regarding her conviction eight years ago?"

"The evidence proving Ms. Nixon's crime against me was so incontrovertible that she had no choice but to plead guilty," I said. "She has neither witnesses nor evidence for anyone to conclude otherwise."

"But aren't you upset that Amanda Nixon has accused you after all this time?"

"People can say anything they want in this great land, but it doesn't have to be true. The appeals court reviewed the case and said it was a fair trial. She had a good lawyer. There was no evidence that what she now claims is true. Case closed."

"So we should say you had no personal response?"

"You can quote my reaction exactly as I just stated it, boring as it may be."

Most of the journalists drifted away after that.

From Dallas I went on to New Orleans. Every day I spent with Amanda Patina exceeded the last. Our weekend was filled with cool jazz, ambrosial cuisine, and passionate lovemaking. It ended with my plea for her to visit me in the Golden State—or wherever I eventually found gainful employment.

CHAPTER 24

It has become appallingly obvious that our technology has exceeded our humanity.

—Albert Einstein

I ARRIVED IN THE BAY AREA HOMELESS and unemployed but far from destitute—thanks to my loving and prosperous mother, who met me at the airport and said the senator would "love" to see me.

The next morning I was contemplating my future and the San Francisco skyline from Rita Mae's floating estate in Sausalito when I received an e-mail from Sacatchy:

> Hey, Bro, now you've toured the world, I have a way-cool opportunity for you—no, it doesn't involve anything illegal. I have a "start-up" in Santa Clara. Actually it's a start-up for start-ups. Your position would be to use your considerable charisma to attract venture capital and deal with investment bankers after we go public. And you'll have a really cool title—Chief Information Officer.
>
> PS: These brilliant geeks in my company are driving me nuts. You can give me your answer over lunch next Monday in Palo Alto. See you then.

After thinking about it for a half-hour?

Hi, Sacatchy. As much as I'm impressed at your written acknowledgment of my charisma, what the hell do I know about business, software, or computer security? And by the way, I didn't know I was going to circle the globe until I did it.

We ended up at the same restaurant where we'd once shared burgers with Amber the militant vegan. The place had undergone a green renovation, figuratively and literally—the menu featured a photo of a now-famous woman who'd chained herself to an old-growth redwood in Northern California, along with a disclaimer: "The non-vegetarian items on our menu feature organic, range-fed beef and chicken. All of the fish were happily swimming in the open ocean before being mixed up in the gentlest of nets. The creatures of nature were raised in the most humane environment before they were mercifully euthanized to be served on our plates."

"Hey, bro, good to see you," Sacatchy said when he arrived. "The place has changed a bit, but it still brings back fond memories."

I tried not to giggle as he studied the menu.

"What can I get you guys?" the waiter asked.

Sacatchy ordered the prairie-raised Organic Bovine Burger With Soy Cheese. I got the Vegan Portabella Soy Fajitas.

"You haven't gone to the dark side, have you?" he asked.

"No, but I'm already feeling more peaceful."

"Speaking of peaceful," he said, "your marriage didn't last long."

"Did you expect otherwise? I assume you're still with Roc-Cindy."

"She's one of the reasons we relocated north. She has a new gig teaching art and design in the city, so I decided to start up a start-up. Everyone seems to be doing it."

"And how's your start-up going?"

"We have office space in Santa Clara, about thirty employees, and a fifty-page business plan. My partner was able to raise almost a million from his family, but we need some big bucks before we actually start producing."

"And what are you going to produce?"

"Software for start-ups. It'll feature computer security and show you how to convince your clients their investments and credit cards are safe."

"Don't you already have a lot of competition?"

"Yes and no. There're a lot of start-up companies dealing in software, but we're one of the only ones offering top security and an easy learning curve. And we're the only company geared towards other start-ups."

"So what would my job be?"

"Initially you'd court venture capitalists and convince them our plan has great potential."

"You think I can understand all the tech-talk?" I asked.

"It might actually help if you don't completely understand it," he said. "If somebody wants a more detailed explanation, you set up a meeting with one of the geeks. Dickster, this is the perfect application for your fantastic verbal skills—which I assume you'll want to sharpen in preparation for entering the political arena."

"I'm going to enter politics?"

"Just a question of when. That silver tongue of yours was made for bigger and better things."

"And the compensation for this fantastic opportunity?"

"At first you'll get enough to live on, and lots of stock and stock options once we go public."

"And when does that happen?"

"Probably in about a year."

"If I take your offer, you realize I may leave at any time to go back to teaching?"

"Not a problem, especially after we get the company up and running."

Seduced by the undulating roar of dot-com success stories, I jumped into bed with Sacatchy and stayed there for the next twenty months.

In the short run, the company prospered. All the venture capitalists were on a galloping quest to lasso the next big thing—all I had to do was convince them that the next big thing was computer security.

"Hey, Dickster," Sacatchy said one day, "the press is here in my office. They want you to show them around and explain what we do here."

Susan Chen was a business reporter from a San Francisco newspaper and I gave her the grand tour. At that point, our operation included about fifty people staring at computer screens and a few more walking around and looking important while everyone devoured coffee and croissants and smiled at our apparent success.

"How's your product different from those of other developers?" Susan asked.

"None of the competition incorporates unfaltering indigenous safeguards that deftly interface with all known existing platforms," I said. "Our state-of-the-art security component embodies a safety code composed of transposition keys capable of universal obfuscation. Our proprietary software could presage the difference between success and failure to a new company trying to become a predominant pioneer in e-commerce in the blossoming environment of trade-secrets fortification." I paused. "Did that make sense?"

She looked up from her frantic note-taking. "Business publications are full of jargon, and nobody wants to admit they don't understand." She smiled. "Maybe you could dumb it down for me?"

"We have this sexy supercool software that's destined to be the next colossal thing in the land of silicon, and so far investors just love us to death," I said. "Don't quote me, though."

"But that's the only thing that's made much sense since I've been here."

"Then steal my words and pass them off as your own conclusion," I said.

She laughed. "Have you ever thought about running for office?"

"Why do you ask?"

"I'd vote for you."

Two days later, the paper published a small article in the business section. The headline? "Success of Start-ups Such as SEXUTEC Based on Psychology More Than Fundamentals."

A few months after the article was published, I was worth a hefty chunk of change. I liked the job, but I wanted to get back to a more meaningful occupation.

"Sacatchy, I have to quit."

"You jockeying for a raise?"

"The pay's fine, but I miss teaching—and I don't think this tech expansion is going to last much longer."

"So in less than two years you're an authority on the industry?"

"Just a feeling I have. Besides, at this point you can easily get along without me."

I not only resigned, but I also sold over 90 percent of my stock. I was now a millionaire and a half, but I kept the source of my newfound wealth on the down-low with my family, friends, and associates. I did offer to pay my mother and grandfather back for their bad investment in my education at Stanford, but they resoundingly rejected my offer. Instead, I split my cash between savings and a few conservative investments.

I almost succeeded in my conscious attempt at pushing my newfound wealth into the deep recesses of my mind. Having a healthy bank account, however, did give me the swagger if I moved on to bigger things eventually. At the moment, I yearned for a return to teaching.

In 2000, a few months before I left the dot.com world to become an unemployed schoolteacher, Amanda Patina arrived from Tel Aviv. Having finally accepted my repeated invitations, she'd taken leave from her major news organizations and decided to spend the summer at my San Francisco Mission District loft.

During the five months we cohabitated, she continued to work freelance, while she opted to write a San Francisco restaurant guide.

"How hard could it be?" she said. "All you need are taste buds and a keyboard."

So we tasted our way through half the restaurants in San Francisco—a task more herculean than enjoyable. The book was ill-fated from the title, which she still blames on me: *None Dare Call It Frisco: An Outsider's Culinary Guide to Inside San Francisco.* Sales were less than brisk, and she no longer makes disparaging comments about food critics.

I loved her book.

I loved every second of our cohabitation.

"Dickie, it's been the best five months of my life, and I love you more than ever." I caught the quiver in her voice as she hugged me.

"But?"

"My forte is reporting and interpreting the world's events. You know I'll be back—please don't give up on me."

"Impossible," I said. "Even if I wanted to, which I don't."

So Amanda Patina reestablished herself as a citizen of the world and we reestablished our relationship as part-time and long-distance.

During my tenure among dot-com entrepreneurs, my lifestyle was relatively austere with the exception of a 7-series BMW— Sacatchy had insisted I project a veneer of chic prosperity to potential investors. Because the company had taken care of my lease payments, my brief infatuation with German engineering came to an abrupt halt after I quit. I could have easily continued making payments on my own dime, but I preferred to drive some- thing less ostentatious into a school parking lot. So I turned the lease over to the company and purchased an early-model Toyota Prius, the greenest car in America at the time.

It was August of 2000, and most California school districts were settling their budgets and making final staffing decisions for the coming year. I roamed the length and breadth of the Bay Area, résumé in hand, and within a week had three offers. The most appealing was from my alma mater, Rio de Mañana.

I accepted the offer and was hired for three classes of U.S. History and two of American Government. Only about a third of the teachers had been there when I was a student, and Ms. Hanal wasn't among them.

During the first faculty meeting, all the new teachers were introduced.

"We have a celebrity joining our staff," the principal said. "Coach LaTrudy, would you do the honors?"

My old coach stood up.

"Just over a decade ago, Dick Youngblood was a student here at Rio. I forgave him for a major faux pas on the basketball court, and I even forgave him when he brought my daughter home way past her curfew." Giggles and guffaws. "Since then Dick has earned two degrees from UCLA, served in the Army—for which he received numerous medals, including the Purple Heart—published a highly successful book, and been named a teacher of the year in Los Angeles. Welcome back to Rio de Mañana, Dick."

During the first few days of class, students generally pretend to be interested in anything teachers have to say. I used the opportunity to pontificate on the overarching themes of history and government. By the second week, the upcoming presidential election was much on my students' minds.

"Mr. Youngblood, do you have to be rich to run for president?"

"It doesn't hurt," I said. "Are both Bush and Gore wealthy?"

"Bush's father had an oil company, right?" Gabe said. "What about Gore?"

"His father was a senator, but no oil company," I said.

"Doesn't Bush want to cut taxes for rich people?"

"He does, yes."

"Big surprise," Gabe said. "Rich people want to make it harder to get rich and easy to stay rich."

"No," Will said from the back of the room, "the rich have more money because they worked harder."

"What if they inherited their money?" I said.

The class ended just as we were starting to engage in what President Bush called "class warfare." Although I'd examined this issue as a graduate student, I was now looking at it from the perspective of a citizen—a fairly wealthy citizen, as much as I tried to suppress it. Whether it be James Madison's Republican virtue or Franklin D. Roosevelt's New Deal pragmatism, I was convinced that our system works best when our representatives sublimate at least a smidgen of their self-interest for the sake of common good—I would be that type of representative.

In what I assume was a slow news week, the student newspaper opted to run a brief article on various facts about my life that one of its reporters unearthed.

"Mr. Youngblood," Megan said the next day, "the student paper said you were a student here back in the day?"

"Class of '86."

"Were you really a hero in the Gulf War?"

"I was awarded several medals, but that doesn't make me a hero." I decided to run with this teachable moment. "What if a soldier was very courageous but a lot of innocent people were killed? Is he still a hero?"

"Heroes don't kill innocent people," Jasmine said.

"They do if they're war heroes," another student said.

"What if we were attacked by another country?" I said. "Does that make it OK to bomb their cities like we did at Hiroshima and Nagasaki?"

"We have to protect our country," Jack said. "Didn't General Sherman say something about fighting a population during the Civil War?"

"With the weapons used then, it was easier to avoid civilian deaths," I said, "or 'collateral damage,' as the generals like to call it these days."

"Why do they call it collateral damage?"

"Anyone want to answer Terry's question?" I said.

"Because then they don't have say what it really is," Margaret said. "Killing women and children, even babies."

Time to bring it back around.

"Given the destructive force of the weapons we're using today," I said, "is it even possible to avoid killing civilians?"

The bell rang, allowing my point to resonate. As the students poured into the hallway, I glanced at my reflection in the window. A happy man looked back.

CHAPTER 25

Remember, America, I gave you the Internet and I can take it away.

—Vice President Al Gore, on *The Late Show* with David Letterman

SACATCHY CALLED ME IN LATE SEPTEMBER.

"Hey, bro, how's the teaching going?"

"I love it. How's the company? Still prosperous?"

"Very, but I decided you might be right about the tech bubble. So I sold the company and now I'm kind of rich."

"What are you going to do now?"

"Get back to my first love."

"Roc-Cindy?"

"Yes, but a close second is screwing with the system, which gets me to the reason for my call."

"Why am I not surprised?"

"We have a presidential election in less than six weeks," he said. "It's time for us to step up and ensure the best person wins."

"And I'm guessing it's not W, right?"

"Very perceptive."

"Sacatchy, do you foresee us doing anything unethical in the course of this noble endeavor?"

"Ethics, like art, are entirely subjective."

"I'd say that's far from entirely true, but count me in—tentatively."

"Do you remember the fliers blanketed on key areas just before the primary election in South Carolina? After McCain thumped Bush in New Hampshire, the Bush campaign distributed propaganda that said McCain was mentally scarred from his time as a POW, his wife is a drug addict, and he has an African-American love child. It seemed to work."

"Yep, the compassionate conservative at his best."

"So shouldn't we counter their nastiness with some of our own?"

"And how would we deliver this disinformation on such short notice?"

"On the Internet," Sacatchy said. "It's more or less free, and the old-time politicos don't understand its potential."

"And what will I be doing while you handle the Internet stuff?"

"Got any ideas for an 'information' sheet?"

I thought about it. "A chart has the illusion of fairness," I said. "We can borrow the title from Thomas Paine."

"'Common Sense About the Presidential Election'?"

"Sacatchy, I'm impressed. Polls show Gore has a lock on the Golden State, so I assume we're taking our 'Common Sense' nationally?"

"Yep, to the swing states."

We concocted a chart with a Gore side and a Bush side, with fifteen categories down. For every category, we juxtaposed two photos: unflattering images of Bush, presidential-looking images of Gore. For the Vietnam Era, we had Bush lifting a beer in a Texas bar with far too much enthusiasm to be sober, while Gore looked serious as an enlisted man serving as a photographer, with fire and smoke in Vietnam as the background.

No denying it was effective, especially if the voter didn't have much prior knowledge.

"Sacatchy," I said, "it's been fun to mess with Texas and its current favorite son, but I'm having qualms."

"If I was really unethical, I could go over to that computer and disrupt communication for a large segment of the Bush campaign," he said. "Take about an hour."

"That's not unethical, it's illegal."

"Sure, but could they catch me?"

Sacatchy sent out our document to every political group, newspaper, TV station, and radio station that had a Web site. Within a few hours it was ubiquitous on the Web. After a day, the blogs were abuzz. By the second day, some of the mainstream media had mentioned it. In a weekend TV interview on one of the major networks, the interviewer produced a copy of our chart and asked a major Bush campaign official about it.

The same weekend, I received an e-mail from faninfantaisa@yahoo.com:

> Hey, Dickie, fantastic facts you put out about Bush and Gore. I hope to see you soon. I discovered lately that I can maintain my radical persona but work within the system. Love, your pops, Tri-Y

I replied, but my e-mail bounced back with one of those "unable to deliver" messages.

"Hey, Sacatchy, are you in contact with Tri-Y?"

"Not since your wedding, and then only via the most sophisticated cryptographic algorithms."

I found it amazing that a two-page piece of anonymous propaganda could create such a buzz.

"What happens when the power of the Internet falls into the hands of someone even more unscrupulous than you?" I asked Sacatchy.

"Soon there'll be so many competing political movements that only the naïve and uninformed will be swept up in any sort of radical cause. There will, however, be vast increases in cybercrimes, thereby creating a huge need for geniuses like me to try to keep people's secrets safe."

"Your genius is transcended only by your hubris."

Sacatchy was so emboldened by the success of our chart that he told me he'd planned something bigger and better. As concerned as I was about a Bush presidency, I said no to further Sacatchy schemes.

"Is this your conscience yelling at you again?"

"I agree with Gandhi, I'm happiest when what I think, what I say, and what I do are all in harmony."

"So you'll be coming back as a nonviolent toad in the next life?"

"Jackrabbit."

Although I didn't know it at the time, three weeks before the election Sacatchy sent out a memo from W himself, telling his surrogates and campaign staff to "stop all references to me being compassionate and play up how tough I can be."

A week later Dick Cheney, again courtesy of Sacatchy, sent out another memo: "We have not hit our opponents hard enough on foreign policy. We need to remind the voters that the Clinton-Gore bunch have been milk-toasty towards our enemies. I want North Korea and Iran to be quaking in their boots when we take over. How about we release a statement that we have not ruled out an invasion of either nation?"

Sacatchy was having the time of his life, unfettered by a partner with a Gandhi complex or the demands of running a company. He hacked, pranked, and disrupted communications to his heart's content.

Three weeks after the election and the hanging chads debacle, I got a call from Sacatchy.

"Dickster, we're in trouble."

"What's this *we* shit? And with whom are you in trouble?"

"The Federal Election Commission. They have your name as the co-author of the Bush vs. Gore flier. Also, they think they've caught on to the rest of my escapades. Some of the federal investigators are almost as smart as me."

"But not quite?"

"They actually hacked into my computer. Then they got a warrant and seized half of my gadgets. They found the phony memos, including one to W that I didn't tell you about before, advising him to say, 'God will be very disappointed if Al Gore becomes president,' but they missed the one in which a speechwriter advised Bush to mumble some profanities about reporters, then pretend he 'didn't know the microphone was on.'"

"So, what do *we* do?"

"Get a lawyer. I have one, but you surely don't want to slog through the same legal bog as me."

Five days later the headline read, "Former CEO and CIO of SEXUTEC Under Investigation." I thought of calling the senator but remembered that I could easily afford a flaming-hot lawyer all by myself. Soon I'd contracted with Tyson Hall. I explained my limited involvement with Sacatchy Sun, and she ran with it. Within a few days, I was in the clear.

Sacatchy wasn't as fortunate. He was convicted of violating federal election law and sentenced to six months in a federal prison and fined ten thousand dollars. He did, however, convince the judge that rather than paying a fine he could easily afford, he'd be willing to spend a hundred hours upgrading the court's computer system.

Within a week of his stay in prison, he finagled an audience with the senior warden. Within two weeks, he not only redesigned the prison computer system, but he also vastly improved the loudspeaker and alarm systems. He then took up temporary residence at the warden's home, where he converted all the electronic devices, from the television to the washing machine, into technological marvels that could be controlled by a single remote. Within six weeks he was released for "good behavior."

CHAPTER 26

I can hear you. I can hear you. The rest of the world hears you. And the people who knocked these buildings down will hear all of us soon.

—President George W. Bush

ONE MORNING BEFORE I LEFT MY SAN FRANCISCO loft, I turned on the TV and watched the planes fly into the Twin Towers. Later, in class, my students and I watched that footage again and again. I could see the questions on every face. I tried to help them make some kind of sense of what had happened.

I gave up.

"Class dismissed," I told them after fifteen minutes. "Maybe tomorrow we can discuss this."

"Mr. Y, why do they hate us?"

"Thomas, they don't all hate us," I said. "But a lot of them see the United States as sort of a global bully."

"Hey, Mr. Y, why can't the U.S. be united all the time like we are now?"

"The last time we were this united was probably during World War II. Is there such a thing as being too patriotic?" I asked them.

"Hitler's Germany was pretty patriotic," Shawn said.

Less than two years later we "shocked and awed" Iraq and deposed Saddam Hussein.

"I guess we showed those Iraqis," Matt said in my first-period class.

I looked at him for a moment. "What did we show them?"

"We stopped them from making all those weapons and planning more terrorist attacks!"

"How many of you believe the Iraqis were hiding weapons of mass destruction?" I asked the class.

About six hands went up, some tentatively.

"And how many of you believe there is no evidence of Iraq hiding weapons or planning attacks against the U.S.?"

About twelve hands went up, most of them confidently.

"Raise your hand if you've seen any evidence of either of those things," I said.

Not a hand went up.

"So why did we attack Iraq?" Jason said.

"Good question. By next Tuesday, everyone bring in an article from a newspaper, newsmagazine, or online source, printed out or on a flash drive. Be prepared to explain to what degree your piece is fact, opinion, political spin, or propaganda."

For two class periods, we analyzed and evaluated each contribution. Many were starting to become intelligent, skeptical consumers of the media.

"Mr. Y," Charlotte said from the back of the room, "why aren't more teachers like you?"

Scattered groans and more than one eye-roll. "Suck-up," someone whispered.

"What do you mean, Charlotte?"

"You seem to really care what we have to say."

"Maybe other teachers don't have dedicated students like you to inspire them." More groans, but I also caught a few smiles.

"What about me?" Adam said. "I'm way dedicated."

Amid a chorus of chuckling, it was a fun day in G-5 at Rio Mañana High School.

* * *

After the invasion of Iraq, my publisher contacted me.

"I think there might be a fresh market for *Was the Gulf War Really a War?*" he said. "Let's bring it back."

Soon after my book was reintroduced, National Public Radio interviewed me.

"Do you think the U.S. learned anything from the first Gulf War, Dick?"

"If anything," I said, "we've learned that people have very short memories."

"How have you been handling 'no WMDs in Iraq' thus far in the classroom?"

"It's been a huge challenge for teachers not only to explain the issues but to teach kids to question information without turning them into cynics."

"Let's say you're in Congress," my interviewer said. "What would you do?"

"I wouldn't vote to commit American soldiers to a war unless our security was directly threatened."

In the few days after my interview, I received several (mostly positive) e-mails from listeners. By far the most gratifying was from Maria, my former student at Millard Fillmore:

> Hi Mr. Youngblood,
>
> I heard your voice on NPR as I was driving near the Nation's capital. If I hadn't been on the inside lane of the beltway I'd have pulled over and given your words my complete attention.
>
> I owe you, Mr. Y. Because of your class I was inspired to pursue a career in journalism, and I just landed my first job with the Washington Post after graduating from NYU.

You turned history into a fun exciting adventure. More importantly, you seemed to really care about your students (you even laughed at our sometimes silly humor). Although, you didn't declare your candidacy in that interview, I look forward to seeing you in Washington DC when you arrive as an elected member of Congress. I can never thank you enough. Love and Peace,

Maria Marquez.

CHAPTER 27

Have you folks been following the controversy with John Kerry and his service in Vietnam and the Swift Boat campaign? It all took place in Vietnam and now it just won't go away. I was thinking about this—if John Kerry had just ducked the war like everybody else, he wouldn't have this trouble.

—David Letterman

EARLY IN 2004, I VOLUNTEERED TO ASSIST the Democratic Party, where I quickly became one of the regional directors for John Kerry's campaign. I was starting to realize that politics was part of my soul. It seemed inevitable that I'd become a candidate at some point—but could I actually make a difference?

Although my job was primarily organizing other volunteers and distributing information, on occasion I participated in policy meetings.

"The campaign needs to hit Bush/Cheney much harder on the WMDs," I said.

"The problem there," the California campaign manager said, "is that the senator voted for the resolution supporting the Iraq war."

"Because of the lies—excuse me, the bad intelligence," I said. "And we need to hit the Swift Boat people harder." I sent a few smart suggestions to the higher-ups in the campaign, and each time the response was the same: they were "taking it into consideration."

The campaign was in full swing when I got a call from Sacatchy.

"Hey, Dickster, the Kerry campaign is way too nice."

"Agreed. What's your solution?"

"We need to make a video."

"Call it 'Is Our President as Dumb as He Seems?'" I said.

"How about 'Oh, Why Can't We See Where the WMDs Could Be?'" Sacatchy said.

"I'll be your cheerleader," I said. "But I'm on the bench when it comes to production."

"At least one of us learned his lesson."

"What have you got in mind for your video?"

"Clips—lots of them—with just four words."

"Could they be *weapons of mass destruction*?"

"You're amazingly astute, Dickster."

"Let me know when you've got a finished product," I said. "Maybe I can convince the Kerry campaign to back it."

Sacatchy collected the clips and enlisted the aid of an unemployed film-school graduate. The viewer was treated to a collage of Bushies justifying the invasion of Iraq. "Weapons of mass destruction," Collin Powell crooned at the United Nations. "Weapons of mass destruction," Donald Rumsfeld barked on national TV. Big Dick Cheney touted the dangers of Saddam's weapons of mass destruction with terrifying authority. The president cited the importance of destroying the WMDs before Iraq could establish complete "nucular" capability.

None of the clips had been altered by a single word.

My new friends in the Kerry campaign loved the video but were still trying to drive on the high road. More likely, they didn't want it to be again pointed out that Kerry had voted for the Iraq invasion.

"Sorry, Sacatchy," I said. "They're not interested at this time.

I'm beginning to think that if Bush wins, the blame can be placed on timid higher-ups in the Kerry campaign."

"I guess I'll have to do some heavy Internet lifting myself."

Sacatchy sent the video out to each of the PACs and other organizations that supported Democrats and then posted it on YouTube. It became the front-page feature of his new site: "WMDs Where Can You Be?"

Of course, by 2004 posting on the Internet was preaching to the choir. Democrats laughed their liberal asses off while Republicans increasingly looked to Fox News and conservative radio talk shows as their only source of the so-called truth. Which meant that the only people watching Sacatchy's video were the people who already agreed with its message.

"Victory is in our hands," Senator Kerry said at a leadership meeting on a post-convention sweep through California. "Keep up the hard work and we'll have a new administration in January. Thank you! Any questions?"

I jumped to my feet. "Hello, Senator, my name is Dick Youngblood. Do you and your advisers plan on a more pointed reaction to the Swift Boat Veterans for Truth charges?"

Someone whispered something to Kerry.

"Hi, Dick, I just spoke to your grandfather in Washington a couple days ago. How'd you come to be a Democrat?"

"Must be a recessive gene."

"In answer to your question, we believe a more detailed response would give the Swift Boaters more credibility and put us on the defensive."

"Senator, I'm afraid the tabloid qualities of these charges are appealing to a lot of people whose news sources, let's face it, don't give them facts. If you lay out all the evidence, remind people what men in your unit said, you can sound strong without coming off as defensive."

Senator Kerry smiled. "Thanks, Dick. I'll take it into consideration."

As the campaign matured, I became more and more frustrated with these spineless responses. If I learned anything from the Kerry candidacy that might apply to my upcoming campaign, it was that I will not be yellow-submarined the way he was Swift Boated.

CHAPTER 28

I'd jump in front of a bus for you … as long as it's not moving.

—Anonymous

IT WAS SEVEN O'CLOCK ON A MONDAY morning, September 11, 2006. I was standing in line at my local non-chain coffee shop, waiting patiently for my towering nonfat whipped mango cappuccino, looking up at the flat-screen TV.

"Al Jazeera reports that a group identifying themselves as Jihadists Against Jesus claims to have kidnapped two American journalists," a reporter said. "CNN's investigation, however, reveals that neither Amanda Patina nor Clay Katona are U.S. citizens."

The phone in my pocket buzzed.

"Dickie, have you seen the news?" Rita Mae's normally soothing tones sounded tightly wound.

"Just now." My throat was so tight I could hardly speak.

"Call your grandfather—"

"I'll call him from Cairo."

By late afternoon on September 13, I was on an Air France red-eye to Cairo. According to Al Jazeera and CNN, neither the Egyptian government nor the U.S. embassy in Cairo had ever heard of Jihadists Against Jesus. They had, however, shown the video the JAJ released online shortly after the kidnapping: it showed Amanda Patina and Clay Katona, sitting in front of a black curtain and looking despondent while a voice off camera recited a fairly typical manifesto.

I closed my eyes and tried not to cry.

After a precarious taxi ride from the airport, I tossed my bags into my hotel room and jogged through the crowded back alleys toward the U.S. embassy. After a security pat-down, I was finally let in.

"How can we of service to you, Mr. Youngblood?" a young woman asked while scrutinizing my passport.

"I'd like to talk with someone, probably in your security division, about the recent kidnapping of those two journalists."

"What's your interest in this?"

"Amanda Patina's my … she's my girlfriend."

"Have a seat out in the lobby," she said. "I'll see if someone from Security is available."

A few minutes later a young Asian woman appeared.

"Mr. Youngblood, I'm Foreign Service Officer Jenna Kam. I'm so sorry," she said with a deep sincerity, "but there's very little we can do in this case, since neither Amanda Patina nor Clay Katona is a U.S. citizen."

"She's lived in the states, she's worked in the states," I said. "She went to Harvard—we met in California!"

Ms. Kam touched my shoulder. "We'll alert our operatives to be on the lookout for any information on the so-called JAJ."

I took a deep shaky breath. "What else can I do?"

"The local police and the EIS are investigating, but you might be able to put some pressure on them by talking to the Indonesian embassy."

For all Ms. Kam's warmth, I felt cold as I made my way through the throngs of Cairo. I'd never felt more helpless.

Time for a long-distance phone call.

"Grandpa, I need your advice."

"Dickie, where the hell are you?"

"Cairo," I said. "You heard about Amanda Patina?"

"Your mom called. I'm sorry, son."

"I need to do something," I said. "There are brick walls everywhere."

"You've been to the embassy?"

"They say they can do almost nothing." My voice caught. "She's not a U.S. citizen."

I waited through an uncharacteristic pause.

"You really love this girl, don't you?"

"More than I could ever explain." I suddenly realized we'd been together, figuratively if not physically, for nearly seven years. "Is there anything you can do?"

Another long pause. He took a breath and cleared his throat. "I'll see if I can move her up the priority list."

Three hours later, the senator called back.

"Dickie, go back to the embassy and ask for a man named El Fuente. He's CIA, but, of course, we don't have spies in our embassies, do we?"

"Of course, Grandpa."

I ran most of the way to the embassy, only to find the gate blocked by American soldiers.

"My name is Richard Youngblood," I said. "I need to see a man named El Fuente. It's urgent."

The guard pulled out a cell phone and spoke in low tones with his back to me. Then he slid the phone back into his pocket and turned to me.

"Mr. Youngblood, El Fuente is in transit. He'll meet you here tomorrow at 0900."

* * *

I arrived at the embassy early and was ushered into a large conference room with only one inhabitant.

"Mr. Youngblood, I assume." El Fuente held out his arm and gave me a bone-crushing handshake. "I want you to know that the kidnapping of Amanda Patina has become an issue of the utmost importance to the United States."

"How much help can we expect from the Egyptians?" I said.

"I've been assured this case is among their top priorities. And an intelligence officer from the Indonesian embassy will be joining us shortly."

Soon a large bronze man was ushered into the room. He introduced himself as simply, Gema.

"Gentlemen," he said, "tomorrow the Indonesian Embassy will issue a statement demanding the release of the international journalist and Indonesian citizen, Amanda Patina."

"I like it," El Fuente said. "Even though CNN already spotted their screw-up, this corroborates it."

"Why the hell were they even targeted?" I asked. "Everybody but the JAJ seems to realize they're not U.S. citizens."

This elicited a look of mischief in El Fuente's handsome face.

"As you Americans, my new fellow citizens might put it, I have a feeling we're not dealing with the fastest fuse lighters in the bomb-making class here."

Though it didn't make global headlines, the story was featured in several publications, including a French daily with the headline "Terroristes Incompetents." For the next day or two we had high hopes, but there was nothing—no word, no further videos, no communication of any kind.

The JAJ was silent.

For the next few days I wandered through the streets of Cairo looking up at empty windows and wondering if Amanda Patina was being held somewhere close by. I kept calling the embassy. Kept getting the same response: nothing yet.

Most of the people in Cairo were friendly, and quite a few spoke English. Almost half the people I talked to had heard about the kidnapping, and a few smiled or laughed when I mentioned the Jihadists Against Jesus. But when I showed them Amanda's picture, they only shook their heads.

Someone directed me to a supposed leader of the Muslim Brotherhood. I also spoke with a Cairo police officer who stood on the corner, whispering out of the side of his mouth. But nobody could—or would—tell me anything. What I needed was an Egyptian Sacatchy.

After five frustrating days, I had only one option left. As an American citizen and the grandson of a U.S. senator, I had to be more valuable to the JAJ than an Indonesian journalist.

I arranged a meeting with El Fuente and then spent most of the night tossing and turning. My plan was reckless, but it was all I had.

"I'm going to make an announcement," I told El Fuente the next morning. "I want to trade places with Amanda Patina."

"Are you nuts?" El Fuente said. "Then we'll have to rescue you."

"At least we can draw them out in the open," I said. "Right now we can't even find them."

He studied me. "You really willing to do this?"

"It scares the hell out me. But yes."

After a minute, he nodded. "Officially, the embassy will deny any involvement," he said. "The United States does not negotiate with terrorists, except when they do."

My voice sounded really thin when I said, "I'll do it today. This afternoon."

"Slow down. The Egyptians say they've got a lead. Let's give them a day, OK?"

I went back to wandering the streets of Cairo, feeling deflated—courage interruptus. I called El Fuente every few hours, with no results. So I sent a press release to CNN, Al Jazeera, and the

Egyptian newspapers. Nothing fancy—I only stated who I was and that "I'm willing to trade places with Amanda Patina." I found out later a story appeared in *The San Francisco Examiner* with the headline "Marin County Teacher Offers to Trade Places With Kidnapped Journalist." The article went on to say I was a high school teacher at Rio de Mañana, the grandson of Senator Lambright, and romantically linked to Amanda Patina.

Three hours after I delivered my press release, a message was delivered to my hotel:

> Mr. Youngblood, please meet Mr. Awad in front of the statue of Omar Macramé in Tahrir Square tomorrow at 2 PM to discuss the details of a possible exchange. Please come alone or there will be no exchange. If we believe the United States government is involved, there will be no exchange. Mr. Awad will approach you by identifying himself. We know what you look like.

Two hours later I met El Fuente at a small coffee shop far from the U.S. Embassy.

"Seems they're interested," he said. "When you meet Awad, insist the exchange take place in a public place where both you and Amanda Patina can see each other. He'll probably say that's not possible—stay strong on this point but don't close the door to negotiation."

"Why would they believe I'm not working with the U.S. government?"

"Say you tried but there was nothing they could do. Keep insisting that you're acting alone. Of course, US agents will—hang on." He pulled out his cell. "Got it." He slipped the phone back into his pocket. "Let's go."

"Where?"

"To the embassy. Something's come up."

* * *

We sped back to the embassy, where El Fuente led me straight to a conference room. There, sitting at the table, disheveled but smiling, were Amanda Patina and Clay Katona.

I held Amanda so tight she couldn't breathe until I finally let go, tears in my eyes.

El Fuente, Gema, and two stern-looking agents from the Canadian embassy sat down.

"I'm sorry to interrupt your reunion," El Fuente said, "but we need to speak with Ms. Patina and Mr. Katona while details are still fresh."

We took a seat around the conference table.

"Please tell us the whole story," Gema said.

"We were held in a dilapidated apartment building about five floors up," Amanda said. "We had almost no contact with our captors. A couple of times a day, food and water were delivered by an Egyptian woman who seemed a bit confused—perhaps by the man in the hallway with a rifle."

As she spoke, I tried to picture myself in this situation. I couldn't. I was trembling while Amanda seemed so courageous.

"Did you see the man?"

"I did," Clay said. "He was massive, way bigger than our original captors."

"Please continue," El Fuente said.

"Clay and I were in different rooms," Amanda said. "The doors were locked and the windows were nailed shut. I was dozing off earlier this afternoon when I heard scraping noises outside my window. Eventually someone pushed the window up a few inches. I looked out and there was Clay with this smiling man who gave me a shush sign and a thumbs-up. He pried the window the rest of the way open with a crowbar and I joined them on the ledge outside."

"He had to break part of the window to get me out," Clay said.

"So we crept along this ten-inch ledge until we were able to jump the gap to the roof of the next building," Amanda said.

"Someone fired at us," Clay said.

"How many shooters?"

"No idea," Clay said. "We were moving pretty fast at that point."

"The man took us down a staircase, through several alleys, and finally to a waiting taxi." Amanda turned to me and smiled. "When I asked him who he was, he said, 'What color is the submarine?'"

I grinned as I connected the Y's. "My *dad* rescued you!"

"Ms. Patina and Mr. Kotona," El Fuente said, "as international reporters, I'm sure you'll understand that the identity of the agent must be kept secret to avoid putting his life in great danger as well as limiting his intelligence-gathering abilities."

"What are we supposed to say?" Amanda asked.

"You can write about the entire experience—just refer to your liberator as Agent X or something."

She smiled. "How about Agent Y?"

El Fuente rolled his eyes. "Definitely not."

"He saved my life," Amanda said. "Of course I agree."

"My lips are sealed—forever if necessary," Clay said.

"Dick, I assume you can agree to this also?"

"Absolutely." I was still reeling.

After all the questions, the debriefing, the interviews, and a good night's love-sleep, Amanda Patina and I flew to San Francisco, where we spent three incredible weeks at my San Francisco loft.

"Would you really have traded places with me?" she asked on our second morning together.

"Of course."

I didn't mention the relief I felt at not having to test my commitment to this declaration.

"You're nuts," she said. "Did you stop to think how I'd feel if they actually took you up on your offer?"

"I'd still have wanted you to be free."

CHAPTER 29

I don't want to be invited to the family hunting party.
—*President Barack Obama, after being informed that he and*
Dick Cheney are eighth cousins

I RETURNED TO RIO DE MAÑANA and a hero's welcome. One class even gave me a standing ovation. I was tempted to embellish the facts and make myself a hero, but I didn't.

Some media outlets suggested that my "courageous offer" to trade places with Amanda Patina had something to do with her escape. As far as I know, the two events were not connected, but I'll ask Tri-Y someday.

Right after the publicity hit, I received an e-mail from Lily Livinsky:

> Hey Dickie! Hero again, huh? Don't let it go to your
> head. You're still not as famous as some of the fossils I'm
> digging up. Love and sound bites, Lily Livinsky.

During this period of time, Amanda Patina and I enjoyed a spectacular weekend in Carmel, the picturesque village that is California's prime claim to quaint. The ostensible purpose for our little rendezvous, not that we needed one, was to celebrate the contract for her new book, *Democratic Movements in Arabia: The Wave of the Future?* We had dinner at Casanova, seated in a cozy alcove with a fireplace. The food was first-rate and our wine glasses seemed to refill themselves.

"Amanda, dear, are you trying to get me drunk?"

"It's a technique I perfected to glean information. You didn't even notice my filling your glass until the last time."

"But my life is an open book, at least to you."

"I doubt it. What do you think about when I'm not around?"

I was curious about this curious question. "Since you've gleaned so much information, you tell me."

"Running for office."

"Politics is a persistent mistress," I said. "At first it was periodic lust that turned into the occasional fling. But I've been thinking about a two-, four-, or even six-year commitment." I sipped my wine. "You're not jealous, are you?"

"Hardly. I can do things for you that nothing in politics could equal." She giggled with a devilish grin. "Really, why do you have such an attraction to the political life?"

"Every time a politician gives a speech, I ask myself why she or he didn't say X instead of Y, wasn't more firm, more artful, more diplomatic. I constantly ask myself how I could bring about change where others have failed."

Amanda leaned back and studied me. "When did you start thinking so seriously about this?"

"A few months ago I heard a rumor that my congresswoman may retire after her next term expires."

"Have you substantiated the rumor?"

"Apparently she's still undecided."

My soul warmed as I watched the reflected fire flicker in Amanda Patina's lovely eyes.

"Should I go for it?" I said. "If the door opens?"

"I'm not sure you have a choice," she said.

"Everybody has a choice. Want to be the girlfriend of a congressman?"

"Maybe I should become a citizen first."

* * *

With the freeing of Amanda Patina, my life was so peachy that even the San Francisco fog couldn't cloud my outlook. My notoriety was on the wane, but I was still famous in room E-5 at Rio de Mañana. The only thing missing was a daily dose of Amanda Patina.

"Dickie, I'm stuck and lonely again this weekend," she said on the phone one Tuesday morning.

"Where this time?"

"Bora Bora."

"Damn, guess I'll have to read my students' essays on the plane."

"Think you can get a flight?"

"I'll charter one if I have to."

I was increasingly alarmed at the low priority placed on education. California classrooms were rapidly descending into static anarchy, and bare-bones budgets were being stripped yet again.

After several trips to the capital, I was drawn to a new organization called ACERT, the Association of California Educators for Revival of Teaching. The "revivalists," as they were often referred to, sought to reform public education. Founded three years back with just two hundred members, ACERT's numbers had exploded to more than twelve thousand. Its ultimate goal was to have control of education in the same way the California Bar controls the legal profession.

On my third sojourn to Sacramento, ACERT offered me a job as a public advocate. I took the position but knew it would be hard to leave my students.

"Mr. Youngblood, why are you leaving?" one of them asked.

"Yeah, why?"

"I'll miss you all," I said, and they knew I meant it. "But I have a chance to help make schools better all over California."

They got it.

* * *

At first my new job was a bit mundane, to the point that I sometimes wondered if I'd made the right decision. Gradually, though, my silver tongue turned platinum and I began talking to legislators and testifying before the Senate and Assembly committees.

At ACERT, I had the option of creating my own job title. Some of my colleagues opted for "legislative advocate," but I decided to keep things simple (and keep myself humble). I was simply a lobbyist.

I was proud of each small victory I helped win for public education, but as new opinions and ideas darted around my mind, I yearned for a broader influence. I kept a close eye on the legislative and congressional districts in California, looking for an opportunity to run for office no matter what Congresswoman Demore decided.

In 2008 I reestablished my volunteer role with the Democratic Party as one the regional directors of the Obama campaign. On the policy front, I particularly pushed for an emphasis on his ideal of health care for all. But I was also responsible for developing personalized e-mails for potential donors in many of the western states. We received more donations (mostly small) than any presidential candidate in history. This, I realized, was the real power of the Internet: fund-raising.

But big money still talked, and with the Citizens United Supreme Court decision two years later, it would roar. In the meantime, Obama's charisma and the Republican vice presidential candidate, who was giving late-night comedians job security for years to come, increasingly brightened Democratic prospects.

A couple of weeks after the 2008 election, I was having dinner with Sacatchy and Roc-Cindy in downtown Sacramento.

"When are you going to run for office, Big Daddy Dick?" Roc-Cindy said.

"I can hardly wait to work on your campaign," Sacatchy said.

"No thanks," I said. "I've seen the effects of negative campaigning. The system responds just fine to well-funded and well-organized interest groups."

"Except not everyone has a lobbyist."

"And not everyone has a PAC," I said, "which makes money even more the mother's milk of politics."

"The country needs you," Roc-Cindy said. "Go for it!"

"OK, you two are the first to know." I stood up. "Tonight, with the utmost humility, I hereby declare my candidacy for an undisclosed office on some near but as yet undisclosed date. I pledge to you that upon my election, the ignorant will become educated, the sick healthier, the undocumented will become documented, carbon will become healthier than a mist of broccoli, the poor will become powerful, the polluted converted to pristine, war will become peace, job offers will be as plentiful as fast food advertisements, and the frowny will turn smiley. Oh ... and I promise to win. On to victory!"

Sacatchy and Roc-Cindy stood up and gave me a two-person standing ovation. A few people at adjacent tables also applauded while everybody else laughed or looked completely confused.

"Why not run for the next election?" Roc-Cindy asked.

"Politics isn't just about issues and money," I said. "It's also about timing."

Early in my career as a lobbyist, I'd become acquainted with Mickey McWhirr, the self-described "secretariat for the proletariat." He was an eighty something professional protestor and permanent fixture around Sacramento. He was also a disbarred lawyer who'd taken too many shortcuts defending clients.

"Hi ya, laddie," he said as I approached the Capitol one fine morning. "I know you're not a legislator, so you must be a lobbyist or a lawyer."

"Dick Youngblood." I held out my hand. "Lobbyist for ACERT. I've heard about you."

"All good, I'm sure. Here, I've got a sign for ya." He rustled through his large canvas messenger bag. "Ah, yes, in Scottish blue and white."

The sign was professionally painted in huge letters: "STOP THE CASTRATION OF PUBLIC EDUCATION."

"It's yours if you promise to put it up in your office."

"Deal."

I snagged the sign and ran up the steps.

As I was heading out of the Capitol a few days later, there he was with two painted signs in merely big letters: "License Parenting, not Marrying," and "Let's Keep Track of Who's Funding the PACs."

"What's with the rhymes?" I asked

"Let's go across the street for a wee dram and I'll enlighten you, Dick."

"My treat."

When we got to the pub, Mickey in well-rehearsed finesse, literarily jumped up onto the barstool. The bartender slid a shot of single-malt in front of him.

"Fill in the blank, my friend," he said. "'Tippecanoe and _____ too.' And I didn't even grow up here."

"Tyler?"

"I rest my case."

"I don't think 'I like Ike' or 'All the way with LBJ' would work today," I said.

"Why not?" Mickey said. "How about, 'Youngblood guarantees real action to stop the pain of gridlock and faction.'"

"I'll use it when I run."

He handed me his card. "Mickey McWhirr: the power of the rhyme outlasts its time."

* * *

Finally in 2009, the headline for which I'd been waiting: "Janet Demore to Quit Congress at the End of the Term." I had just become a homeowner in her district, and in the interest of full disclosure, the location of my new condo had been intentional. She was a moderate Democrat, but the Tea Party had increasing strength in less-than-urban parts of the district. The question was not whether to run but what were my chances of winning. Although I wasn't quite ready to toss my sombrero into the circle, I resigned from ACERT and started looking for supporters.

CHAPTER 30

Hawaii is not a state of mind but a state of grace.

—Paul Theroux

AN E-MAIL FROM AMANDA OPENED up a delightful prospect:

> Dickie Dear, how about a long weekend on the Big
> Island, so I can take a break between Bangladesh and
> the Philippines? We can raise our Aloha spirit to a
> whole new level. A hui hou kakou, Amanda

After two days of sampling Hawaiian culture—the highlight of which was Amanda Patina's private hula—I decided to take a hike while she worked on her next article. I headed down then up a switchback trail looking for the mythical kahuna of the Waipio Valley. I remembered Tri-Y's referring to it when I was very young as the magic that kept him coming back to this astonishing gorge.

I stopped a hundred feet or so above the valley floor, lost in wonder at the view of a waterfall and the infinite shades of green that framed the surf and the black-sand beach below. A sudden shower chose that ineffable moment to blow in, turning a downward trickle near me into a roaring falls.

The bare root to which I clung became a slimy rope. I lost my grip and tumbled down the cliff toward the rocks below, which I'd have surely reached had I not lunged for a treetop along the way.

I crashed through the leafy canopy and landed chest-first on a substantial limb of one of Hawaii's indigenous hardwoods, the koa. Once I'd caught my breath, I congratulated myself on my luck. As I looked through the trees to the other side of the valley, I saw the steep road I'd driven my rental Jeep down just a few hours ago.

It seemed like a good place to make a final decision when it came to survival. (Circumstances like mine tend to encourage melodramatic thinking.) Maybe I was egomaniacal, but I was convinced my views on education, poverty, immigration, and human rights were the most rational course for a pluralistic society. I even believed I could make significant inroads in breaking congressional gridlock—which meant I had to get elected. Which meant I had to stay alive.

Just because you're an egomaniac doesn't mean you're wrong.

I yelled for help, but that seemed to exacerbate the pain in my ribs, which I self-diagnosed as broken or cracked. Singing seemed to cause less pain, so I ran through a few pop/rock classics from the eighties before finally settling on *the* Hawaiian classic:

> Aloha 'oe, aloha 'oe
> E ke onaona noho I ka lipo
> One fond embrace
> A ho 'I a 'e au
> Until we meet again.

I sang until the rain subsided and evening started to fall on the Waipio Valley. I sang even though I suspected Queen Lili'uokalani was doing a reverse hula in her grave as I slaughtered the song's melody and no doubt the meaning of her lyrics.

I stopped singing only when I remembered my mini-pack, still securely strapped to my back. I carefully wrestled it from my back to my front and was rewarded with a half-full water bottle, two smashed granola bars, and the ultimate prize: a little airplane bottle of Bacardi. At some point I must have dozed, lulled by the ebb and flow of the trade winds and the rum. At dawn I resumed singing "Aloha Oe."

"Hey, brah. Whadda hell?"

I looked down and saw a familiar face—the same man I'd spoken to the day before.

"What you doing up there?" he said. "Stay there, I'll be back."

"Where would I go?"

Soon there were people gathered below. Eventually a military-looking helicopter arrived and two soldiers descended with a stretcher of sorts. As I was carried away, I waved "bravely" to the cameras (according to a cable news channel).

I was whisked off to the hospital in Hilo and diagnosed with one cracked rib and one broken rib. My treatment consisted of spending the rest of the night in the hospital and "taking it easy" with the assistance of some nifty narcotics. I was meditating on my adventures when Amanda Patina blew into my hospital room.

"You looked really cute up that tree."

"I didn't see you among the concerned citizens on the valley floor."

"Who do you think called in the military?"

She told me she had "taken care of" hospital bureaucracy as well as my rental Jeep at the bottom of the Waipio Valley. She then gave me a deep kiss and departed.

The next morning, she drove me to the Kona Coast. For several days she overachieved as my nurse, but not without taking breaks for scuba diving and hiking. I read, pondered my place in the universe, and watched the waves roll in through a haze of Vicodin chased with occasional sips of wine.

A few days later, with decreased pain and increased restlessness, I celebrated with Amanda Patina at Huggos Restaurant in Kailua. We sipped Mai Tais with plenty of rum and cute umbrellas. With the surf crashing just below and the sunset making its spectacular exit for the day, I finally detailed my plan.

"I'm going to write an autobiography," I said. "Then I'm going to run for office."

"Do you think the voters are ready for high-def Dick?"

"I guess we'll find out."

"Most voters probably have families and kids. Might be hard for them to identify."

"I'm still up for it. Let's go procreate."

"I'm sure you're up for lots of things, but neither of us is really up for parenthood."

After more days of rest and recuperation—the most restorative factor being Amanda Patina's special therapy—my ribs and my ego were pretty well healed. Once I was able to skip a block down Kona's Alii Drive on my own, she bade me adieu.

"Ciao, Dickie, and go for it," she said before she left. "California politics will need some entertainment after the imminent demise of Arnold."

CHAPTER 31

Politics has never been for the thin-skinned or the faint of heart.

—President Barack Obama.

ON MY WAY HOME FROM HAWAII, I flew into San Francisco, retrieved my Prius, and drove to Rita Mae's floating estate in Sausalito.

"Dickie dear, you looked adorable up in that tree. Everyone in my office saw it."

"Your office?"

"I forgot to tell you—I have an actual office now, in the corporate headquarters for Natural High Enterprises. I'm the CEO."

"I knew you were doing well, but ... wow!"

"It took off when I started organizing yoga retreats for business leaders. Now we're offering franchises for Natural High Yoga Centers." She smiled. "Soon they'll be all over the western U.S."

"Was my story a comic episode on Fox's weather report or mildly entertaining fodder like the animal story at the end of a newscast?"

"They played it pretty straight at first, but as they found out more about you, it got funnier. I loved it—once I was sure you were all right, of course."

"I guess that's as good a way as any to start my campaign."

"Your what?

"I'm going to run for Congress." I could hear my voice taking on resonance.

"As a Democrat?"

"I can't believe you even have to ask," I said. "I'll be running in a district where the incumbent just retired."

She walked over, placed her hands on my shoulders, and wry-smiled at me. "Maybe I didn't give you enough attention when you were growing up?"

"You were the epitome of perfect parenting. I just want to put my thumbprint on the country's future."

"But you have skeletons, dear. And, let's not forget, a grandfather."

"That's why I'm writing an autobiography," I said. "I'll tell the whole, honest, absolute truth and publish it right before the election."

She laughed. "Good luck on the honesty part, sweetie."

"Now that you're so prosperous, can I depend on you for a campaign contribution?"

"Depends," she said. "How do you feel about the overregulation of business? I'm practicing to be a full-blown capitalist."

"I'm for what you're for, Mom!"

"I can't wait to read your book," she said, "but isn't it a bit presumptuous for someone just beginning his political career to be writing an autobiography?"

"Some may see it as the act of a brazen egomaniac, but that's better than getting pulled off the campaign track revisiting the yellow submarine or my radical father. I'll just say, 'Read my book—now let's talk about immigration reform.'"

"Speaking of your father, did you detect his footprints in the islands?"

"On the big island, Waipio Valley—where I was stuck up the tree. I think he was there just before me. One of the locals remembered seeing a man with a silvery hair and a big grin."

She turned toward the window but seemed to be looking way beyond the bay. "Are you still getting e-mails from him?"

"A vignette every once in a while, always from a different e-mail address." I walked over and stood beside her. "He always seems to know what I've been doing lately, but when I try to reply, they come back."

I hugged her. She smiled.

"Maybe he really is magic," one of us said.

After visiting Rita Mae, I drove home to Sac Town—an appellation used by the young and the hip. In the parking garage beneath my newly acquired condo, my next-door neighbor, Andi, was just slithering out of her Porsche.

"Dick, I'd join you in a tree in Hawaii any old time."

"Sacramento is the city of trees. Let me know when you want to go climbing."

"I can hardly wait. Also, I have good news and bad news about your bird."

About a month earlier, Andi had given me a mynah bird I named Sacatchy. I taught the bird to say, "Dick is cool," whenever someone entered the room.

"Good news first," I said.

"He came back?"

"He was gone?"

"I took the cage out onto the balcony with my good bird, Nixon, and somehow the door got open," Andi said.

"So what's the bad news?"

"He came back, and now all I can get him to say is 'Bite me, Dick.'"

"Really?"

"Could I make up something like that?"

About the time I was preparing to work full time on my campaign, I got a call from Sacatchy.

"Hear you're running for Congress, bro. How about a fat donation for your campaign?"

"How did you know? I'm just now starting the paperwork."

"I know all, Dickster. And thanks to your apt moral guidance over the years, I'm feeling like a solid citizen these days."

"Sacatchy, it might be best if I keep you away from my campaign."

"Surely, and I say this with all modesty, you can use someone of my vast intellect and unique talent."

"If you look back, you'll see we've usually been on the losing side," I said. "This time I plan on winning. Besides, I'd rather not draw attention to our past escapades."

"And how will they know about these escapades?"

"They'll be documented in my autobiography, which will be published before the election."

"I thought you said you wanted to win."

"I want to find out if you can get elected by being open and honest."

"You were a history teacher," he said. "Surely you don't need to publish a book to know the answer to that question."

With the filing deadline approaching, it was time to formally announce my candidacy.

"We need loads of people, loads of press, and boatloads of enthusiasm," my campaign manager said. "There's nothing more pathetic than delivering a speech to an audience of fifty in a venue that holds hundreds."

"You're right, Emily," I said. "So let's do it outside. Someplace no one would expect a big crowd."

"What do you have in mind?"

"The Tower Bridge."

The Sacramento landmark bears a vague resemblance to London's Tower Bridge, which also starts and ends with two towers. Between the towers is a wide center section—my ideal campaign launching pad—that can rise to make way for medium sized vessels.

"How on earth—"

"I've got a plan. You just get the press there. Oh, and twenty or thirty enthusiastic Young Democrats with signs. I'll do the rest, unless you know someone who runs the bridge."

"You're on your own on that one."

Trying to get permission for a press conference on the Tower Bridge was a fun test of my political skills. Diligent research turned up a bill, languishing in congressional stacks, to refurbish small aging bridges on the federal dime. I invited the Department of Transport's deputy director to lunch, during which I assured him that once I was in Congress, advancing this bill would be among my highest priorities.

I had a big grin on my face walking across Capitol Park when I saw Mickey McWhirr that afternoon.

"Hey, Mickey, bring your friends to the Tower Bridge next Friday at ten in the morning," I said. "I'm going to announce my candidacy."

"About time, laddie!" An enthusiastic group of supporters and some media people began assembling near the east side of the bridge soon after nine o'clock on that crisp Friday morning. As quoted in *The Sacramento Bee*, Emily referred to me as the "undeclared front-runner." Mickey McWhirr was on hand with a sign saying "Hot Scots for Free Thoughts" and three bagpipers. A few supporters dressed in green waved signs: "Micks for Dick." A three-person mariachi band's sign read "Si Ricardo."

Once we had close to forty people and two television cameras, I whistled for attention. "Ladies and gentlemen, please follow me."

When we got to the middle of the bridge, I signaled the bridge operator. The gates stopped traffic and we began our ascent via platform to the top—accompanied by both the bagpipers and the mariachi band. The television cameras and my new supporters were soon treated to an awesome view of the Sacramento River and the city skyline.

The bands stopped playing. The Young Democrats started chanting: "Youngblood, Youngblood, Youngblood, Youngblood!"

The platform stopped moving.

I turned to face the audience.

"Citizens of California, my name is Dick Youngblood. Thank you so much for coming out on this dazzling Sacramento morning. It's my pleasure to announce my candidacy for the Democratic Party nomination to represent the Fifty-fourth District in the United States House of Representatives. I do so with humility, but more importantly, I do it with a sense of purpose—I believe I can help make this country a better place to live.

"I want an America that's strong but at peace. I want to bring into the American community eleven million people who live and work here yet are living in legal limbo. I want jobs in California and a growing economy in all fifty states. I want an America where our candidates get elected not because they have superior financing but because they have superior solutions. And I want an America that's a world leader in addressing climate change.

"Being atop this amazing structure, we're reminded that the river and all of nature needs to be protected for us and for our children. I chose the Tower Bridge to announce my candidacy for a reason: it serves as a symbol of the bridges I'll build as your congressmen during a time when our country has never been so divided. I will bring back the art of compromise as the epitome of public service. Thank you all for coming."

"How did I become 'the undeclared front-runner'?" I asked Emily when it was all over.

"I asked ten people on the street if they'd vote for you," she said. "Three said yes, two would vote for any Republican who ran against you, two had never heard of the district, one had no intention of ever voting again, one wanted Bill Clinton, and one wasn't sure what state he was in."

"Oh."

"Cool press conference," Sacatchy said on the phone the next day. "Do you know who your opponents are going to be?"

"As of yesterday, on the Democratic side there's a one-term assemblyman named Austin Treadwell and a female city council-person named Julia King. So far the Republicans have a former mayor of West Sacramento named Judy Muransky."

"Your main Republican opponent will be none other than Rob Banks."

"He hasn't filed yet."

"He will, trust me."

"When did he move here?"

"I told you you'd have a need for my talents," he said. "Rob moved to the Natomas area of Sacramento about eighteen months ago, which would make his residence in the district a little longer than yours. He works for a Sacramento law firm that specializes in defending businesses against suits by consumers and employees. He's a recent member of the Sacramento Chamber of Commerce, the Rotary Club, and the Sacramento Theater Association. He has a wife and two kids and they all attend the Church of Christ. What've *you* got, bro?"

"Let's see, I'm a homeowner, condo actually, and my girlfriend is an internationally acclaimed reporter. I also have a mynah bird named Sacatchy who used to say, 'Dick is cool,' but now says, 'Bite me, Dick.'"

"Smart bird."

"I've also joined a runners club and have high hopes of running a marathon someday. On the religious front, I attended a Hindu ceremony in San Francisco a couple of months ago, and I often walk by a really impressive Catholic church."

"I think you need to do some work on this whole community thing."

* * *

I actually took Sacatchy's advice. By the time I filed for office during the first part of February, I was a card-carrying member of at least four new civic organizations. I also assembled a campaign committee that included some impressive volunteers. There's a wealth of talented politicos willing to expend superhuman effort for nothing more than the vague hope that their candidate will win.

A few days after the announcement, I received an e-mail from Lily Livinsky, who still sent me verbal barbs from whatever corner of the globe in which she currently toiled:

> Hey Dickie, your decision to run for Congress is strong evidence confirming my hypothesis that social progress is doomed as long as people, whether they be ancient Mongolian nomads or California politicians, never seem to learn from their mistakes. You know I love you and will be back to vote for you in your final election, which in your case will probably be the primaries, especially if you insist on writing your "honest autobiography." Hui lou jian, Lily "Amanda" Livinsky (I just declared myself an honorary Amanda.)

I replied:

> Hi Lily, great to hear from you. I'm still the eternal optimist so I'll see you in November for the final election. I like your new name. Love, Dickie

Many years ago, a California politician called money the "mother's milk of politics." Thanks to Citizens United, the multi-billionaire Koch brothers, and super PACS, money is also the first and greatest ethical dilemma of any aspiring politician. While I put campaign reform near the top of my legislative agenda, I knew I had to win to make change—so I started my campaign by lending it $400,000. This made my egalitarian soul uncomfortable, but I reasoned that at least the only person I'd owe in this particular instance was myself.

Obviously, I couldn't fund my campaign alone, so I still had to suffer the indignities of sucking up to special-interest groups. Education groups, including ACERT and the California Teachers Association, knew I was on their side and showered me with modest contributions. And since I was deeply committed to immigration reform, including a pathway to citizenship for undocumented workers, I also received contributions from immigration groups.

"How's the campaign going?" Andi asked as she slid into her Porsche. I'd never seen a woman get in and out of her car with such style.

"It's moving along," I said. "Any chance you could start pushing me with Prozac?"

"I'm betting Prozac patients have a lethargic voter record. By the way, I saw another charming photo of you and Amanda Patina at a fundraiser in San Francisco. Does that mean I should stop flirting with you?"

"Absolutely not. My ego needs soothing after my bird says, 'Bite me, Dick,' for the tenth time in a row." I folded my arms. "Level with me, Andi. Who really taught him to say that?"

"You think I'm that devious?"

"I'm working on a conspiracy theory," I said.

"Politicians always get paranoid when election time rolls around."

She started to walk away but turned back. "Speaking of paranoid, there was a woman peeking in your window a few days ago. When she saw me, she went to your door and rang your doorbell. I told her you weren't home but I could deliver a message when you got back. She seemed a little strange, so I gave her the look."

"The look?" I asked.

"Like this." She lifted her chin and narrowed her eyes, making her expression so vitriolic I shivered.

"That look would make me blab for sure."

"She said she was a reporter with TRBB, a wire and Internet service. Said she wanted to interview you."

"Did you get her name?"

"I asked, but she changed the subject."

I was starting to have a bad—and familiar—feeling.

"What'd she look like?"

"An inch or two shorter than me, huge sunglasses, and lots of phony red hair."

"How'd you know it wasn't real hair?" I asked.

"Didn't match her complexion."

"You do great work for a drug dealer."

"I'm a pharmaceutical representative, thank you very much. So who is she—jilted lover?"

"Not exactly."

Reluctant to slog through the sordid saga of Amanda Nixon, I put off contacting my lawyer, Tim Escuella , for a couple of days. When I finally called, he was concerned.

"I'll contact the police, but maybe the campaign needs to hire some security."

"So I can walk into a meeting with an entourage? No thanks."

"Do you have an alarm on your condo? A gun?"

"I don't like guns."

"Given the voters in your district, I advise you to change subjects whenever the subject of gun control surfaces," Tim said.

"I won't raise the subject, but if it surfaces I'll have to say what I believe."

"Which is?"

"People do kill people, usually people with guns. Which brings me to my next point ..."

He agreed to find Amanda Patricia and keep track of her whereabouts.

My main opponent in the primary was Assemblyman Austin Treadwell. Though he had an encyclopedic knowledge of California politics, he had less money than I did, and during his one term in the California legislature, he'd distinguished himself by achieving virtually no media attention.

"Looks as if we'll be the main candidates," Treadwell told me over the phone. "I wondered if you're willing to enter into a joint pledge to keep the campaign honest and positive."

"Absolutely, and may the best person win," I said. "Of course, whoever wins will have a tough time sticking to the high road if the Republicans choose Rob Banks."

"You know him?"

"Know of him would be more apt."

As the campaign increased in vigor, I rather enjoyed meeting every Kiwanis Club and Chamber of Commerce between Sacramento and Napa Valley. I even enjoyed shaking hands, smiling, and actually kissing babies, all faithfully documented by the press. Most of all, I became skilled at saying the same thing over and over with a new spin each time.

"Keep it fresh, Dick," my campaign manager said. "Keep it fresh."

I even hit the streets, stepping into the local Starbucks or fast food outlet: "Hi, I'm Dick Youngblood and I'm running for Congress," or "Hello, I'm Dick Youngblood and I hope to be your next representative in Congress."

As the campaign continued, the questions got tougher.

"How're you going to save Social Security and Medicare?" older voters asked.

"I'll stay on the job until I'm eighty to save more for you."

Sometimes this response resulted in waves of laughter, more often a smattering of chuckles. "In seriousness," I'd say, "although it won't affect those who're already retired, it's simple math. If there are more retired people in the future, we need to increase contributions or raise the retirement age. I believe that Democrats, Republicans, the AARP, and any other interested group can save Social Security and Medicare by practicing the crucial art of compromise."

"How are you any different from all the other double-dealing bozos?"

This was the most difficult question. It was also my favorite.

"If you ever catch me double dealing," I said, "call me, e-mail me, write me, and I'll explain why I changed my mind. Basic trust is at the heart of every political relationship. If you can't trust me, there's no reason for me to be your congressman. But the only way democracy works is through what Teddy Roosevelt described as the 'splendid art of compromise.' The Republican Party and especially its Tea Party seem to have forgotten this."

It was right before the primary election that videos of me began to appear on YouTube, all of which originated on the political blog "You Can Fool Some of the People All of the Time." They started with a photo of me up a tree in Hawaii and were followed by a compilation of clips from what seemed to be my entire life.

The video was often revised but almost always featured "Yellow Submarine" as background music and usually began with me at four years old standing proudly by my grandfather while "doing the Nixon." There might follow a three-second clip of me at nine after my rescue from Red Emma and/or a headline from the Rio de Mañana student newspaper: "Wrong Way Richard Shoots the Winning Shot Into Opposing Team's Basket." Usually there were a few seconds of animals descending on White Plaza at Stanford with me in the center of the melee—I didn't even know who'd filmed that one. The most sensational clip was of me rising out of the concrete with blood oozing from my inner thigh, followed by a quick one of my mynah bird saying, "Bite me, Dick," followed by a final chorus of "We all live in a yellow submarine."

I found the YouTube videos irritating, but my escalating angst was focused on just two people: Rob Banks and Amanda Patricia Nixon. My lawyer had contracted with a private investigator, who found out she'd come in on a flight from Miami and spent six days at the Hyatt Regency in downtown Sacramento before showing up at my condo. In late May, just before the primary, I received an e-mail from notonyourlife77@gmail.com:

> Know what Billy Graham said at Nixon's funeral? He said there was a democracy about death.

I forwarded it to Tim and asked him to see if he could trace it back to Amanda Nixon. He called me a few days later.

"As I'm sure you guessed, the e-mail address doesn't exist anymore, but an FBI official admitted that Amanda Patricia Nixon is under investigation for questionable purchases made in the past few months."

"Where is she?"

"They believe she's in the Sacramento area. Again, I implore you to have your campaign hire security for you."

"I told you, I don't want to show up at every meeting with a retinue. It screams arrogance, especially on the part of someone who's yet to be elected."

CHAPTER 32

The hardest thing about any political campaign is how to win without proving that you are unworthy of winning.

—Adlai E. Stevenson

WE WON IN THE PRIMARY, WITH THE official count at Youngblood 52, Austin Tredwell 41. A few days later, I got an e-mail from Lily:

> Hey Dickie, congratulations on your victory—I voted for you by mail. Good news, I'll be back to vote for you again in person. My life in here in a Mongolian archaeological dig is mostly humorless, so what better place to get a laugh than watching the climax of your campaign? My parents recently moved to Napa, so I made their address my home of record. If by some quirk of karma you happen to win, I hope to serve as one of your whiniest constituents. Love and fossils, Lily "Amanda" Livinsky.

It was July fourth in Sacramento. The temperature was soaring toward a hundred degrees, and I was on my way to shake hands at four separate Independence Day picnics and barbecues.

I got into my Prius and hit the power button, but instead of a gentle hum I heard a rapid *bang-bang-bang-bang-bang* from underneath my car. It was then that I noticed the three-by-five card on my windshield.

> Happy Fourth of July, Dickie! Next time the bang will be bigger.
>
> Love, Amanda Patricia.

I jumped out of the car just as the last of a string of firecrackers exploded.

What to do? I called Sacatchy.

"I need your help."

"I think a bit of groveling is in order," he said. "Seeing as how you refused my gracious offer of assistance last time we spoke."

"Sacatchy the Magnificent, I apologize with the utmost humility. Please assist me."

"I knew you'd come back to me. I have to admit I was feeling just a little bit rejected."

"No one with your ego feels rejection for more than a second or two. The problem again is Amanda Nixon." I filled him in on everything up through the firecrackers under my car. "I'd also like you to check out any possible connection between her and the Banks campaign. Her timing couldn't be better, from their perspective."

"I'm on it, like, yesterday."

And indeed he was. He called less than a week later.

"Got something for you, bro."

"What'd you discover, Your Omniscience?"

"Amanda Patricia Nixon has been on three flights to Sacramento since January. The first was a round trip from Atlanta for a couple of days. The second was in June from Miami. She stayed here about a week, then flew to Dallas. Two weeks ago she flew back in from Miami, and unless she decided to walk home, she's still here. The first flight she might have purchased herself, but at least one ticket came courtesy of the credit card of one of Banks's wealthy supporters."

"Anything else?"

"She has a handgun and a lot of curious stuff in her hotel room."

"Curious how?"

"Two sets of handcuffs, materials that could be used in explosive devices, and five bottles of prescription medications: two anti-psychotics, one bottle of Prozac, and two bottles from India—we're not sure what those are. I've got a sample of both if you want them analyzed."

"Dare I ask how much of this information was obtained legally?"

"All of it except the stuff in her hotel room, which I did not personally enter."

"Then who did?"

"The maid."

"And she did this because?"

"She thinks I'm cute."

My first TV spots appeared just after the primary. They were positive and direct, with some New Age guitar in the background when I talked about the environment. The music became more patriotic when the ad mentioned my service record, and I talked about our need to maintain security for the nation, all against a backdrop of rippling American flags.

E-mails began flowing in almost immediately, one from a guy who'd fought with me in the Gulf War, two from former students at Stanford, one from someone I couldn't remember but who said I had her support "one thousand percent." I even received an e-mail from Judy LaTrudy:

> Hey Dick, I'm impressed! I wish I could vote for you, but I'll look forward to voting for you for senator or president. I'm now part owner and the Managing Editor of *Erofit Magazine*. Since I last talked with you

a few months ago, I got divorced, and I have plans for husband number two. I sent the maximum contribution to your campaign treasurer and I'm thinking of sending another under the name of my ex-husband. Remember, voters, girlfriends, wives, and campaign managers may come and go, but I'll always be your first. Love and Lots of Votes, Judy

I would have been touched even if she hadn't mentioned contributing.

Dear Numero Uno Judy, Thank you for remembering. Your generous contribution is fantastic. At the risk of being a bore, I'm running my campaign on the basis of honesty–so it would be unethical for me accept a contribution from someone I know didn't actually send it. But thanks for nice thoughts. I fondly remember every detail of our high school romance, and I'd love to see you sometime—when I run for the Senate, will you campaign for me? Love, Peace, and Victory, Dick

Throughout August, the pace and intensity of the campaign increased, as did the tension. Once I'd overruled every member of my staff on the issue of publishing my autobiography, everything else seemed easier. As for Rob, in an interview for a Sacramento newspaper, he "clarified" his stance on the issues. He was for improved health care, but I was for socialism. I was for higher taxes, which apparently meant I didn't care about the federal deficit.

Unlike most candidates on the outer edges of the right-wing continuum, Rob didn't seem to be groveling for moderates— probably because he was increasingly funded by the Tea Party. I suspected he wasn't all that in love with its dogma. Over cocktails, my finance guy, Nick got Rob's finance guy to admit, off the record that "Rob was no longer sleeping with the Tea Party," but he couldn't afford a divorce. The only thing Rob seemed genuinely fired up about was gun control.

"If everyone had a gun, everyone would be afraid to use them," he said at a rally out in Yolo County. "I'm proud to be a member of the National Rifle Association, and I agree with the executive director of the NRA: what we need is "more good guys with guns." He paused. "My opponent, Mr. Youngblood, is suspiciously silent on the issue of gun control."

A few days later I was speaking to a group of fifty or sixty students at Sac State, about half of them Young Democrats, a few of whom were working on my campaign. There were also representatives of the local media in the audience.

"How many of you have heard my standard stump speech during this campaign?"

About half the hands went up.

"In that case, I'm going to try something new," I said. "Please shout out any question you have, but try to make sure your questions start with 'What is your answer to ...' or 'What is your position on ...' or 'How do you plan to deal with ...' I'll respond with very short answers, and we can cover a lot of territory that way. Ready?"

"What is your answer to violent crime in American society?" the president of the Young Democrats said.

"More guns," I said. "Next?"

A moment of shocked silence into which came some scattered applause and a few giggles.

"Mr. Youngblood, how do you plan to deal with the high dropout rate in public schools?"

"Guns for teachers."

The giggles got louder.

"How do we maintain a strong defense with dwindling finances?"

"Bigger guns."

"What is your answer to illegal immigration?"

"More guns at the border."

"What would you do about the national deficit?"

"Shoot it."

By this time, the audience had gone from a delirious giggle to a spurious chant: "More guns, more guns, more guns, more guns!"

Eventually I managed to quiet the crowd.

"It seems really silly when we say it, but I worry that candidates like Rob Banks have their long arms in the deep pockets of the NRA. Rob says there's no public record of my owning a firearm. That's the point—I could have an arsenal of assault weapons in my spare bedroom, and thanks to the NRA, nobody would know."

The next day Rob told a reporter: "I have a wife and children who eat dinner together almost every night and attend church together on Sundays. My opponent has a 'girlfriend' who calls herself a 'citizen of the world.'"

The headline read: "Banks Draws Invidious Comparison Between His Family and Opponent's Girlfriend."

Within minutes after the headline appeared, I texted the gist of the articles to Amanda Patina, who was covering a news story in Bangkok. An exhilarating email exchange followed:

> Dickie, it seems that a forty-one-year-old politician's having a global girlfriend may be a detriment to your traditionally inclined constituents. How about I become your fiancée?

> Are you proposing?

> YES! I would love to advance to the status of fiancée.

Amanda Patina's periodic appearances as my fiancée began to coincide with major events. As the campaign matured, her natural charm was reflected in the poll numbers, but it was alarmingly close to the election.

"Mr. Youngblood, did you really criminally conspire to defeat Rob Banks as student-body president at Stanford?" a reporter asked at a press conference.

"We liked to call them pranks."

"Were you asked to leave Stanford as a result of your actions?"

"Yes."

"And wasn't your co-conspirator, Mr. Sacatchy Sun, convicted of a felony a few years ago involving an election?"

I didn't like where this was going. "Yes."

"And weren't you investigated for your activities with Mr. Sun?"

"I was."

"Mr. Youngblood, didn't you recently assist or recommend Sacatchy Sun in obtaining employment with the state of California?"

"I did."

"Has Sacatchy Sun helped you in your current election bid?"

I paused. "He provided me with information, yes."

"Information about what?"

I decided to try for a bit of sympathy.

"He's provided me with some information on the where-abouts of Amanda Patricia Nixon," I said. "She was convicted of attempting to kill me twenty years ago, served her sentence, and recently threatened me again." I held up a hand. "As far as all the other questions you've asked, my autobiography will be published before the election. Everything else will also be explained truth-fully, believe it or not."

After reading accounts of this press conference, the media con-cluded that I was in trouble. A local TV station's interview with Amanda Patricia on the noon news in Sacramento didn't help.

"The truth is, Mr. Youngblood tried to kill me." She stared straight into the camera and her eyes were as clear and resolute as her words. "I pled guilty because I was told it was the only way to avoid a very lengthy prison sentence."

Anybody who didn't know the facts would be impressed. Hell, *I* was impressed and I was the fucking victim!

"Can you tell us what really happened that night, Ms. Nixon?"

"I attempted to wrestle the gun away from him and it discharged into his thigh. I'm sure if my grandfather was a U.S. senator, it would be Mr. Youngblood who served six years in prison."

The tabloids had a field day, jumping on the story with surprising vigor considering it was simply a congressional election.

A new poll placed me twelve points behind Rob Banks. My campaign was in a disagreeable dither. Should we ignore? Answer forcefully? Dismiss the charges as "not worthy of a detailed response"? I was all for answering forcefully, but my advisers persuaded me to wait a few days.

I was speaking at a rally in Caesar Chavez Park, in downtown Sacramento, in front of a hundred supporters and about ten Tea Partiers booing from the back row. Ten members of the Westboro Baptist Church had turned out with signs indicating I'd been born in Mendoza, Argentina—a giant ho-hum to those in the audience who knew something about the U.S. Constitution. A lone sign in the back said, "Youngblood's Girl Friend is NO American!"

It was a warm day in late September, ninety-six degrees with not a cloud in the sky. I was enjoying the spirited response to my speech when out of the crowd emerged Amanda Patricia Nixon wearing an unstylish and unseasonal raincoat.

I pulled my iPhone from my pocket and surreptitiously dialed 911, still talking. She hadn't moved, just stood there with that oh-so-familiar deranged smile.

"What this nation needs are real jobs for the eleven million undocumented immigrants who mow our lawns and clean our hotel rooms at substandard wages," I said.

Amanda moved toward the stage.

"What this nation needs is a political system not based on the size of campaign coffers."

She mounted the steps. She seemed to be reaching for something under her coat.

"Please step back!" I yelled to the audience. "This woman may be dangerous!"

She lunged toward me.

"See you in paradise, Dickie!" she screamed. I winced, but instead of the big bang I expected, there was just a sad puff of dust as she shrieked and sank to the ground.

"Call 911," I said. Within a minute or two, I heard sirens.

Even before the ambulance showed, a doctor and a nurse appeared from out of the crowd. They tore away her raincoat and saw the remains of a homemade bomb.

Within a week, Amanda Nixon was out of the hospital and safely in the hands of the Sacramento police, again charged with attempted murder. Now the headlines read: "Amanda Nixon Attempts to Suicide Bomb Candidate Youngblood." *Entertainment Tonight* referred to me as "courageous candidate Youngblood." Not only did I now look as sympathetic as possible, but my name recognition was also at an all-time high.

CHAPTER 33

Don't run a political campaign that would embarrass your mother.

—Senator Robert Byrd.

ONE DAY IN MID-SEPTEMBER, I stepped out of my humble hybrid in the parking garage below the L Street Lofts and Condos and spotted Andi's iPhone on the ground where her Porsche was usually parked.

I picked it up and scrolled down her list of contacts. Sure enough, there was Sacatchy's number. I now had some proof to support my mynah-bird conspiracy theory.

I opened the door to my condo.

"Bite me, Dick!" said Sacatchy the mynah bird.

"Hi, Dickster." said the actual Sacatchy, sprawled on my couch with his feet on my coffee table and reading a copy of the latest *Congressional Record.*

"How'd you get in?'

"What ever happened to *mi casa es su casa?"*

"No, *mi casa es mi castillo.*"

"This is America. You don't get a castle until your third term."

"You kidnapped my bird. Don't even try to deny it."

"It was Andi's idea."

I sat down. "To what do I owe the pleasure of this break-in?"

"I have some information for you."

"About?"

"Banks's next sound bite."

"Sounds like a major detour from my journey on the high road."

"Killjoy."

Our conversation was interrupted by a call from Andi. "Hey, Dick, I have a big problem," she said. "I lost my cell phone sometime this morning. Have you seen it?"

"Can you call your phone to see if someone picked it up?"

"I'll try that."

Seconds later her phone, now on my kitchen counter, started singing Billy Joel's "Captain Jack."

I answered. "You've reached Andi's phone. I can get you high tonight."

"Dick, you asshole!"

"Found it where a Porsche used to be," I said, "and it contains some incriminating evidence."

"What? I'll be over in a minute."

Moments later she walked in and gave Sacatchy a hug.

"How about you two go reprogram my bird?" I said.

"Too busy," Andi said. "I'm organizing a big drug confab here in town."

"Is that where pharmaceutical reps get together and conspire to keep their drugs as high-priced as possible and as many people taking them as possible?" I said.

"It's a conference and trade show for Pharm West. Speaking of which, how would you like to join a panel discussion on public policy?"

"I think we should clamp down on direct advertising of prescription drugs to the consumer. Still want me on the panel?"

"Not a chance, but I'll still vote for you."

A few days later, I was taking part in a question-and-answer session at a special meeting of the Sacramento chapter of the Rotary Club.

"Mr. Youngblood," a fortysomething guy in an expensive suit said, "how do you rectify the dichotomy between your call to control the spending of wealthy contributors versus the fact you lent your own campaign large sums of money and took substantial donations from the unions?"

"I'll play hardball on the field as it exists, but after I'm elected I'll work even harder to level the playing field. Reforming campaign financing will be one of my highest priorities. Many of our citizens seem to have forgotten the corrupting role that money plays in politics, which has only been exacerbated by the Supreme Court's Citizen United decision."

"Mr. Youngblood," the bald man in the first row said, "your opponent says you'll vote to raise taxes. Is that correct?"

"Many Republicans would rather drive a railroad spike through their mother's heart than vote to raise taxes. But we have to do something about the federal deficit, and that means limiting tax deductions and/or raising the tax rate on the richest among us."

"Mr. Youngblood, I'm an attorney with the Pacific Legal Foundation. How would you react to the charge of your opponent that you and the Democratic Party continue to push for policies that take away our freedom?"

"For Rob Banks, freedom means the rich become freer to get even richer. What about the freedom to marry anyone you want? What about a woman's freedom to make decisions about her own body? What about the freedom to breathe clean air? You can't shout 'freedom, freedom, freedom' while staring at freedom through such a tiny pinhole of a definition."

A few days later, I agreed to participate in a debate with Rob Banks at UC Davis. There were four student interrogators, one each from Young Democrats and Young Republicans, one from a student environmental organization, and one from a Christian political organization.

"Mr. Youngblood, what is your position on the sanctity of marriage?" a smiling young woman in a long dress asked.

"I don't understand how so many Californians voted against allowing couples to legally affirm their love for each other."

"So you didn't support Proposition Eight?"

"If the courts don't strike it down, I think we need a new proposition to repeal it."

"Mr. Banks, would you like to weigh in on the subject of gay marriage?" the moderator asked.

"I believe marriage is traditionally between one man and one woman."

"And people used to believe marriage was traditionally reserved for people of the same race," I said. "I think my opponent is confusing tradition with dogma."

Muffled applause, mild boos, and a few raucous "Woots!"

"Mr. Banks," the Young Republican on the panel asked, "would you vote for increased taxes to deal with the looming federal deficit?"

"Absolutely not," Rob said. "The last thing we need is more government taking even more of the *people's* money. I'm for smaller government, needing less money and taking—you might say stealing—less money from its citizens."

A small group of young Tea Partiers in the back went wild with applause. Unfortunately, they weren't close enough to hear Rob's off-microphone comment: "Maybe that'll get the fucking Tea Party off my back."

"Mr. Youngblood," a journalist in the front row said, "what's your solution to reduce the deficit?"

"'Taxes are the price of civilization,' as Justice Oliver Wendell Holmes Jr. once put it. There is simply no example in history where a weak government created a strong economy. I believe the people who benefit the most should pay a higher rate. No one in this nation got rich by themselves."

"Thank you, gentlemen," the moderator said. "This is the part of the debate where the candidates can ask each other one question and up to two follow-up questions on the same subject. Mr. Youngblood, you're first."

"Mr. Banks," I said, "what do you intend to do with the eleven million people currently living in limbo in the U.S.—including the children born here and those who were brought here at a very young age?"

"Deport as many as possible," Rob said. "This will discourage others from jumping our borders. As for children of illegal immigrants, they shouldn't benefit because their parents broke the law."

"You're saying that law enforcement should take a timeout to arrest and deport eleven million people? Do you have any idea how much time and money that would take?"

"If law enforcement had done their job, we wouldn't have this problem," he said. "I'm also in favor of decreasing legal immigration until we get the economy running full throttle again."

"Are you acquainted with statistics showing that immigrants start businesses at a higher rate than native-born citizens, thereby creating wealth? And while we're on the subject, is there any truth to the charge that the gardening company that mows your lawn and trims your roses hires undocumented workers?"

"I don't know anything about the company that does our gardening," Rob said.

The moderator raised a hand.

"Mr. Banks, it's your turn."

"Mr. Youngblood, what do you really value besides getting elected?" Rob asked.

"I value a society where the street cleaner's vote counts as much as a CEO's. I value a society where health care is affordable and easily available. I value the rights of women to maintain control over their own bodies, and I value the rights of all people to marry anyone of any gender—if that doesn't fall under equal opportunity, I don't know what does."

"Sounds like you're outlining a basic prescription for socialism. Isn't that correct?

"Yes, Rob, equal protection of the laws is a radical socialist idea from the Fourteenth Amendment to the United States Constitution. Did you run across that in your law-school studies?"

The audience chuckled.

"Don't you dare lecture me about the Constitution! I'm an attorney and you were a ... a high school teacher! You talk about reining in the power of special interests, yet one of your most recent jobs was as a lobbyist. How do you account for this inconsistency?"

"I proudly served as a high school teacher and a lobbyist for the Association of California Educators for Revival of Teaching. I want to decrease the power of all groups equally—yes, equally. And please, let's avoid labels like 'socialist.' In another era, you'd have called me communist, and if it wouldn't make you look like a complete dolt, I'm sure you'd love to call me a terrorist."

The majority in the audience went crazy with applause.

"Mr. Banks and Mr. Youngblood," the earnest girl from the better-dressed side of the room said, "will you please explain to us how your faith and values will guide you as a United States congressman?"

"I have the utmost faith in the Lord," Rob said. "We have to recognize there is evil in the world and we have to deal with it forcibly. I attend church regularly with my family and we need to get back to a time when Christian values and American values were the same."

Now it was my turn.

"I notice Mr. Banks didn't mention the Christian principles of compassion or the stories of Jesus administering to the poor," I said. "I think the founding fathers were amazingly wise to write freedom of religion into our First Amendment. Anyone can believe anything they want in this great country of ours, and tolerance and celebration of cultural differences is a value I hold dear."

"But Mr. Youngblood," the representative of the Christian Association asked, "don't you think the voters have a right to know how you stand on the issue of faith?"

"All I can say is that there are times I've had doubts about God," I said. "Then again, I'm sure he has doubts about me."

Parts of the audience chuckled.

The debate ended at that point and I assumed the subject of religion was closed, at least for the day, but as I was walking out of the hall, a freshly scrubbed young woman with a reporter's badge chased me down.

"Mr. Youngblood, you didn't really answer the question about faith. Do I assume that you're not affiliated with any particular religion?"

"On the contrary, I'm a Wikipedian, in fact an Evangelical Wikipedian."

The next day I got a call from Emily.

"You're one lucky bastard," she said. "And what in the hell is an Evangelical Wikipedian?"

"I promise to hold off on more verbal mischief until after November 6," I said.

"And stay away from Sacatchy until after the campaign."

"Whatever you say, Mommy. So what's the latest polling data?"

"Ten days ago, Rob was up twelve points. That poll was taken right before the attempted bombing. A quick poll taken yesterday puts you only five points down. Soon we'll see the impact of your book. Good thing your publisher keeps stalling."

"Why's that?"

"People won't have time to read it all."

CHAPTER 34

I will not deny that there are men in the district better-qualified than I, but, gentlemen, these men are not in the race.

—Speaker of the House, Sam Rayburn

THE BANKS CAMPAIGN LAUNCHED A TV commercial featuring a list of the charges and accusations against Yuri Yablonsky Youngblood: draft dodger, expatriate, anti-war demonstrator, and friend of the Weather Underground. It hinted at his association with Castro, the Sandinistas in Nicaragua, and the current regime in Iran. It ended by saying, "Richard Youngblood, candidate for United States Congress, has yet to disavow his father's treasonous activities."

The next day, as I was leaving a meeting of Helicopter Parents for Higher Standards, a reporter cornered me.

"Are you ready to denounce your father?"

"Rob Banks is bottom-feeding in the cesspool of political hypocrisy," I said. Of all the charges he'd leveled at me, this was the only one that brushed a nerve. "He extols the virtue of family values then turns around and wants me to denounce my father?"

Three weeks before the election, a new conservative super PAC called Futures United filed with the Federal Elections

Commission. The first anti-Youngblood ad showed selective video clips of me in the Davis debate saying the last church I attended was Hindu. It went on to show me shaking hands at a local Starbucks with an "avowed atheist," followed by a clip of me conversing with two apparently Muslim women on a street in Sacramento. "How can Dick Youngblood purport to represent the values of the Fifty-fourth Congressional District?"

I doubted if the ad would hurt me all that much, but it seemed completely incongruous with democracy that voters wouldn't find out who was behind these public charges until the election was over—super PACs can choose to report on a monthly or quarterly basis.

The last blast from Futures United appeared a few weeks before the election. It opened with a clip of me walking on J Street in the evening (against ominous background music).

"Dick Youngblood is often seen prowling the streets of Sacramento late at night," the narrator said. "What's he looking for?" The word *mysterious* flashed on the screen in big letters at the bottom of the screen. "Mr. Youngblood was investigated for election violations in 2000." *Criminal* flashed on the screen. "His fiancée calls herself a 'citizen of the world.'" *Unpatriotic* went by—after a quick flash of the only unflattering picture of Amanda Patina in existence.

"Who is the real Dick Youngblood?" asked the narrator as *mysterious*, *criminal* and *unpatriotic* came back into view.

"Hey, Dick," a reporter asked me, "who do you think is behind Futures United?"

"Not a clue. Why don't you guys go find out? Secrets like these might be the greatest threat to democracy today."

On October 20th, I woke up at 6:30 a.m., laced up my bouncy new running shoes, and charged off on a thirty-minute run as the sun rose over McKinley Park. As soon as I got home, I flipped on the local news station.

"… Central Intelligence Agency is holding a rare news conference in the next few minutes," the anchor said. "All they'll say is that it concerns Yuri Yablonsky Youngblood, otherwise known as Tri-Y. A radical icon of the sixties and seventies, Tri-Y is the father of California congressional candidate Richard Youngblood."

I stared at the TV, remote still in hand. Since when did the CIA hold press conferences?

My mind treading the waters of confusion, I waited. Finally, the cameras focused on a podium in front of CIA headquarters, in Langley, Virginia. There was the deputy director of the CIA and a man with a cropped beard, blue blazer, and no tie.

Tri-Y. He looked tan and healthy as he grinned at the cameras.

"This is an unusual occasion for the agency," the director said. "We are here to introduce and shout kudos to one of our most important—and, until today, most classified—secret agents. For the past eighteen years, Yuri Yablonsky Youngblood has provided us with an abundance of information that has helped keep our nation safe." The director glanced back at my pops. "Although we counseled him against such a public 'coming in from the cold,' he was insistent. I'm honored to introduce Yuri Yablonsky Youngblood."

My pops stepped up to the podium with great aplomb to a small wave of applause.

"Good morning! For the past forty years, my life has been largely a secret, sometimes even to me. I'm sure psychologists now have a term more sophisticated than 'adrenalin junkie,' but it's an apt description for now. From the day I dodged the draft, I've been on the move, always with a new mission and a new scheme. I believed I was helping people end injustice, overthrow dictators, and improve their quality of life.

"When I found myself in the Middle East at the same time my son was serving as a soldier there, I came upon some information—information I realized the United States needed to have. After a year or two, I formalized my relationship with the CIA." He beamed. "Any questions?"

"Mr. Youngblood, Les Tranker with *The Washington Post*. Does your coming out at this time have anything to do with your son's congressional campaign in California?"

"The timing may have been a factor."

"Are you going to write a book?" another reporter asked.

"Why not?"

"Tri-Y, did you really rescue your son with the help of a yellow submarine?" a TV reporter from *Entertainment Tonight* asked.

Try-Y paused. "Dick got the story straight, but I think they called it a chameleon submarine—it changed colors to fit the mission."

There were a few muffled groans and wows as the news corps typed away on tablets or spoke into cell phones.

"While I'm up here," Tri-Y said, "I'd also like to thank the men and women of the press for keeping my legend alive. If anybody's still interested in the mythology and reality of my life for the past four decades, you'll have to read my book. Thank you! Oh, one more thing: I wholeheartedly endorse my son, Richard Youngblood, for the United States Congress."

A reporter from *The Sacramento Bee* asked the last question after my speech the following day at the monthly meeting of the Sacramento Bar Association. "How surprised were you by your father's press conference?"

"Astonished doesn't even begin to cover it."

"Have you spoken with him since?"

"I hope to soon. I've kind of been searching for him since I was a kid."

"Do you think his announcement will help or hinder your campaign?"

Someone in the back of the room stood up. "May I comment on that question?"

It was my pops, looking almost like a member of the bar

himself in a pinstripe suit. There were a few gasps and a smattering of applause.

"Please do, Mr. Youngblood," said the president of the Bar Association.

"During all of these years as a fugitive," he said, "I often regretted not spending more time with my son. I had to watch him grow up mostly from a distance, but I'm proud of the man he's become. In my experience, rebels are almost nonexistent in societies where the government really listens to its people. My son will help reestablish that kind of government, and for that, he really is my hero."

Resounding applause followed, and I walked out alongside my father.

"Nice speech," he said. "Let's do lunch."

As we entered the eatery, heads turned. For the first time ever, our encounter didn't feel rushed—though I still worried he might vanish at any moment.

"Pops," I said after we ordered, "why now? Really."

"Let's just say it's my way of making up for all the years I wasn't around." He smiled. "Besides, when your body tells you it's time to quit, you listen."

"Won't living like the rest of us be a huge snooze for you?"

"Maybe I'll run for office." He tried to maintain a straight face but broke into exuberant giggle. "Seems to be the thing to do."

"Someday I want to hear about those envelopes, not to mention all your other mystical appearances in my life."

"Well, I can't tell you everything." He winked. "Otherwise you won't have any incentive to read my book."

"Want to do some more campaigning this afternoon?"

"Sure, but I think I'd better keep my mouth shut until we see the reaction to my mini-lecture this morning."

"You trying out to be my new campaign manager?"

"Why, you having problems with Emily?"

"She's starting to love me again, thanks to you."

* * *

255

I gave speeches at two more venues that day, and in each case I waited until I was finished to introduce Tri-Y. Naturally, all the questions were directed at him, which suited me just fine.

"If I keep campaigning with you, I might be the one to get elected," Tri-Y said as we were walking through Capital Park.

"Let's make our last stop a banquet at the Hyatt. By the way, do you know that guy in blue blazer and red tie? I'm pretty sure he's been everywhere we have today."

"Temporary security, courtesy of the company." He nodded across the street. "Bet you didn't even notice the guy in the tree at two o'clock."

After my speech at the fund-raising banquet, Tri-Y stood up, silver hair glimmering, and offered a toast.

"It is one of the greatest privileges of my life to raise my glass to the next congressman of the Fifty-fourth District. He brought me back to America, and now it's time for him to lead us all to a better America. Here's to Richard Milhous Nixon Youngblood."

We exited the hall accompanied by a spirited cacophony of clinks and clapping.

The next day I delivered my standard speech to the faculty at Sacramento State. After a few innocuous questions, a woman in the back wearing a safari hat and large dark glasses stood to her full height, which made her only slightly taller than those still seated.

"Mr. Youngblood, what actions will you take to restore federal funding for research grants in science and technology?"

It could only be Lily Livinsky.

"Dr. Livinsky, even if we tripled the budget for these grants, it wouldn't come close to the cost of preliminary study for better drone aircraft, yet I believe it's a hundred times more important."

Lily and I met outside later, and when we hugged I realized how long it had been.

"How's the campaign going?"

"It was dicey for a while, but I think we're on the comeback trail."

"What can I do to help?"

"Funny you should ask," I said. "Tomorrow I have a long-standing commitment to speak to the Public Employees Association, but I just received a request to address the faculty at UC Davis. Would you consider being my surrogate?"

"Can I say whatever I want?"

"You might look over my campaign literature first."

The evening after her appearance, Lily and I met for dinner.

"How'd it go with the Davis academics?" I asked.

"Fantastic! After I told them who I was, most of the questions were about me."

I grinned. "Did you find time to mention my name, at least?"

"I said you deserved their vote because you're almost as smart as I am."

The next morning I rose before the sun, put on my running shoes, consumed a half a cup of coffee, and was out the door. As I jogged toward McKinley Park, I heard someone running behind me.

"Hey, Dickie," Tri-Y pulled up beside me, decked out in full running regalia. "Think you can keep up with an old man?"

"I promise not to get too far ahead," I said.

"Looks like a lesson in humility is in order."

For the first two miles, I tried for answers to as many mysteries as I could get.

"How did you arrange the meeting in Budapest with me and Amanda Patina?"

"In those days, Internet security was fairly lax, as I'm sure your friend Sacatchy's told you. When do I get to meet him, by the way?"

"I'll make it happen, but it may put western civilization in peril."

After a couple of more questions, he picked up the pace to

a level that made casual conversation impossible. At the end of four miles, we both slowed—though unlike me, he was barely breathing hard.

"Good thing there's no voters around," he said. "See you soon, Dickie."

And he jogged off into the sunrise.

Two days after Tri-Y's coming out, it was Rob's turn to tread the shark-infested political waters when he delivered a speech at Sacramento State.

"Mr. Banks," a reporter said, "after the recent press conference at CIA headquarters, would you like to revise your comments about your opponent's father?"

"Until further information is released, I stand by my previous statements."

"Are you suggesting the CIA is being less than truthful about Tri-Y?"

"I'm suggesting that we don't have all the facts," Rob said. "It was only a few years ago that Mr. Youngblood's grandfather, Senator Lambright, was on the Senate Intelligence Committee."

"Are you suggesting a conspiracy between Senator Lambright and the CIA?"

"I'm suggesting something kind of ... smells, doesn't it?"

CHAPTER 35

(published after the election)

History doesn't repeat itself—at best it sometimes rhymes.

—Mark Twain

I INTENDED TO RELEASE MY AUTOBIOGRAPHY at least a month before the election, but delays held back publication until just two weeks before the big event. Rob scrambled to turn my own life against me.

"Dick Youngblood's so-called honest autobiography," he said in a speech to the Federation of Republican Women, "shows his dangerous disregard for the values and traditions on which the great state of California and the United States of America are founded. His pattern of sedition, immaturity, and moral turpitude began in early childhood and clearly continues to the present day."

The comment drew an interesting question from one of the small-business owners whose group I addressed the next day.

"Mr. Youngblood, even though this is a small-business forum, I'd be interested in your reaction to Mr. Banks's assertion that your life, as detailed in your autobiography, shows lack of character, values, and maturity."

"He's losing and he's desperate," I said. "He didn't dispute my integrity when I revealed some less-than-flattering events in my past. At the end of the day, the most important trait a politician can have is honesty. Because I've exposed my past, blemishes and all, I think the voters know they can trust me."

My answer was quoted in its entirety in several Northern California publications.

Two days later, Rob spoke at the Sacramento-area Ninety-Nine Percent Club.

"Mr. Banks, I'm Julie Tanaka, from the *Sacramento News & Review*," a young woman said. "My question concerns an incident documented in the recently published autobiography of your opponent. I realize this happened a long time ago, but when you were running for student-body president at Stanford, did you really say you 'love your animals sautéed and your women in bikinis'?"

"That's just one of many inaccuracies in Mr. Youngblood's so-called honest autobiography."

"But you've also used his words as evidence of his lack of maturity," Ms. Tanaka said.

"He lies when he has to and he's truthful when it makes him look good."

"So is it true that you said gays won't achieve equal rights because of their aberrant behavior?"

"I … don't remember saying that, no." Rob glanced around. "Next question?"

"Hi, Rob. Tom Altruis, political writer for the *San Francisco Chronicle*. On several occasions, you've referred to your opponent's proposals to increase the power of market incentives as 'too radical for this district.' Can you elaborate on that?"

"To Dick Youngblood, 'market forces' is code for bigger government and higher taxes."

"Can you cite a specific example of how Mr. Youngblood's proposals will mean bigger government and higher taxes?"

"All we need to do is examine how government has grown under every Democratic administration in the recent past. Next, please."

"Mr. Banks," Tom said, "should I report that you don't have an example?"

"No! Next, please."

"Hello, Mr. Banks, I'm Raul, an unemployed college graduate. Two weeks ago you said your opponent lacked the character to be a congressman because of his disdain for tradition. Can you give us one example?"

"Just read between the lines of his criticism of U.S. foreign policy."

"But can you give us an example?"

"Well … I don't want to misquote my opponent, so I think we have to move on."

"I'll move on, Mr. Banks," Raul said. "Did you ever serve in the military?"

"No, I was studying in law school and raising a family."

"How about the Peace Corps? Job Corps? Teach for America? Have you ever performed any public service outside of politics?"

Banks's bumbling performance was shown on local and some national outlets just nine days before the election. All the hits seemed to be in my parade.

The next day I got a voice mail from Rita Mae.

"Dickie dear, your grandparents want to invite you to dinner tomorrow night in Sausalito. I'm sensing positive vibes—and bring your campaign manager."

I not only invited my campaign manager, but I also invited Sacatchy.

"So what's the deal here, Dick?" Emily asked as we motored toward the Bay Area in my Prius.

"I'm not sure, but the senator has something important to say. Also the enchanting Amanda Patina will make an appearance."

"Why is almost every important woman in your life named Amanda?"

"Want to be an honorary Amanda?"

"Ha, sign me up!"

* * *

In Sausalito, media types were circling the iconic fountain near the restaurant where our little reunion was scheduled to take place. The senator was chatting with anyone and everyone. Beside him were my mom and grandmother, and there was my new fiancée sauntering toward me in all her magnificence. I hadn't seen her in three weeks, and part of me wanted to whisk her off to the closest hotel. But since all eyes were quickly on us, we kept it to a hug and a kiss.

The senator stepped up to the fountain.

"Ladies and gentlemen, thank you all for coming. The reason for this makeshift press conference is first to introduce my family and welcome back to America Richard Youngblood's father, Yuri Yablonsky Youngblood."

Tri-Y materialized from behind the fountain, waving and smiling.

"It is also my great honor," the senator said, "to endorse my grandson, Richard Youngblood, as my choice for congressmen from the Fifty-fourth Congressional District. Even if he weren't my grandson, there's no doubt in my mind that he's the best candidate. Richard and I don't agree on every issue—we're not even members of the same political party—but like all informed leaders, his approach to public policy will be thoughtful and pragmatic. He's what the Fifty-fourth Congressional District needs, but more importantly, he is what the country needs. Thank you."

Within seconds, Amanda Patina left my side and ran to greet Tri-Y.

"I never had the chance to thank you for saving my life, so thank you, from the bottom of my heart." This was followed by the most enthusiastic of hugs.

"I always thought Yuri was in on your escape," Rita Mae said, "but Dickie seemed to change the subject whenever I brought it up." She was standing next to them with a smile brighter than her laughing Buddha's.

There were about ten of us seated in the warm light of the Italian bistro. The wine flowed freely and the mood was celebratory.

Tri-Y and Sacatchy ended up seated together at the end of the table, and somewhere between the entrée and the dessert, Tri-Y excused himself. Within a minute, Sacatchy followed.

I glanced out the window. Under a street lamp I observed conspiratorial body language followed by belly-bouncing laughter.

The last speech I gave before the election was at a Democratic Party banquet in Sacramento to honor Northern California politicians of the past, present, and future. It was the Saturday night before the election, and all the statistics, as well as the anecdotal evidence, seemed to be in my favor.

"Thank you to the Democratic Party and to everyone in this room for supporting my candidacy," I said. "Contrary to the beliefs of the Mad Tea Partiers and their Republican cohorts, this nation was founded on a sense of community as much as on the principle of individualism. One shouldn't come at the expense of the other, and I'll fight for a fair balance between the two.

"Some of you have read my autobiography. As Gandhi said, 'Happiness is when what you say and what you do are in harmony.' And we will all be in harmony when the Democratic Party has record-breaking success on Election Day! Thank you."

As the applause grew louder, I briefly raised my hands in double victory signs.

After the banquet, I decided to walk home. I was headed east on J Street and the younger demographic was out in force. According to the pollsters, this group was mine—if it actually showed up to vote.

In my walk, I registered six nods, two handshakes, one "Hey, Congressman," one "Hi, Dick," and one "You've got my vote." As I neared the line in front of a nightclub, I got smiling waves from three stunning females.

"Hey, Dick, come in and party with us!" one of the cutest said.

"Thanks," I said as I held up my hands, palms outward. "But have fun without me."

My phone buzzed in my pocket.

"Hi, I'm Mike Turnbell, an assistant district attorney in Los Angeles County. I have some news about Amanda Patricia Nixon. You're aware the venue for her upcoming trial was moved down here?"

"That's what I heard.

"She was released on bail this afternoon."

I stopped walking.

"Wasn't bail something like a half a million dollars?"

"It was, but she got a smoking-hot attorney who must have convinced the judge her bombing was a prank gone wrong. He got the bail reduced to twenty thousand dollars and someone paid it."

"Where is she now?" I glanced up and down the street.

"The judge instructed her not to leave Los Angeles County, but the police decided to follow her for the first twenty-four hours. They lost her when she got near LAX, and by the time they picked up her trail, she'd already landed in Sacramento. We contacted the Sacramento police, but you might want to call them yourself. And beef up your security."

"Thanks, I'll sleep with one eye open."

As I approached the H Street Lofts and Condos, I stopped and looked up. My lights were blazing. A silhouette moved past the window shade.

Only three people had a key to my condo: my housecleaner, Andi, and Amanda Patina. Amanda Patina was in Seattle, Andi was away until Monday, and my cleaning lady was never here this late. I supposed it could be Sacatchy, who didn't seem to need a key, but what would he be doing here?

I listened at the door and heard furniture moving. I *wanted to* burst in to confront the intruder, but I hadn't stayed alive for forty-one years by letting testosterone dictate my every action. A

911 call could have resulted in a tabloid splash—the last thing I needed three days before the election.

I ran down the street to the closest pub and ordered something to calm my nerves. As I gulped a Sierra Nevada Pale Ale, I called Emily and explained the situation.

"For now, call the cops and wait for them before you barge in. OK?'

"Got it," I said. "You call the press—if it *is* Amanda Nixon, I want plenty of witnesses."

"Yes, sir."

I called the police, finished my beer, and headed back to my building. As I neared my front door, I tried to peek in the windows.

Something cold and hard was thrust into the middle of my back.

"Hi, Dickie," Amanda Nixon said. "Don't turn around or I'll shoot you right here."

I opened my mouth to tell her the police were on the way but then stopped. I didn't want to force her trigger finger. I had to keep her talking.

"Hello, Amanda," I said. "How'd you get out of jail?"

"I found a real lawyer and a fair judge."

"And what are you doing here?

"I'm throwing you a little pre-election party."

"Wouldn't a post-election party be better?"

She jabbed the barrel of the gun hard into my kidneys.

"Inside, *now*."

I went inside. My living room, I now saw, had been generously decorated with my campaign signs and bumper stickers. The furniture had been rearranged around a podium.

"How did you get in here?"

"I have my ways."

"And what are we going to do at this little party?"

MIKE C. ERICKSON

"You'd probably enjoy making 'strange political bedfellows,' wouldn't you?"

I kept my voice as gentle as possible. "That was over twenty years ago," I said.

"Before you tried to kill me."

"Amanda." I slowly turned to face her. "Whatever you're planning, there's still time to talk it over—"

"No more talking, Dick. Remember the hanging chads?" She beamed. "We're going to have a hanging Dick."

In the past twenty years, my understanding of firearms had improved considerably. Amanda was holding a Magnum. I also noticed a small pistol stuck down her blouse, providing a fierce decoration to her cleavage. And unlike on the night outside the Nixon Library, she had the Magnum aimed squarely at the center of my chest.

I heard noise outside—the police? Whatever it was, Amanda was too involved to notice.

The beat of my heart was moving into hummingbird rhythm while sweat bathed my forehead. She pointed at the podium.

"Go on, Dick, give me one of your famous campaign speeches."

To the podium I went. After months of campaigning, all I needed to do was open my mouth and the words spilled out, but not my crisp, succinct stump speech. I was long-winded from the get-go.

"We need to return to a time when people cared not only for their own family but their fellow citizens, whether they're rich or poor, young or old, men or women, black or white ..."

Amanda Patricia set a chair up beside me, climbed onto it, and pointed the gun at my temple as I went on. And on. Anything to stall, stall, stall.

"I am here today to better represent our history,' as Abraham Lincoln once said. His words have more truth today—"

"That's enough."

"Don't you want to hear the rest of my speech?" I said. "In some ways Lincoln was almost prophetic—"

266

"Shut the fuck up, Dick."

She reached out and tugged a piece of cord I hadn't noticed. A noose fell from the ceiling and dangled in front of my face.

She slipped the noose around my neck, but the noose was far too loose. She'd have to tighten it—a task that would require coordination and the use of both hands.

I watched her try to hang on to the Magnum by looping her two smallest fingers through the trigger. After less than a minute she gave up and jammed the gun against my temple.

"No more games," she said. "See you in the afterlife, Nixon."

"Amanda—"

The door burst open. Amanda gave a little shriek as four police officers, followed by Tri-Y, barged into the room.

"Everyone freeze!" one of the cops said. "Put your hands where we can see them!"

"Not a chance!" Amanda screamed and then pulled the trigger. *Click. Click.* She stared at the gun and turned it on the police. *Click, click, click, click-click-click.*

Tri-Y held out his hand—filled with bullets. "Missing something?"

She grabbed the small pistol from its nest in her cleavage and pulled its baby trigger.

Click, click, click.

Around the fourth click, Sacatchy stepped out of my second bedroom.

"You might need these." He opened his palms to reveal eight smaller bullets.

Within seconds the police had Amanda Patricia in handcuffs. Someone congratulated me for my courage. A flash went off.

Emily approached me. "Looks like your charmed life continues. Didn't I tell you to wait for the cops?"

I brushed her aside and marched over to the corner where Tri-Y and Sacatchy were giggling.

"Why didn't you guys just take the guns?"

"What's the fun in that?" Sacatchy said. "We could actually hear you sweat from the second bedroom."

The basic facts made the 11 p.m. news, but the headline the next morning in *The Sacramento Bee* was far more satisfying: "Candidate Youngblood Saved by Father and Best Friend: Attacker Held Without Bail."

The article went on to say that police were still investigating but that this event settled "once and for all who is the aggressor and who is the victim in the saga of Richard Youngblood and Amanda Nixon."

In the same newspaper, the editorial page included a ringing endorsement for me. It cited my "integrity, service to country, and an unprecedented unique attempt at openness" as factors that would make me a fine congressman.

On Election Day I arrived at my midtown Sacramento polling place before 8 a.m. The media recorded it for the morning news, which according to Emily could net me a small ballot box of additional votes. Afterward I drove out I-5 to Sacramento International Airport to pick up Amanda Patina, who was flying in from Seattle.

"You faced death and won—again," she said after she gave me a hello hug and a deep kiss. "You might have a huge karmic debt to repay, but let's hope it's in your next life."

"I hope to be a jackrabbit in the Texas hill country in my next life."

"Why a jackrabbit?" she asked as we got into the car.

"What could be better? Romp, play, have sex."

"Speaking of which …" She leaned over and fondled my ear with her tongue.

"You're worse than driving with a cell phone."

"How about this?" Her fingers danced along my inner thigh.

"Perhaps I should address this problem as a congressman."

"So you're going to win?"

"That's what they tell me."

"You got my vote. I sent in my ballot two weeks ago."

"But you're not a citizen."

"I've been working on citizenship for the past year."

"Congratulations," I said. "But you don't live in my district."

"I do now."

"Where?"

"With you, of course."

I felt a warm glow wash over me. "Really?"

"And sometimes in D.C.," she said, "if you actually win."

"I'm not sure two thong panties and a toothbrush prove residency."

"I'll move some more stuff in, but you'll have to clear out a closet."

I spent that evening cloistered with Amanda Patina, Emily, Tim, Andi, Lily, and a host of officials and volunteers from my campaign in a suite at the Hyatt Regency watching the returns. Most people at the big party in the ballroom on the first floor were concerned about the entire Democratic slate.

The first returns showed Rob Banks with a substantial lead. By 9 p.m., his lead had dropped to seven points, and by ten I was down by only two points.

Suddenly, across the bottoms of the screens of CNN, NBC, and even Fox, were the words, "Congrats Dickie, you won."

Thirty minutes later, two local channels named me the winner.

The networks later announced that they were investigating the unauthorized congratulatory advertisement. My own investigation consisted of a phone call to Roc-Cindy the day after the election.

"Hey, Big Daddy Dick, congrats on your victory."

"Thanks," I said. "Any ideas on the whereabouts of our mutual friend?"

"I just talked to him. His phone was cutting out but he said something about Yemen."

"Did he say when he'd be back?"

"After Myanmar. Oh, and I asked if Tri-Y was with him, but all he said was 'no comment.'"

As soon as Banks conceded, we all went downstairs to celebrate. I stood at the podium with Amanda Patina by my side, thanked my campaign workers, and described in the most glittering of generalities how our victory would give us hope for a new tomorrow.

After the last handshake, Amanda Patina, Emily, and I walked out into the cool Sacramento night.

"Well, Dickie, you did it," Emily said.

"No, we did it," I said. "Thank you so much. Next time I'll heed more of your sage advice."

"Ha, don't lie to me, Congressman Integrity."

As Amada Patina and I walked away hand in hand, a photographer took our picture. We'd already been compared to Barack and Michelle and once even to the Kennedys.

"Do you want to get a cab or walk?" I asked.

"What would Lincoln do?"

"I think he'd prefer to walk."

We headed east on J Street. I tried to think of Jefferson or Lincoln, but my memory was drawn to Mickey McWhirr and our last conversation, which followed a speech to the League of Women Voters. I left with the uncomfortable feeling that I'd exaggerated my role in assisting public education.

"Hey, Mickey," I said as I passed him on the steps of the Capitol. "Do you think it's possible for a politician to be completely honest?"

"Well, laddie, I think this is the best advice I can give you." He held up a sign in the black and red that adorned my campaign literature, only the letters were huge: "HONESTY IN GOVERNMENT: IF NO ONE REALLY TRIES, DEMOCRACY WILL SURELY DIE."

ACKNOWLEDGEMENTS

Like most first-time novelists, I have a plethora of people to thank and acknowledge, not the least of which is **Arlene Rose,** my esteemed colleague and walking dictionary. Long before there were computers on every desk and smart phones in every pocket, there was the distance of three classrooms to ask Arlene what something meant. More importantly, she encouraged me to write.

I also would like to recognize **Judy Murray** who excelled as my very first editor, and **Smokey Murphy**, who more than any other person, was my cheerleader for this entire project.

I would like to acknowledge the Chief Information Security Officer for Yahoo.com, **Alex Stamos**. He is one of my most famous former students, but he was a much better student of mine than I was a student of his. In a phone call a while back, he tried to enlighten me about the history of computer hacking and security. Sorry, Alex, the mistakes are all mine, but I have the perfect excuse: if it doesn't make sense, that's because it's either humor or satire.

I would a like to thank **Erin Brown** of Erin Edits who was the first to assist me in excising superfluous stories.

My colleague, **Donn Miller** was the inspiration behind the Lexus story. I can hear him chuckling.

He probably doesn't remember, but my workout friend, **Jonathan Brown,** not only enlightened me about California government and the role of lobbyists, he also bought my lunch. I think he will like my novel if he practices deep breathing during the parts that could possibly be tainted by a liberal bias.

Throughout the whole process, I felt the amorphous influence of the eminent barrister and self-anointed, great grammarian, **Ron Erickson**. He's also my brother.

I must also recognize the encouragement of a multitude of former students and members of the academic decathlon teams that I taught and coached for many years. If I start naming names, someone who was the ultimate influence will feel left out. You know who you are. To all of you who have ask how my book is coming along, as well as my fellow coach, **Geni Aymeric**, thanks for your support.

To the real Amandas with whom I am acquainted— you are all wonderful young women and I apologize for tarnishing your name. None of you were models for the Amandas in my novel. I just love your name.

I want to also acknowledge the gang at **Harp's Lounge** who may or may not even know that I wrote a novel. Thanks for keeping me laughing and preventing me from taking myself too seriously.

I would also like to thank **Katelyn Schirmer,** graphic designer and former captain of my Academic Decathlon team. She designed the quirky, yet artistic, cover for *Pianist in Bordello*.

Above all, 1 would like to acknowledge the immense role of my content editors **Renni Browne** and **Shannon Roberts** of The Editorial Department. In the process of deleting, rephrasing, and revising for almost three years, I earned a self-declared degree in writing fiction— taught by the masters. I also received invaluable advice from **Morgana Gallaway, Doug Wagner, Karinya Funsett-Topping,** and **Beth Jusino** from TED, as well as fantastic assistance from **Liz Felix** and **Jayne Ryder**.

ABOUT THE AUTHOR

Mike C. Erickson grew up in the idyllic college town of Logan, Utah, but because of a twist of fate he graduated from high school in Honolulu. He left Hawaii brimming with aloha and enrolled at Utah State, where he was awarded two degrees and self-proclaimed minor intellectual status, which was of dubious value when the US Army invited him to vacation in South-East Asia. Ten days after leaving Vietnam, he began decades of dispensing pearls of wisdom as a high school history teacher, academic decathlon coach and on occasion, as a community college instructor in the Sacramento area. Mike and his wife Trudy, have two grown sons and a grandson to be born about the time that this novel is published. When not in Hawaii or a more exotic locale, they live in Gold River, California. This is his first novel.

To contact the author, go to his website: **mikecerickson.net**.

Made in the USA
San Bernardino, CA
11 May 2018